✣ THE ✣
REVENANT EXPRESS

A Newbury AND Hobbes Investigation

❧ THE ❧
REVENANT EXPRESS

A Newbury AND Hobbes
Investigation

GEORGE MANN

TITAN BOOKS

THE REVENANT EXPRESS: A NEWBURY & HOBBES INVESTIGATION
Print edition ISBN: 9781781160060
E-book edition ISBN: 9781781166451

Published by
Titan Books
A division of Titan Publishing Group Ltd
144 Southwark Street
London
SE1 0UP

First edition: February 2019
2 4 6 8 10 9 7 5 3 1

A CIP catalogue record for this title is available from the British Library.

Printed and bound by CPI Group (UK) Ltd, Croydon, CR0 4YY.

For my sister, Irene Duncan-Curmi

CHAPTER 1

♕

LONDON, AUTUMN 1902

Some days, she liked the rain.

As a child she had often sought its purifying qualities, enjoyed the play of it upon her upturned face. Out in the garden of her parents' home, heady with the scent of damp, fresh earth, she had allowed it to wash away all concerns; for her desperately unwell sister, her bickering parents, her ailing grandmother. She had not forgotten the comfort of those days, and even now, she still enjoyed the thrill of being caught in a sudden English downpour.

Today, however, was not one of those days. Today she would have rather been at home, curled up by the fire, or else in her barely used office beneath the British Museum, shuffling papers; anywhere but in Stoke Newington in a torrential downpour, standing amidst a gaggle of police constables and overeager civilians who had yet to be persuaded to clear the area.

Veronica angled her umbrella in order to look for Sir Charles Bainbridge, sending a cascade of pooled water over the brim, spattering her shoes. She sighed.

Bainbridge was standing a few feet away, muttering in low, fractious tones to another man she didn't recognise. When he saw her looking, he gave a weak smile and raised a hand in brief salute. He looked hassled, which, Veronica allowed, was quite understandable, given the circumstances. All of the furore, all of the noise and bluster and milling crowds, centred around the thing on the pavement, the object that she had so far studiously managed to avoid. The people around her had already dubbed it—in hushed, scandalised tones—"*the monster*." She could ignore it no longer. Bracing herself, she turned her head to regard it.

She stifled a gasp. It was even worse than she'd imagined. The creature was, without doubt, one of the most ghastly things she had ever seen.

It had once been a human being—although she couldn't easily ascertain whether a male or female—but now its body was so bloated and malformed as to be almost beyond recognition. The victim appeared to be on its back, its belly distended to at least three or four times its natural capacity. The flesh had burst, and from deep within the intestines strange plant-like growths had erupted, pushing out through the ruins of the person's clothes.

Tendrils, resembling masses of thick, ropey vines, were splayed across the pavement, spilling out from the corpse as if feeling their way towards the gutter. Pink tumours, resembling bulbous, fungal growths, nestled amongst the vines like sickly blooms, ready to burst open at any moment and dissipate their spores.

The flesh of the face was terribly misshapen, as if the same gnarly growths had formed beneath the skin, bulging out, warping the features into something less than human. The result was that the victim looked as if it had suffered from a severe case of elephantiasis, or that the corpse had been preserved mid-metamorphosis, frozen in a state of change. Perhaps most bizarrely, fresh green shoots had emerged from the fingertips of the right hand, which rested on the paving slabs nearest to Veronica, as if the dead person were reaching out to her in silent desperation.

She swallowed, feeling bile rise in her gullet.

Two constables were holding umbrellas above the remains, attempting to protect it from the storm, but despite their best efforts, raindrops were still bursting upon the creature's hide, trickling over the exposed flesh and giving it a glistening, glossy appearance. While she watched, a man in a white smock nudged one of the constables out of the way and began poking around in the corpse's mouth with his index finger.

Veronica shuddered.

"Horrible, isn't it?" muttered someone nearby. The voice was familiar. She adjusted her umbrella and turned to see Inspector Foulkes standing just a few feet away, regarding the corpse with a thoroughly disgusted look on his face. He turned his head, his expression brightening slightly when he saw she was looking. He was a tall, bearded man in his late thirties, a good policeman who, in recent months, had begun to appear rather downtrodden by the interminable horror of his profession.

"It is, rather," she confirmed.

They were silent for a moment.

"How are you, Inspector? Is your family well?" she asked, in an effort to dispel the pall of gloom that had seemingly settled over them. Neither of them, however, could tear their eyes from the sight of the unusual corpse.

"Oh, very well indeed, Miss Hobbes. And your sis–" He caught himself mechanically reflecting her question. "That is, I mean to say…" He looked pained. "Oh, I'm sorry, Miss Hobbes. Things must have been very difficult for you, since your sister passed, and I… I…" He trailed off, unable to find the right words.

Veronica smiled. "Why don't you step out of the rain for a moment, Inspector? This umbrella's big enough for two."

Foulkes sighed with barely concealed relief. "Thank you, Miss Hobbes," he said, with feeling. He edged closer and she held the umbrella aloft to accommodate him. As a result, she felt the patter of raindrops against the back of her plush red evening cloak. The garment, she knew, would never be the same again.

Foulkes blew into his cupped hands and tried, unsuccessfully, to wipe the dripping water from his eyes with his damp sleeve.

"What is it?" she asked, nodding in the direction of the body. "What's happened here? I've never seen anything like it."

"Nobody seems to have any idea. It's as if his body has been infested with these growths, plants that appear to have germinated in his guts," Foulkes said.

"A parasite?" asked Veronica.

Foulkes shrugged. "Perhaps. I think Sir Charles is hoping that you and Sir Maurice are going to help to answer that particular question."

"Hmmm," said Veronica, as noncommittally as she could. She looked up to see Bainbridge concluding his conversation with the man he'd been talking to.

He stalked over to join them. "Foulkes, get rid of these people," he said, waving a hand at the crowd. "Close both ends of the lane until we know what we're dealing with."

"Very good, sir," replied Foulkes. He glanced at Veronica with a look so forlorn that she had to stifle a laugh. He looked like a drowned, moping puppy. Sighing heavily, he stomped off to speak with one of the uniformed constables.

"It's good to see you, Miss Hobbes," said Bainbridge, taking her by the hand. He seemed distracted. "Where's Newbury?" he asked, peering over her shoulder. The lapels of his heavy woollen overcoat looked sodden, and rain was spraying from the brim of his bowler hat. Droplets had settled in his grey-speckled moustache. He seemed beyond the point of caring.

Veronica sighed. "Otherwise engaged," she replied. She

tried to keep the disappointment from her voice.

Bainbridge frowned, his shoulders sagging. "Oh, don't tell me we're back to that? We're not going to have to drag him out of one of those despicable Chinese smoking dens again, are we?"

Veronica shook her head. "No. Not that. He's gone north. He received word that Lady Arkwell had been operating out of a small mining town near Durham, and took off at once. That was two days ago."

"Oh, perfect," snapped Bainbridge, leaning heavily on his cane. "Stuck in the rain with a... a... well, I don't know what it is, and Newbury's nowhere to be seen." His moustache twitched in frustration. "This Arkwell woman is becoming another of his ruddy obsessions."

"Hmmm," murmured Veronica, by way of agreement. She fought back a sharp stab of jealously, cursing herself for such petty emotions.

Newbury had, indeed, become rather obsessed with his pursuit of the female agent in recent weeks, and Veronica had seen very little of him, save for the brief episodes during which he attended to her sister's health at Malbury Cross. He'd taken to turning down many of the cases that would otherwise have captured his interest, and now, he was absent even when his oldest friend, Sir Charles Bainbridge, was in need of his help.

"What the Devil are we going to do now?" barked Bainbridge in consternation. He was being somewhat unreasonable, expecting Newbury to be available at his beck and call, but all the same, Veronica knew it was derived from concern for his friend, and for his investigation, rather than any real sense of entitlement.

Veronica put a hand on his arm. "I'll do my very best to assist in any way I can, Sir Charles," she said, pointedly.

Bainbridge's eyes widened as the nature of his unintended

slight suddenly dawned on him. "Oh, quite so, Miss Hobbes. Quite so." He gave a forced smile. "And most welcome such help will be."

Veronica bit her tongue. "So," she said breezily, despite the sinking feeling in the pit of her stomach, "what would Sir Maurice do?"

Bainbridge's face creased in an unexpected grin. "Other than drop to his knees in that filthy puddle, poke the corpse with the end of his pen, and utter ominous and obtuse noises, you mean?"

Veronica laughed. "Other than that, yes."

"Well, for a start, I believe he'd be interested in whatever Dr. Finnegan here has got to say," replied Bainbridge, taking her gently by the elbow and leading her over to where the man in the white smock was still hunched over the corpse, poking about in its mouth with his ink-stained fingers. He didn't look up or appear to acknowledge their presence.

Veronica gave the man a brief appraisal. He was in his middle to late fifties, with wild, wispy grey hair that clung to his balding pate in thin cusps. He wore thin, wire-framed spectacles on the end of his nose, and was reviewing the body with something approaching glee. He was wearing his cotton smock—once white but now stained with patches of faded brown, which Veronica recognised as spilt blood—over a loose-fitting brown suit. His left trouser pocket bulged dramatically, as if he were harbouring something alive inside of it.

"Why's his pocket... well, *moving* like that?" whispered Veronica, leaning closer to Bainbridge in order to be heard over the sounds of the storm. He smelled of damp cloth and lavender.

"Ah. That'll be his ferret," replied Bainbridge, apparently nonplussed.

"His ferret!" remarked Veronica, unable to contain her bemusement. "Here, at a crime scene?"

"A *potential* crime scene," replied Bainbridge. "We're unsure what happened, yet." He shrugged. "Finnegan's an eccentric old blighter, but he does a solid job. He's one of our best surgeons. Newbury's fond of him."

"Hmmm," said Veronica, grinning. "That explains a lot."

"Guinea Golds," announced Finnegan, suddenly, stepping back from the body and arching his back, his hands on his hips. He sighed heavily, and flexed his neck from side to side. He spoke with a clipped Irish brogue.

"I'm sorry?" said Veronica.

"No need," said Finnegan, shaking his head. "It's not your fault the poor beggar had a fondness for cigarettes, now, is it?" He peered at her over the top of his rain-spattered spectacles and offered her a wide, gap-toothed grin. What was left of his hair was now plastered to the side of his head with rain, but he seemed not to notice. "Or is it?"

"It's most definitely not," said Bainbridge, interjecting. "Dr. Finnegan, this is Miss Veronica Hobbes. She's assisting with my enquiries."

"Delighted to meet you, my dear," said Finnegan, thrusting out his hand.

Veronica glanced at the corpse, then back at the hand. She took it gingerly. "A pleasure to meet you, Dr. Finnegan," she said.

"Owen, my dear. Owen. I insist!" He retracted his hand and rubbed emphatically at his temples, as if trying to encourage his brain. He swatted at a sudden burst of movement from his pocket, frowning at the unwanted distraction. "Not now, Barnabas. Can't you see I'm busy?" The pale brown head of a ferret popped out momentarily from the pocket, glanced around nervously with little beady eyes, and then ducked back inside.

Veronica gave a polite cough. "So, tell me, Dr. Finnegan–Owen–have you any idea what it is, yet?"

Finnegan nodded enthusiastically. "Why, it's a corpse, my dear," he said, by way of reply.

"We can ruddy well see that!" said Bainbridge, impatiently. "What can you tell us?"

Finnegan offered him a fierce, quizzical glare.

"About the body, I mean!" clarified Bainbridge, the exasperation evident in his tone.

Finnegan gave a brief nod. "It's a man, in his late twenties, I'd estimate. He was once a heavy smoker, and seriously malnourished. He carries an old wound to his left shoulder. He's been infected with the revenant plague for some time–" At this Veronica took an involuntary step back, and Finnegan watched her, appraisingly. "But curiously the infection has not run its full course," he continued. "His damaged flesh appears to have been healing."

"*Healing?*" echoed Bainbridge, astonished.

"Yes, it's really quite remarkable," replied Finnegan. "His body seems to be rejecting the plague."

"Like Sir Maurice," said Veronica. "He's somehow established a tolerance for the infection, through previous exposure. Immunity, if you will."

Finnegan shook his head. "No, not immunity. This poor sod had already succumbed to the plague. It's more that he appears to have been making steps towards recovery. Look here." He prodded the dead man by the left ear, easing back a ragged flap of torn skin. "The necrotic flesh has peeled away, but there's fresh, pink growth forming underneath."

"This is unprecedented," said Bainbridge. "Is it related to all of this bizarre flora?" He waved the end of his cane to indicate the eruption of vegetation emanating from the dead man's belly.

Finnegan wavered for a moment. "I don't know. It may be entirely unrelated, or it may be that whatever species of plant infected him had a bearing on the progression of the disease." He removed his glasses, wiped them on the front of his already sodden smock, and replaced them. He frowned at the fact he still couldn't see through the smeared lenses.

"Forgive me, Dr. Finnegan, but is it really possible for a plant to take root inside a person's body?" asked Veronica. "It seems... somewhat unlikely."

Finnegan nodded. "Yes, quite right, Miss Hobbes. Highly unlikely. I wouldn't testify to it, but I have a theory that what we're dealing with here is a microsporidia infestation."

"A what?" blustered Bainbridge.

"A parasitic fungus," explained Finnegan. "But I'll have to take it back to the lab to confirm."

"Well, you'd better get on with it, then," said Bainbridge, shaking his head.

Finnegan turned and glanced over his shoulder, beckoning to two uniformed constables who were sheltering in a nearby doorway beside a wooden cart. Reluctantly, they stepped out into the downpour and slowly wheeled the cart over. Finnegan was just about to start issuing instructions when Veronica interjected with another question. "Just one more thing, Dr. Finnegan. This parasitic fungus—assuming that's what it is—I take it it's not native to the British Isles?"

Finnegan looked thoughtful. "No, I would imagine it originates in a more tropical climate," he said. "Otherwise we'd have likely seen it before."

"So, do you think there might be foul play at work?" Veronica pressed.

Finnegan shrugged. "Who'd want to murder a plague revenant?" he said. He turned and began conversing with the constables in low, precise tones.

"It's a good point, Miss Hobbes," said Bainbridge, from over her shoulder. "The poor fellow does seem the most unlikely of targets for a murder. Damned odd though, isn't it?"

Veronica nodded, although she was watching the three

men manhandle the bloated corpse onto the wooden cart in preparation for ferrying it away to Finnegan's laboratory. "Something about it doesn't sit right with me, Sir Charles. I can't help thinking there's more to it than meets the eye."

"Perhaps you're right," said Bainbridge, in a conciliatory tone. "Finnegan will have more for us in the morning. Right now, I think we could both do with getting out of this damnable weather."

Veronica turned to him, and smiled. "I can't argue with that," she said.

"Come on," said Bainbridge, indicating the other end of the lane with the tip of his cane. "I have a police carriage waiting. I'll drop you at home."

"Thank you," said Veronica, looping her arm through his as they negotiated the slick cobbles. "And tomorrow?"

Bainbridge laughed. "Tomorrow I shall send for you as soon as there's word. We can question Finnegan together. If you're still unsure after that—well, we'll have to see."

Behind them, Finnegan and the two constables trundled off into the downpour, bearing their unusual cargo along with them.

CHAPTER 2

♛

PARIS, SUMMER 1903

The rich tang of oil and smoke stung her nostrils as she shoved her way through the unyielding crowd. The people here, she decided, were not at all like those at home. Their continental attitudes were both heady and enticing, and scandalously obtuse.

In London, a woman would never be left to drag her own case across the platform, but here at the Gare du Nord, everyone was so engrossed in their own noisy business—hurrying to be the first to board the train—that no one stopped to pay her even the slightest modicum of attention as she hauled the leather trunk across the concourse.

Not that she minded, particularly. It was quite exhilarating not to be patronised. She simply wished they'd get out of her way in order for her to pass.

Amelia searched the platform for Newbury. She couldn't see him amongst the bustle of people and the billowing steam that issued in hissing jets from the immense, shuddering engine. It was a remarkable feat of engineering: at least twice the size of the typical, domestic steam engines she'd seen back home in England, with sleek golden skirts and fat, snaking pipes of gleaming brass. Hastily erected scaffolds had been pushed against the sides of the vehicle, and men in blue overalls clambered over the tank and engine housing, wiping streaks of soot and sweat from their shining red faces as they prepared the machine for the first leg of its tremendous journey across the continent.

Behind the engine stretched the train itself, two stories high and so long that its tail disappeared somewhere beyond the far end of the platform. Already, passengers were milling about inside the carriages, haggling over compartments and fighting to be the first to the best seats. Thankfully, Newbury had reserved them a first class suite on the lower level of the train, close to the front, so she wasn't going to have to join in with any of the distasteful bickering.

Nevertheless, she couldn't help but feel a slight pang of apprehension at the thought of such a long journey, and, perhaps more pointedly, to such a far-flung destination. She'd heard tales of St. Petersburg, of an icy fantasia filled with frost-rimmed palaces, wondrous clockwork machines and magical creatures, and the very thought of it left her feeling breathless and excited all at once. Not to mention a little guilty, given the cause of their mission. She had to keep reminding herself that she was not there for her own gratification. More than anything, she wanted to help her sister.

"Remarkable, isn't it?" said a familiar voice, startling her from her reverie. She turned to see Newbury standing at her shoulder, regarding the train with a tired, weary expression. He looked handsome in his top hat and black suit, although there were dark rings beneath his eyes, and more lines than she had noticed before. Amelia knew that his concern for Veronica, along with the ongoing impact of her own treatment, was taking its toll on him. He'd lost weight, and where once he had appeared fit and lean, he now seemed painfully thin. He'd already told her that he was having trouble sleeping.

"Confirm to me again, Sir Maurice, that this journey is absolutely necessary," she said.

Newbury looked over, his expression firm. He put his hand on her arm, gripping it intently, and she wondered for a moment if he wasn't clinging onto her as much for his benefit as hers. "Amelia, it is *entirely* necessary. If we are to help Veronica then we must undertake this journey. Only the artisans of St. Petersburg can provide us with the intricate mechanisms we need to replace your sister's heart." Amelia nodded. "And besides," continued Newbury, "if I am to make such a journey, you understand that you must accompany me. It is the only way we can continue with your treatment. We will be gone for some time."

"Very well," said Amelia, forcing a smile. "Then we must continue as planned."

"I've booked us adjoining cabins," said Newbury, "that open into a shared living room. We should be comfortable." He smiled. "Come on, let's try to settle in while our fellow travellers board." He gestured to a nearby porter and the man, sweating profusely, obligingly took Amelia's luggage and swung it up onto his trolley. Muttering under his breath, he struggled across the platform towards the train, trundling their bags behind him.

Amelia looped her arm through Newbury's and they followed behind, pausing as the porter checked their tickets for the carriage number, and then started off again, full of bluster, in the opposite direction. Amelia suppressed a chuckle at the look of consternation on the man's face.

"As unenviable a job as I could imagine," said Newbury.

"Really?" countered Amelia. "I can't think the firemen would agree, shuffling all of that coal, hour after hour, in such infernal heat." Up ahead, the engine issued a hissing gush of steam, as if to emphasise her point. A small huddle of women, clutching their hats as if they expected to lose them in the sudden gust, stepped back in surprise.

"Ah, but at least they're warm," said Newbury, with a grin. "And besides, they don't have to deal with all of these *people*."

Amelia shook her head, laughing. Newbury was being as contrary as ever; while he clearly enjoyed his solitude, she knew he couldn't bear to be without the bustle and attention of other people for too long. In this regard, at least, he wasn't so different from everyone else. She, on the other hand, was finding the whole experience rather invigorating, after spending so long cooped up indoors in Malbury Cross, pretending to be dead. It felt good to be out in the world again.

"Ah, here we are," said Newbury, leading her over to where the porter had parked his trolley on the platform and was—rather indelicately—unloading their bags, tossing them up onto the train through an open door. She felt Newbury tense as he watched his leather suitcase slide across the floor on its side.

Up close, the vehicle was even more impressive than it had seemed from across the platform. The lustre of the green paint had not yet been dulled by the weather, and the carriage gleamed in the thin morning light. It towered above her, its two stories reaching a good twenty feet above the platform.

They were to board here, it seemed, in order to locate their rooms: the third carriage in line behind the engine's tender, close to the very front of the train. Amelia leaned to one side to enable her to peer over the porter's shoulder. Through the windows she caught glimpses of plush interiors and fittings that gave the impression of a sumptuous gentleman's club, rather than a passenger train. It looked most inviting.

All around her, people were clamouring to board; a woman in a mink coat barked commands at another porter to hurry along with her oversized case; a young couple slipped aboard carrying their own bags, paying little attention to whatever else was going on around them; a tall man with a bushy grey moustache and a military bearing was mustering two small boys, who whispered conspiratorially to one another in hasty French.

All of it seemed so new to Amelia, and must have seemed so mundane to Newbury, she thought, who had seen so much of the world. Veronica, too, had travelled widely and seen wonders in all corners of the globe. This journey, then, this small, new experience, felt to Amelia like something of a triumph, as if she were finally leaving her old life behind and starting out again, with something new.

"Come along, then," said Newbury, taking her arm. "Let's take a look at where we'll be staying."

Amelia nodded and allowed him to guide her up the steps.

The vestibule was not at all what she had been expecting, even after peering through the windows at the grandeur of the cabins on either side. It resembled the hallway of a large London house, only somewhat smaller and more contained, with a chequerboard marble floor, a spiral staircase encircled with impressive wrought iron railings, tall potted plants, and portraits of stately looking people she didn't recognise. To her left, a passageway led away into the carriage, and this is the direction in which their porter had disappeared, dragging their bags behind him. She followed, single file behind Newbury in the confined space.

"This is it," said Newbury a moment later. "Suite seventeen." He indicated the open door, and Amelia peered in.

The suite comprised three interlinked rooms—two small cabins that adjoined a larger, but still modest, drawing room. Additionally, each room had a door that opened directly onto the passageway, which ran the entire length of the carriage, from the lobby area where they'd boarded to, presumably, the vestibule that linked them to the next coach in the train. There would be at least one other suite of rooms on this lower level of the carriage, she guessed; the length and appearance from the outside suggested as much.

Above them, on the upper floor, would be the social areas– the observation lounge and the like. She'd read about them in the literature that Newbury had given her as they'd journeyed south from London to Dover. She would explore those later, she decided, once they'd settled in and were properly underway.

The porter had finally finished unloading their bags, placing them just inside the door, and Newbury saw him off with a small coin. Amelia watched the man clatter away with his trolley, still muttering beneath his breath.

She stepped over the threshold, taking in the room in which she would be spending the majority of the coming days. Behind her, Newbury closed the door and turned the key in the lock.

The drawing room was well appointed, with three armchairs arranged around a small card table, a hat stand, an aspidistra in a large terra-cotta pot, a gilt-framed mirror upon the wall, and a window, presently covered by a fine net curtain, that looked out upon the station. The floorboards underfoot were polished and worn. It was cosy and clean, and more than she'd expected. Indeed, it was larger and more comfortable than many of the hospital cells in which she'd spent her formative years.

"Yours is the cabin on the left," said Newbury, with a wave of his hand. "I hope it's comfortable. I know it's not much," he sounded apologetic, "but it'll be home for a while. We'll make the most of it."

Amelia smiled. "It's just fine," she said. She crossed to the door he'd indicated. When she opened it, the hinges creaked in tortured protest. She winced, supposing the likelihood of having them oiled was probably nonexistent. She'd just have to hope that Newbury didn't object if she needed to get up in the night.

The cabin was compact but well appointed, with a bunk, a

luggage rack, a small closet, an external-facing window, and the other narrow door, leading out to the carriage beyond. The room was panelled in dark mahogany, adding to the sense that the place had been designed to resemble the interior of a gentleman's club or country estate, and had a clean but slightly musty smell about it. The sheets on the bed looked crisp, white, and functional.

She sensed Newbury behind her. "I hope it'll suffice," he said.

"It's small, but cosy," she said, with a smile. "And far more than I've grown used to, over the years. It'll seem like a luxury."

"Well, I wouldn't go that far," said Newbury, laughing. He edged past her, approaching the door to the passageway. He slid the bolts. "Keep this door locked," he said, running his hands around the frame as if searching for any possible weaknesses in the structure. "Bolted from the inside. Use the door to my cabin as our only entrance and exit from the suite."

Amelia frowned. He seemed suddenly direct, serious. "Yes, if you insist. But why?"

"It's safer that way," he replied, a little dismissively. He'd already crossed to the window and was methodically examining the frame. "Keep this locked, too."

Amelia sighed. "Very well," she agreed, "although it all seems rather unnecessary."

Newbury turned to her. Again, that determined look: the fixed jaw, the firmness in the set of his mouth, the cold eyes. This was a side of him she'd never seen, and she wasn't much sure she liked it, or at least, what it represented. This, she presumed, was the professional Newbury, the experienced agent—the man who had faced all manner of terrible things and somehow managed to remain alive. Perhaps some of those experiences had left him suffering from a touch of paranoia? No one could experience such horrors and remain undamaged.

"Trust me, Amelia," he said. "It's entirely necessary." There was something about his tone that caused her to shudder: the fact his voice was so calm, level. This wasn't a man in the grip of irrational fear. This was an experienced agent securing a room because he anticipated a threat.

"Is there something you haven't told me?" she asked, and she could hear the slight break in her voice. She'd been right to hesitate earlier on the platform, she realised. This *wasn't* going to be a holiday, an adventure. She was journeying into the unknown, and it was evidently fraught with danger.

Newbury shook his head. He offered her an attempt at a reassuring smile, but it was too late for that–the seeds of doubt had already begun to take root in her mind. "I fear, Amelia, that trouble has a tendency to follow me around."

"But you suspect danger?" she pressed. "You think there's someone on this train who means us harm?"

Newbury crossed to her and placed his hand gently on her upper arm. "Not specifically, no. I'm not aware of anyone on this train who might mean me ill, but neither am I prepared to take chances. Nor do we know any of the other passengers, their reasons for being aboard the train, or even whether they're travelling under assumed identities. Do you think they suspect your real name is not 'Constance Markham,' for instance?" He paused, and then continued, more softly. "In my line of work, Amelia, one has a habit of making enemies. Experience has shown me that it pays to be prepared, to expect them to strike at any moment. That way we won't be caught unaware. If the trip proves uneventful–well, what have we lost?" He paused for a moment to let the question sink in. "I didn't mean to frighten you."

"But that's no way to live, always looking over your shoulder," she countered. "And besides, I've never seen you like this. You don't take precautions like these when we're in London, or Malbury Cross." She was careful to keep any note of accusation from her voice, but he was correct to be contrite—he *had* scared her.

"You're right. Of course, you're right. It's just that London is my home, you see. It's familiar. It's home turf. If anyone tries to catch me out, well, at least I know what I'm about, where to go and from whom to seek help. Out here," he waved his hand about him to indicate the cabin and the wider world beyond, "out here we're on our own. Everything hinges on our mission, you see. *Everything.* And so we must take the necessary precautions." He looked her in the eye. "Do you understand?"

Amelia wanted to say no, that she didn't understand, didn't even *want* to understand. She could have no part in this horrible business of suspecting everyone else on the train of malign intent. Yet, despite all of that, she felt herself nodding. She had to trust Newbury's experience, and she knew his intentions were sound, whatever his methods: to help Veronica, no matter what. He was right in that, at least. They couldn't allow anything to get in the way of retrieving Veronica's new heart. "Yes, very well," she said. "I understand. I'll do as you ask. Although I'm damned if I'm going to conduct myself in a manner that treats everyone I meet as a suspect."

"I would never expect that of you, Amelia," said Newbury. "You're far too considerate for that."

She chose to take his comment as a compliment, despite the fact she knew what he really meant was that he considered her gravely naïve. In contrast, she couldn't help thinking how desperately sad it was that Newbury should feel this way. It must be a terrible thing to find oneself unable to trust other people, to always look for the worst in everyone. Perhaps, she decided, this was her role for the duration of their trip—to help cure Newbury of this deep-seated paranoia, to show him there were still good people in the world. Despite everything, despite what had happened to Veronica, she believed that wholeheartedly, and she would prove it to Newbury, too.

The carriage jolted suddenly beneath her, and Newbury, smiling, reached out and caught her elbow, steadying her as she lurched to one side. "It seems we're on our way," he said.

Her response was drowned out by the screech of a shrill whistle from the platform, the scrape of wheels against the iron track, and the increasingly feverish chugging of the engine as they pulled away from the station.

Amelia sighed. Their journey into the unknown had begun—in more ways than one.

CHAPTER 3

If this was to be his lot in life, then Clarence Himes had absolutely nothing to fear from eternal damnation in the afterlife.

All those years hearing talk of hellfire and brimstone on a Sunday morning, the vicar preaching that a life of sin and misdemeanour would lead to condemnation and torment in the next life–at no point had the young Clarence imagined the waking Hell he might first be forced to endure as a working adult. None of it had prepared him for this.

He slumped against the door frame, mopping his brow with the filthy sleeve of his overalls. It was unbearably hot, and the work was relentless, feeding the insatiable machine with enough fuel to keep the boiler going, to continue driving several tons of engine, carriage, passenger, and needless, ostentatious junk halfway around the world.

He blinked away the sweat running into his eyes. Not only was it hot, but the boiler room was dirty, confined, and stank. How had he ended up here, hurtling across France in a grimy sweatbox, all for the sake of a pittance?

And then there was the work itself–well, he knew there had to be consequences. What they were doing, it was just plain wrong, no matter which way you looked at it. Somehow, it was all going to come back to haunt him. He knew it, with the same sort of certainty and conviction that evangelical vicar had shown all those years ago.

From across the other side of the compartment Clarence's comrade in arms, Henry Sitton, grinned at him inanely, his face under-lit by the bright amber glow of the furnace. Sitton's eyes were lost in shadowy relief, and his smile seemed to take on something of a sinister aspect. "Nearly time for elevenses," he said, patting the front of his overalls. "I'm near famished."

Clarence made an appalled face. "I don't know how you can eat anything in here, let alone cook it on a skillet over *that*." He emphasised the last word with a wave of his hand toward the furnace. "It's not right, Henry."

Sitton grinned wolfishly, like a child enjoying the effect of his outrageous behaviour. "What harm can it do, eh? It's just a couple of sausages and a few rashers of bacon. You need to keep your strength up on a journey like this. Mark my words, you'll soon be wishing you'd listened to me. I've done this trip before, remember." Sitton clapped his hands together, but the thick leather gloves he was wearing deadened the sound.

Clarence shook his head. "You can count me out," he said, grimacing as he watched Sitton slide his gloves off and pull a shovel from the bucket beside the fire. He reached for the little parcel he'd stashed earlier in the cubbyhole where they stored their personal effects, and began hungrily unwrapping the waxy paper.

"I don't see why you can't just make up some sandwiches like everyone else," said Clarence, watching, fascinated, as Sitton carefully arranged three rashers of bacon and two sausages on the filthy shovel. "You could eat them in your bunk, instead of in here, surrounded by all that." He nodded at the heap of fuel in the corner, suppressing a shudder.

Sitton shrugged. "It burns just as well as anything else," he said, nonchalantly. He wiped his hands on his overalls, smearing grease and soot, and then slid the shovel into the furnace. Almost immediately, the sausages began to hiss and spit.

Clarence decided he needed to change the subject. "So, if you've done this trip before, you've already been to St. Petersburg. Tell me, is it true what they say?"

Sitton laughed. "And what is it they say, Clarence?" He smirked ungraciously, as if amused by Clarence's apparent naïveté.

Clarence felt his cheeks flush. "Well," he said. "You know. There are stories. They say it's not at all like London, that there are enormous palaces carved from the very ice itself, and frost-fingered sprites that come for your children in the night. That the city guard ride the streets on bears instead of horses, and that weird mechanical birds drift over the rooftops, spying on the people below."

Sitton shrugged. "I wouldn't know about any of that," he said, "but you're right on one count. It ain't nothing like London, that's for sure. Frigid cold and full of stinking foreigners." He slid the shovel from the fire, examined the blackening stumps of his sausages, and returned it to the flames. "My advice to you, Clarence, is to do as I do and mind your own business. Stay on the train and keep your head down. It only takes them a day or so to turn everything around and replenish all the stocks for the journey home. Why risk venturing out? Even if it was true, I can't imagine why you'd want to see it. The only thing you'll find in a place like that is trouble, mark my words."

Clarence nodded, as if acknowledging the sage advice of the other man, but his heart wasn't in it. He'd keep his own counsel. He'd heard all manner of fascinating tales about St. Petersburg, with its frost-limned minarets, shimmering palaces, colourful bazaars, strange creatures, and even stranger people. He was damned if he was going to work his way halfway across the world only to sit in his tiny bunk and pass up the opportunity to take in the sights. A day wasn't long, but it was something. It was *his,* and he would use it to explore. The thought of that day was the only thing keeping him going; the promise of a brief respite, and a break from the dreadful monotony of his labour.

Sitton was over by the furnace again, retrieving his makeshift meal. To Clarence, it looked decidedly burnt, but then he couldn't even conceive of wanting to eat it. Not there, in *that* room, with *that* smell. Even the thought of it was enough to make his stomach heave.

"Do me a favour, Clarence, and throw another one on the fire, would you?" said Sitton, around a mouthful of bacon. "It's looking a bit low." He smiled, showing his teeth, which were mottled with little flecks of burnt meat. "I'd do it myself, but…" He trailed off, shoving another mouthful in. It was obscene, and Clarence resented being treated like an underling. Nevertheless, he supposed he didn't really have a choice, not if he wanted to keep the peace. There were countless days left of this journey, and he'd have plenty more shifts alongside Sitton. They'd have to work together in this confined space. It wouldn't do to fall out or make things difficult.

Gritting his teeth, Clarence pulled his scarf up to cover his mouth and yanked his gloves from the hook on the wall. They resisted for a moment, caught on the brass peg, but came away when he gave them a second sharp tug. Turning his back on Sitton, he thrust his hands into the soft, worn leather, pulling each one right up to the elbow. Then, with a heavy heart, he approached the heaped stack of fuel in the corner.

Flies were buzzing around the mouldering carcasses, and he waved at them ineffectually in disgust. He swallowed, but his mouth was dry. This was always the worst bit, handling it, and he fought back the bile rising in his gullet.

He reached down and grabbed the nearest hunk of bone,

hefting it from the pile. Decaying flesh still clung to it in trailing ribbons, and the scent was thick and cloying. He averted his gaze so that he didn't have to look at it.

He turned and staggered over to the furnace, stepping around Sitton, who was still scooping the last of the bacon from the shovel. As he swung his arms back to toss the hunk of carcass into the furnace, he felt a sharp prick in the palm of his left hand, and let out a hiss of pain. He dropped the misshapen lump of fuel into the flames and stepped back, not daring to look down at his hand. If the glove had torn...

His palm was throbbing. He looked over at Sitton, who didn't seem to be paying him any attention. Bracing himself, Clarence glanced down at his glove. There was a long gash in the leather, probably torn when he'd wrenched it from the hook. There, in the palm of his hand, was an angry scratch about an inch long. Blood had swelled to the surface, causing a line of shiny, irregular beads. The soft flesh was puckered and raised.

His heart felt like it was thudding against his rib cage. He thought he might swoon in panic. The heat suddenly seemed unbearable. What was he going to do? What if he ended up like one of *them*? There was still a chance, of course, that nothing would come of it. He tried to regulate his breathing. It was just a scratch. Nothing but a little scratch, just like every other cut or graze he'd ever had. In a day or two it would be as if nothing had ever happened. It had to be.

"You all right?" asked Sitton, and Clarence turned to see the other man staring at him with a quizzical expression.

"Yes, fine," blurted Clarence, surreptitiously hiding his left hand behind his back. It wouldn't do to let Sitton know what had happened. "I'm absolutely fine."

"You look as white as a sheet. I told you, you should have had some of those sausages." Sitton's expression softened. He crossed to stand before Clarence. "Listen, you'll soon get used to it. Give it a few days and you'll think nothing of it. They're just hunks of gristle and bone, after all. What else is to be done with them? All this death, it's a terrible waste, of course it is, but at least we're putting it to good use." He sounded as if he was trying to convince himself. He patted Clarence on the shoulder. "Now, why don't you go and get a little fresh air? I can manage here for a while."

Clarence nodded. "Thank you, Henry," he said. "I just need a moment. I'll return shortly."

"Mind that you do," replied Sitton.

Clarence opened the door to the vestibule and slipped through, closing it behind him. Away from the roar of the furnace, the clean, cool air was immediately refreshing, but he felt little sense of relief.

The sting of the scratch in his palm had long since passed, but now there was a different pain—a tight, twisted knot in his stomach. It was a familiar sensation: fear.

CHAPTER 4

The blade cut, smooth and sharp, parting pale, unblemished flesh.

Glossy blood swelled to the surface as the incision spread across his left breast in a straight, purposeful line. He watched with detached fascination, knowing that in a matter of moments sensation would follow—pain would blossom and, for a few seconds at least, it would consume him in its exquisite embrace.

He exhaled slowly, flushed with anticipation. He welcomed the cleansing pain, the purity of it. It came upon him like a wave, rising until it was almost unbearable, until it filled him utterly. He revelled in it, gritting his teeth and trembling, closing his eyes and throwing back his head, his arms outstretched. He wanted to scream, to cry out in ecstatic prayer, but circumstances dictated he could not. Anything that brought undue attention would be a distraction from his goal.

His breath came in ragged gasps. He felt the warmth of his own blood trickling over his body, spattering onto the tiled floor—splashes of crimson against the pearly white porcelain; obscene, vital.

The pain receded and the moment passed. His hands dropped to his sides. He open his eyes, was appalled by the sudden, stark mundanity of his surroundings, the drabness of the compartment. It was as if the intensity of the past few moments had somehow bleached the world of all its vitality.

He glanced down at the knife, still clutched in his left fist. He turned it over, examining the polished ivory blade, now slick with a dark and violent red. His lifeblood trickled through the intricately etched channels inscribed on its surface, highlighting them slowly as the fluid ran; whorls and eddies describing visions of Hell, of minutely carved parapets and towers sprouting like fingers from an endless sea of flame, of angels and demons battling for supremacy, locked in an eternal stalemate.

The bone seemed to draw the blood into itself, channelling the fluid as it picked out each of the tiny details in its surface, slaking its thirst, feeding.

The blade had been carved from a splinter of human femur, sometime in the distant past, long before the forging of the world. So the tale had been laid out for him by his masters: that the Horned Beast himself had fashioned the weapon from the thigh bone of Adam, in the youthful days of the human realm, when Heaven and Hell were already ancient beyond imagining and all battles had already been lost and won.

Humanity, he knew, was nought but the plaything of Gods: a simple pawn in the great game of the universe. All he and his brothers could do was hope and strive for an echo of that greatness, to do the bidding of the Master in the hope that one day they might help to turn the tide of the war and shatter that eternal stalemate. They were good for nothing else; all else was sin.

He lowered the blade, placing it reverentially on the ground before him. Everything was silent but the gentle creaking of the carriage as it rocked back and forth, the distant sighing of the engine. In the confined space of his cabin, he could almost believe he was at the very centre of the universe, communing with the Master himself.

There was, however, work to be done. The Keeper reached for a fresh cotton handkerchief that he had placed on the tiles during his preparation rites, and dabbed at the wound in his chest, removing the sticky blood that had already begun to coagulate around it. He ignored the pain—he had done this so many times before that he had become well accustomed to it. His body was covered in ropey, silvery scars; a map of his pain and worship. That was the role of the Keeper: to feed the blade, if not through the blood of others, then through the sacrifice of his own.

Tonight, he had given it but a taste of what was to come. The moment of revenge was almost upon them.

Soon he would retrieve what was rightfully theirs, what the nonbeliever had taken from them. Even now, he could hear the echo of his brother's instructions:

"Pick your moment well, Keeper, and then strike without mercy. Retrieve what has been lost, and do not suffer the thief to live. Ensure he pays for what he has inflicted upon us."

This, the Keeper knew, was how it should be. That payment would not come only as death, but in the utter deconstruction of the man and his sanity. Plans had already been laid, victims carefully selected.

Within hours it would begin. The blade had needs, and the Keeper would tend them well.

CHAPTER 5

"Ah, good morning, Miss Hobbes. Come in. Find a seat. You'll have to forgive me for a moment…" Bainbridge trailed off, distracted. He hadn't even looked up at the sound of her knocking, presumably ascertaining the nature of his caller by virtue of her distinctive, polite cough.

He was standing, hunched over his desk, his palms splayed on the worn leather writing surface. He appeared to be studying a fan of yellowing newspaper clippings and what Veronica took to be recent typescripts of police reports. His brow was furrowed, so that his bushy, greying eyebrows were knitted together across the bridge of his nose. The worry lines on his face appeared deep and well worn; crevices in an ancient, stoic, rock face.

He was brooding, she decided, irritated by something he'd read.

Dutifully, she did as he'd suggested, closing the door behind her as she entered his office. It was a disconcerting sort of place, devoid of personal effects, save for a small portrait of Bainbridge's late wife, Isobel, in a gilt-edged frame on the desk. Veronica had visited Bainbridge here many times before, and it never failed to astound her how unlike Newbury he was in his habits. For a start, his papers were all filed neatly in a lacquered walnut cabinet in one corner, rather than heaped idly upon the carpet. Surfaces were uncluttered by needless trinkets and esoteric junk, and there were no discarded plates, crockery, or wine bottles slowly mouldering away in the corners. Nor was there a constant fug of sweet-smelling smoke hanging over everything like a smothering blanket.

No, what Bainbridge's office lacked was personality, character. The same critique could not be levelled at the man himself, of course—Veronica found him as pleasant and infuriating a man as she had ever known—but something about the room made it feel devoid of life. It wasn't *lived* in.

Perhaps, she considered, that was the lot of a policeman, the only way to retain a sense of perspective, to avoid everything being coloured by the dreadful things they saw. Perhaps Bainbridge needed to keep the place empty, soulless, in order to draw a separation between this, his life as a chief inspector, and his real life as a man.

Or, she considered, dropping into a chair beside the cold hearth, perhaps he was simply too busy.

He emitted a heavy sigh. "Forgive me," he repeated, wearily, as if he knew the apology was redundant, but felt the need to say it anyway. He looked over, smiling warmly. "You look well."

The compliment was welcome, but Veronica didn't feel she could return it. He looked tired and beaten down. Diplomatically, she steered the conversation in a different direction. "Is there anything I can do?" she said, inclining her head to indicate the stack of papers he'd been reading.

Bainbridge gave an exasperated shrug. "Two reports of missing nurses in St. Giles, amongst other things. Just trying to make sense of them. Something's not right, not adding up."

"Go on," prompted Veronica. "Tell me."

He seemed to weigh up the idea for a moment before continuing. "The circumstances are almost identical. Both women had recently taken on extra shifts at a new hospital, well-paid evening work in addition to their other positions. Both of them went to work last Tuesday and never returned home. Neither has been heard from since."

"So they've been missing for over a week?" said Veronica, surprised. That didn't bode well. But then, these things rarely did. "Have you enquired at this new hospital where they worked?" she asked, realising immediately that it would, of course, have been the first place Bainbridge's men would have looked.

Bainbridge shook his head. "That's just it. We can't find the place. No one seems to know exactly where it is. Even the women's families are unsure, and we can't find any record of a new institution in the area. All we have is the half-remembered name of their employer, a Dr. J. Reynolds, or Renfrew. Something like that. It seems as if the whole operation was very secretive, which only adds to my suspicion that something untoward has occurred."

"How odd," said Veronica. "I don't suppose there's very much you can do without further information."

"I fear not," said Bainbridge, frowning. He came around from behind his desk. "Damn infuriating."

"And the other things?" she prompted.

Bainbridge looked confused.

"You said 'amongst other things.'"

He gave a dismissive wave of his hand. "Oh, the usual business. I've been going over early newspaper reports of the plague revenants, seeing if I can't turn up another mention of this strange mutation we saw yesterday. I have to admit, Miss Hobbes, the whole thing has me feeling rather unsettled."

"Everything about the revenants has me feeling unsettled," agreed Veronica. "Did you find anything? In the newspapers?"

Bainbridge shook his head. "No. Nothing. There's no

mention of anything even closely resembling the monstrous cadaver we saw yesterday."

"And Dr. Finnegan? Has he reported on his findings?" she asked.

"Not yet," replied Bainbridge. He looked around, reaching for his cane, which was propped against the edge of his chair. "But he should be expecting us. If you've the stomach for it, his laboratory is in the basement."

Groaning inwardly, Veronica stood. It wasn't a question of whether she had the stomach for it—she knew that she did—but all the same, it didn't mean she particularly relished the idea of spending more time in the vicinity of the ghastly corpse. "Very well, Sir Charles," she said, placing a hand on his arm and trying to sound enthusiastic. "Lead on!"

The passages in the basement were functional and stark, and felt almost abandoned compared to the hustle and bustle of the upper floors where Bainbridge's office was located. Down here, amongst the winding corridors, it would be a simple matter to lose oneself without happening upon another soul for days on end. Veronica considered this as she hurriedly followed Bainbridge, intent on remaining close to him as he navigated through the warren. Every corridor looked the same: vast stretches of glazed brown tiles covering the walls and ceiling, punctuated only by the occasional locked door or dimly glowing lamp fitting. Underfoot, terra-cotta tiles caused every step to ring out like a gunshot. She was amazed that Bainbridge could tell where he was going, but he was like a sniffer dog, following a trail.

"Finnegan's laboratory is just around this next bend," he huffed, a little out of breath. His voice seemed amplified by the echoing tunnels. "He likes the solitude down here, hiding amongst the storerooms and archives. Hopefully he'll be able to shed some further—" He stopped abruptly, peering at something on the ground a few feet ahead of him.

"What is it?" asked Veronica, as she was forced to lurch awkwardly to one side to avoid a collision. She leaned against the wall to steady herself. The tiles were cool and smooth beneath her palm.

"Over there," he said, pointing with his cane.

At first she couldn't discern what it was that had caught his attention, but then a small section of the wall seemed to move, and with a start she realised it was Finnegan's ferret, Barnabas, slinking along against the tiles, almost hidden in the shadows. Bainbridge tapped his cane on the ground, three times in quick succession, and the creature jumped skittishly, gambolling off along the passageway in the opposite direction. Its little claws scratched at the terra-cotta as it ran.

"You startled the poor thing!" said Veronica, admonishingly. "Now Dr. Finnegan will have his work cut out finding it again in these dreadful tunnels."

"Hmmm," mumbled Bainbridge. He looked thoughtful.

"You're worried," said Veronica, reading his expression.

"It's just…" He paused, finding his words. "Well, Finnegan never lets that thing out of his sight. I've never known him to let it run loose around the basement before."

"Perhaps he's so engrossed in his work that he hasn't noticed," suggested Veronica.

Bainbridge nodded, but didn't look convinced. "Come on," he said. "The laboratory is just down here." He indicated the way with a wave of his hand. Veronica glanced after the ferret, but it had disappeared from view, probably holing up in some dusty crevice, waiting for them to leave. With a feeling of mounting trepidation, she followed on.

A hundred yards further along the passage, the door to the laboratory was ajar. It was identical to the many others they had passed as they'd traversed the fusty passages—a dark, mahogany frame with two tall glass insets—only this one also bore a small brass nameplate reading: Dr. Owen Finnegan.

The overbearing stench emanating from inside was acidic and chemical, burning the back of Veronica's throat, but beneath it she detected the rich, pungent odour of rotting flesh. She wrinkled her nose and gave an involuntary cough, cupping her hands around her mouth.

"Finnegan?" boomed Bainbridge, pushing the door aside with his cane. He strode in, full of bluster. "Where are you, man?"

There was no reply. Veronica followed Bainbridge through the door, peering around at the gloomy laboratory. The far wall was decorated with rows of mahogany shelves, each lined with dusty specimen jars, their grisly contents suspended in pretty, colourful liquids. Nearby, a metal trolley bore ceramic pots filled with scalpels and other, ferocious-looking medical tools. Some of them were grimy with old blood.

The corpse of the revenant was spread out upon a wooden table to her left, and it was clear that Finnegan had been busily conducting an autopsy upon it. The chest had been cracked open and prised apart with a brass clamp, revealing what remained of the victim's heart and lungs, now dry and shrivelled like desiccated fruit. The organs were misshapen with yet more of the pink, fungus-like growths.

The vines that spilled haphazardly from the ruptured throat and belly had grown since the previous day, pouring over the edge of the table and cascading to the floor, where they fanned out across the tiles, glistening as if still damp from the rain. Veronica shuddered and took a step back from the trailing growths.

To her right, Finnegan stood with his back to them, his shoulders hunched as he peered at something under his microscope. He was still wearing his heavy coat from the day before.

"Ah, there you are," said Bainbridge. "Stop ignoring me and

get over here. I need you to tell me what the devil's going on."

Once again, there was no response from Finnegan. If he was even aware of their presence, he didn't acknowledge it.

Veronica glanced at Bainbridge, and she caught a glimpse of uncertainty in his eyes. An eerie silence settled over the two of them, a mutual understanding that something was awry.

"Dr. Finnegan?" said Veronica, tentatively. Her heart was hammering in her chest. Why wouldn't he turn around and greet them?

Nothing.

"Answer her, man!" said Bainbridge, feigning annoyance, but Veronica could hear the tremor in his voice.

Slowly, she crossed the room, circling around the end of Finnegan's workbench. Bainbridge watched her, concern wrinkling his brow, as if in premonition of what she might discover.

"Dr. Finnega–" She broke off, startled. "Oh, no..." She stumbled back, upsetting another trolley and sending implements clattering noisily to the floor.

"What?" said Bainbridge, rushing to her side. "What is it?"

She raised her hand, pointing her finger shakily at what remained of Dr. Owen Finnegan. Bainbridge turned his head to follow her gaze, and seemed to freeze on the spot, his hand gripping her upper arm.

Finnegan's face was frozen in shock. His eyes were glazed and staring, boring directly into Veronica, accusatory and afraid. His mouth was open in a silent, nightmarish scream. His lips had blackened and cracked, and dark blood had spilled over his chin, dripping onto the microscope below. Strange growths erupted from deep inside his throat, as if he was in the process of vomiting up a thick bundle of vines and had somehow been frozen in the act, caught in a moment of time. The vines were identical to those growing out of the revenant corpse.

Finnegan's hands rested on the workbench, turned palm up in a pleading or placatory fashion. More of the vines had burst from the soft flesh of his wrists, writhing out across the smooth wooden surface. Some of them appeared to have burrowed down into the pitted oak, taking root.

New green shoots were just beginning to worm their way out through the man's distended belly, poking out through the flesh and clothes as if searching for sunlight and sustenance.

"Good God!" bellowed Bainbridge, swinging her around behind him protectively. "Quickly, cover your face," he said, burying his own mouth and nose in the crook of his arm. Veronica fished in her pocket for her handkerchief and did as he said, holding it firmly over her lower face. It did little to quell the insistent urge to vomit. "Right, out of here, now," he went on, his voice muffled by his jacket. "Get out of here, and don't stop until we've cleared the basement."

"You'll have to show me the way," countered Veronica, unable to recall the circuitous route that had led them here.

Bainbridge nodded and released his grip on her arm. He pushed past her and made for the door, pausing only to ensure she was following.

Breathlessly, Veronica charged after him, keeping the handkerchief pressed firmly over her face. By the time they'd reached the top of the second flight of stairs, she felt dizzy from the sudden burst of energy and the hot, stifling press of the cotton over her mouth. She removed it, bunching it up and dabbing at her forehead with it instead.

She paused on the stairwell, looking up at Bainbridge who, red-faced with exertion, had come to rest on the small landing. He was leaning on the handrail, his face glossy with sweat. Behind him, double doors led back into the office and the main reception area.

"What is that thing?" he said, between panting breaths. The question was obviously rhetorical.

"The speed of it," said Veronica, horrified. "It's utterly consumed him."

"It's spread, infected him. It must have happened when he cut into one of the growths." Bainbridge frowned.

"What are we going to do?" asked Veronica.

"Destroy them," replied Bainbridge, decisively. "Isolate the basement. Get masked men down there to remove the bodies, and then burn whatever they find."

"But what about the evidence?"

"Damn the evidence!" snapped Bainbridge. "Lives are at stake, Miss Hobbes. I cannot risk any more people succumbing to that… that… *whatever* it is!"

"You're right," she said. "Of course, you're right." She climbed the last few steps, placed a hand on Bainbridge's shoulder. "Go on, see to it. Do it now. I can find my own way out."

Bainbridge nodded, duty clearly taking precedence over social propriety. "I'll call on you later, Miss Hobbes, with any news."

"Very well." She stepped to one side and held open the door, and, with a grim smile, he walked through, striding off directly to gather his men.

For a moment Veronica watched him go, and then she allowed the door to swing shut behind her, heading out towards the Embankment and the inclement afternoon. She couldn't help turning over in her mind, however, the disturbing thought that, if the disease could spread that quickly, how many more people out there in London might be unwittingly walking about infected–herself and Bainbridge included?

CHAPTER 6

❦

Amelia tucked her feet up beneath her and sunk back into the warm embrace of the armchair. The gentle rocking of the carriage, the fire in the grate, and the flickering glow of the candlelight were having a soporific effect upon her; she felt her head nodding and her eyelids trying to close, despite the early hour.

She was sitting in the room she shared with Newbury, which conjoined their two cabins. She could barely believe they were hurtling across the wilds of France—for all practical purposes she might well have been back in Malbury Cross, curled up before the fire. Her surroundings felt safe and familiar—boringly so.

Opposite her, Newbury was slouched in another armchair. His face was drawn and pale, his eyes closed, his breathing shallow. Around him lay the assorted paraphernalia of the healing ritual, which he had performed upon her just a short while earlier. Consequently, she was still feeling a little light-headed, and she had a gritty, metallic aftertaste in her mouth. Newbury, on the other hand, looked decidedly unwell, as if the enacting of the ritual had sapped all of his strength, and now there was nothing to do but sleep and recover.

On the floor before the hearth he'd laid out a fine linen

sheet, upon which he'd painstakingly transcribed the familiar concentric circles and arcane markings. Back at home, he would have scratched these out in chalk upon the bare floorboards, having rolled back the rug, but here on the train that was both impractical and dangerous; a porter happening across such evidence of occult practises might well raise an alarm and bring unwelcome questions. Amelia wasn't so naïve that she didn't understand what Newbury was doing for her, the risks he was taking. This way, the necessary components of the ritual could be folded away quickly and hidden from sight.

She supposed she was going to have to tidy them away soon. Newbury didn't appear to be in any fit state to do it. She felt a pang of guilt at the thought. He'd assured her, time and again, that the after-effects of the ritual were only temporary, but nevertheless, it pained her to know that she was responsible for his present condition, however fleeting. And she was beginning to think that it might not be as temporary as he would have her believe.

Incense still burned in a little wooden tray on the mantelpiece, pungent and floral, and the bowl that had held the vile-tasting concoction she had consumed was resting upon the coffee table. The book, bound in brown leather calfskin, lay open on the hearth, its contents as indecipherable to her today as the first time she had seen it. In it were contained all the instructions for the procedure that Newbury was performing, the ritual that was allowing her to be well again.

"Is there anything I can do for you, Sir Maurice?" she said quietly.

There was no response. Not even the flutter of an eyelid to acknowledge that she had spoken.

"Perhaps if I tidy these things away?"

This time, her question did elicit a response. He held up his right hand, palm forward, as if to say: no need, leave it, I'd rather do it myself.

Amelia sighed, unsure what else to say. She hated feeling useless. It was times like this that she longed for Veronica. Her sister would know just the right thing to do, to say.

She wondered whether it was best to stay with him until he recovered. That might take hours, and there was clearly very little she could do to assist him. He obviously needed sleep and rest.

She decided there was only one thing for it. She couldn't just sit there. There was so much outside of the cabin that she wanted to see. So much experience she'd missed. She would retreat to her room to freshen up, and then take a short walk to the observation lounge, just for half an hour. Then she would return and see if Newbury needed anything.

Quietly she got to her feet and slipped away. He would barely notice she was gone and, despite his instructions to the contrary, she was confident there was very little harm in stretching her legs and getting a proper measure of the rest of the carriage.

After leaving their sitting room—by way of stumbling in a rather undignified fashion into Newbury's cabin and out through the door—Amelia traversed the corridor back to the entrance lobby, rocking gently from side to side with the steady motion of the train.

A few people had clearly had a similar idea, and the lobby was sparsely populated with people milling about, smiling politely to one another and passing the time of day.

"Jolly impressive, what?" she heard a bewhiskered fellow say to a younger man who was leaning against the wrought iron window rail and peering out at the flitting landscape beyond. The younger man nodded in agreement without turning his head from the view.

". . . and that's just the sort of business I was hoping to

avoid," said a woman in a shrill voice, walking arm in arm with her coconspirator. The two women were coming directly toward Amelia, an oncoming whirlwind of blue silk and lace, and she ducked out of the way to let them pass, catching only a glimpse of their haughty expressions as they moved on down the passageway past Amelia and Newbury's own cabins.

Amelia drank it all in, reveling in the opportunity to witness such mundane but fascinating interactions. It had been so long—so many years—since she'd had the opportunity to watch people bustling about their normal lives. It seemed to her like another world, as if, for all of those long years spent holed up in institutions, surrounded by doctors and nurses, she'd simply been dreaming her way through life, unable to imagine the bright colours and sounds of the real world.

She really couldn't thank Newbury enough for bringing her here, away from the hospitals, from Malbury Cross. She knew that everything he and Veronica had done—faking her death, rescuing her from the Grayling Institute, hiding her away in that little village—had been for her own good, a form of liberation.But really she knew that the cottage, as sweet as it was, was still just another form of prison. Here, though, with Newbury, she had a chance to see the world beyond the windowpanes. Moreover—this was the world beyond London, beyond England and the Empire. This was a journey into the unknown.

Grinning, and filled with a burgeoning sense of adventure, Amelia crossed to the foot of the spiral staircase in the centre of the lobby. A small white plaque at the foot of the stairs suggested they led to the observation saloon on the upper floor, and she decided to try her luck.

She felt the carriage shudder as she mounted the first step and was forced to snatch at the iron railing to steady herself. She paused for a moment, waiting for the return of the familiar rocking motion, and then took the rest of the steps quickly, finding herself a trifle out of breath at the top.

The saloon was larger than she'd expected, and for a moment she remained at the top of the staircase, taking it all in. It was a huge, open gallery, as large as the carriage itself. The ceiling was polished steel, designed to give the appearance of a vaulted roof, and the walls were made from thick plated glass, lending the room an even airier, open feel. Mahogany armchairs, their seats covered in matching maroon velvet, were placed alongside the windows, and a number of them were occupied by other passengers, some sitting alone, others huddled in little cadres.

Beyond the train, Amelia could see the world flitting by as they roared through the countryside, past fields and tumbledown chateaus, lakes and scudding blue clouds. It was perfect.

She left her perch at the top of the stairs and crossed to one of the windows, searching out a seat.

The armchairs, she saw, were faded, the burgundy fabric wearing thin and pale in large, irregular patches. To Amelia, it seemed as if the many passengers who had come before her had each left something of themselves behind, tiny slivers of light that had brushed off on the fabric as they'd stood to leave. Over time, these patches had grown brighter and more evident as increasingly more people had each shed a little of themselves, so that now the seats appeared to shine with their own inner glow. Each chair told a story, cherishing that which had been unconsciously abandoned.

She knew it was nonsense, of course—in reality, it was simply that the fabric was worn where so many people had brushed against it—but the notion appealed to her, the thought that every soul who had travelled on the train before her had somehow enriched it by gifting a little fragment of themselves.

She chose an empty chair and settled by the window, glancing around at the other passengers.

A corpulent man in an ill-fitting black suit sat opposite her, surrounded by a haze of pungent cigar smoke. The offending object was clenched tightly between his teeth, jutting from his mouth like a stick clamped in the jaws of an angry bulldog. His chair was turned slightly towards the window, so that he was mostly in profile. The flesh of his face was liver-spotted and loose around the jowls. His hands were steepled upon his chest, and his eyes were closed, as if in contemplation. Despite his rather ungainly appearance, he nevertheless managed to look somehow stately, in a way that only the very rich can do.

Beside him sat an older lady, hunched over a novel, her pince-nez resting upon the end of her nose. Her head was wrapped in a paisley scarf, with just a fringe of tightly curled grey hair erupting from the front. Her shoulders were draped in a lilac cardigan, and she was wearing a look of intense concentration.

Further along the gallery, a young couple sat holding hands beneath an occasional table. They couldn't have been much older than Amelia—in their early twenties, perhaps—and the man kept glancing up furtively, as if he expected the girl's father to appear at any moment to offer his disapproval. For her part, the girl seemed utterly smitten, unable to take her eyes off him, constantly playing with her hair or touching the back of her neck. Amelia felt a momentary pang of envy; she could barely remember what it felt like to be in love.

She couldn't quite distinguish the other passengers, save for a pair of businessmen in black suits, discussing rather too loudly the terms of a deal they were hoping to carry out in St. Petersburg, and a slovenly looking fellow who, every few seconds, took another pinch of snuff from a tin on the arm of his chair. Amelia could see that his septum had almost completely disintegrated from overuse, and she had to resist pulling a disgusted expression when he turned to glower at her in return.

"Fascinating, isn't it?" said a whispered voice from behind her, and Amelia turned in her seat to see a woman standing over her shoulder, grinning down at her. She was pretty, in her mid-thirties, her auburn hair framing her face in a neat bob. She was wearing a floral-patterned dress in cream and pastel, pinched in at the waist.

"I'm sorry?" said Amelia, unsure if the woman had mistaken her for someone else.

"Watching people," said the woman in a conspiratorial whisper. "One of my favourite pastimes." She smiled. "I'm Petunia," she added. "Petunia Wren." She held out her hand and Amelia shook it. She smelled faintly of camphor. "May I join you?"

Amelia smiled welcomingly, glad for the company of another woman, and someone who had no idea of her history, her delicate constitution, or any of her other problems. Someone who would treat her normally, like any other woman of twenty. "Of course," she said, reaching over to the empty chair beside her and dragging it closer.

"Wonderful!" said Petunia. "Then we can do it together."

Amelia frowned. "Do what?"

"People watching, of course!"

"Oh, it's not as if I was spying on anyone, you know," said Amelia, suddenly horrified that she'd committed some sort of social faux pas. "It's just… well, it's my first time on a train like this and I–"

Petunia waved her quiet. "Oh, but it is *fun*," she said. "I like to imagine what they're really up to. Take her, for example." She nodded at the old lady reading the book. "What do you imagine she's reading?"

Amelia shrugged. "Perhaps it's all about gardening, or cookery or something."

Petunia grinned. "No, I think it's something much more racy. I bet it's a murder story. Or worse. Maybe it's one of those books you can only buy from under the counter, full of filthy stuff. Maybe she's looking for a thrill." She laughed wickedly.

Amelia felt her cheeks flush, scandalised, but couldn't help herself from giggling.

"Or what about those two," Petunia went on, indicating the young couple. "Runaways, I'd wager. Star-crossed lovers who didn't meet with their parents' approval. Look at the way he keeps glancing up, nervous that someone's going to recognise them. She's the daughter of a marquis, and he's the farmer's lad from the local village."

"Oh, you can't say that," said Amelia. "It has to be happier than that."

Petunia smiled, but said nothing. "And what about you?" she said, looking thoughtful, as if sizing Amelia up. "No, wait! I've got it. You're a runaway, too. You're travelling under an assumed name. You're a rich heiress who's fallen out with her family over a man, a dreadful scoundrel, and now you're fleeing to St. Petersburg to start a new life where nobody knows you."

Amelia laughed, although a little part of her cringed at the woman's guess that she was travelling under an assumed name. Could she know? Surely not. It was just a silly game. Amelia pushed the thought away. "I'm Constance," she said, smiling. "Constance Markham. And you're quite right, in every respect." She paused for moment. "Except about the scoundrel. He wasn't dreadful at all. He was really rather good at it."

Petunia let out a hoot of laughter that caused the rest of the passengers to turn and look at her. Amelia felt her cheeks flushing again under the scrutiny. "Oh, how marvellous," said Petunia, still laughing. "I'm so pleased I bumped into you, Constance. I can see we're going to be the best of friends."

CHAPTER 7

There was no denying it: Clarence Himes was feeling decidedly unwell.

He'd woken with a fever amongst a nest of drenched sheets, and all over his body his flesh prickled with an excruciating sensation that felt as if he were being jabbed by a thousand tiny needles. There was an uncomfortable hollow feeling in his belly, his eyes were hot and dry, and his left hand was throbbing incessantly.

He tumbled from his bunk, landing unsteadily on his feet. His head was swimming. He needed water. His tongue felt as if it were made of cracked leather, and try as he might, he couldn't swallow. When was the last time he'd had anything to drink? He couldn't remember. It was as if his memories were mired in treacle, slow and ponderous to recall.

Clarence tried to think what might be the matter with him.

It had to be a reaction to the heat, he reasoned, dehydration after spending so long toiling at the furnace. A long, cool drink of water would slake his thirst and revive him. His body was craving fluid, making him delirious. Getting to the washroom and scooping up handfuls of water was all he could think about. Until, that is, he felt another twinge of pain, glanced down at his left hand, and remembered.

The skin had swollen and puckered around the scratch on his palm, and thick, yellow pus was seeping from the wound. He sniffed at it and recoiled instantly from the smell. It reminded him of the putrid stench of the furnace room: rotten flesh and decay.

Gingerly, he prodded at the wound with the index finger of his other hand, and immediately regretted it, emitting a sharp howl of pain. His head spun, and he doubled over with an involuntary retch. He gasped for breath, catching hold of the edge of his bunk to prevent himself from toppling over.

Was this it, then? Was this the reason he was feeling so wretched? Had he managed to infect himself with something dreadful, something... terminal? He'd seen firsthand what this plague could do to people, how it *altered* them.

He couldn't allow himself to believe that was going to be his fate. No, he'd been right the first time, surely? He was dehydrated, perhaps even a little under the weather. Hadn't his wife, Jennifer, been suffering with a cold before he'd left for France?

Yes, that was it. He forced himself to take deep, steady breaths. That was the most likely explanation. Of course it was. A glass of water was all he needed. Then maybe another hour or so resting in his bunk. After that he'd be as right as rain and back on his feet in time for his next shift. He could manage with a bit of a thick head and a stuffy nose. They might even help him to ignore that awful stench of rotting meat, and even Sitton might leave him be.

Swaying unsteadily—surely it was just the motion of the train?—Clarence reached for his overalls and hurriedly dressed himself. He winced more than once as he caught his sore hand, or was forced to use it to do up buttons, but within a few moments he was ready. Or rather, he was adequately dressed in order to take a walk to the washroom at the end of the carriage without eliciting concern or indignation from the other passengers.

Still feeling woozy, but driven by a desire to prove himself right, Clarence stumbled to the door, opened it, and lurched out into the passageway. The carriage shook as it bounced over the tracks, and he steadied himself against the window frames as he walked.

He was sweating now, and could feel little beads of it forming around his hairline, trickling down his forehead and cheeks. He wiped at it with the back of his hand, and to his dismay saw that a substantial lock of his hair came away at the same time. He wiped it away on his overalls and carried on.

The passage was dark and mercifully empty, and he realised it must still have been early, perhaps three or four in the morning. He had just the vague impression of movement out the windows as they trundled on, of trees and bushes on the other side of the tracks. It would be a while yet before dawn. Once he'd had his drink—oh, how he needed that drink!—he'd be able to return to his bed and sleep off the unsettling queasiness, the irritating, prickling pain. The thought was encouraging and bolstered his spirit, and he pressed on, rocking back and forth with the motion of the train as he traversed the passage.

The other bunks he passed were all occupied, as far as he could tell, their doors shut tight as his fellow workers made the most of their few hours of rest. That was how it worked: Each of the service staff shared a bunk with their counterpart, and they took it in turns to sleep while the other worked. That way, there was always someone on hand to assist the passengers if required, or to keep the fire stoked, as the engine rumbled on through the night.

The washroom was located at the far end of the carriage, in a small vestibule area that was separated from the adjoining carriage by two narrow doors and a railing. Grateful to find it vacant, he went inside and bolted the door behind him.

It was a confined space, containing only a toilet, a vanity

unit housing a small sink, and a looking glass. Clarence didn't hesitate, and seconds later both taps were gushing water into the bowl. He cupped it in his hands, wincing at the pain from his wound, and brought them up to his lips, drinking thirstily.

The water was warm and stale, but it hardly mattered, and Clarence scooped handful after handful of it from the bowl, gulping it down to ease his burning throat. When, finally, he'd had enough, he splashed it over his face, too, drying it upon his sleeve.

Afterwards, almost hesitantly, he turned off the taps, stepped back, and regarded himself in the mirror. He almost recoiled in horror at the sight. He did not–*could* not–recognise the man staring back it him.

He looked like an apparition, a pale shadow of the man he had been. His flesh was pallid and his lips were pale and cracked. His eyes stared out from dark, bruised pits, and the whites had turned a sickly shade of yellow. His hair was lank, sweaty, and coming away in handfuls, and as he ran his fingers through it he saw that the fingernails of his right hand had split and were peeling away. Blood swelled from beneath them, dripping into the bowl of the sink.

Clarence gave a horrified, strangled gasp and staggered back from the mirror, crashing noisily into the wall behind him. How could this have happened so quickly? Was he dreaming? Was he trapped in a vivid, feverish nightmare?

He had to get back to bed, back to the safety of his bunk. He was so tired, so dizzy, so confused. If he could get some rest, maybe it would all seem better in the morning. He desperately needed to believe that. What other choice did he have?

Clarence slid the door bolt, studiously ignoring the fact that the action caused one of his fingernails to drop off, and staggered out into the vestibule. He was startled to see another man was coming down the passageway towards him.

It was one of the passengers, a tall man with dark hair swept back from his forehead and a thin, unseemly scar across his jaw. He was dressed in a smart black suit, despite the hour, and was staring openly at Clarence.

Clarence ignored him, lowering his eyes and stepping to one side to make way. He expected the man to enter the washroom, but instead he opened the door to the adjoining carriage and stepped through without muttering a word. He left the door hanging open behind him.

Relieved, Clarence started back along the passageway towards his cabin. He would sleep. There was nothing else to be done. And besides, he was feeling so very tired.

CHAPTER 8

The Queen was in one of her intransigent moods; she wouldn't allow Veronica to get a word in edgeways. It was clear she'd already made up her mind concerning Newbury's lack of involvement in the present case—nothing Veronica could add would have the slightest effect on her opinion.

She was as animated as Veronica had ever seen her, hunched forward in her life-supporting chair in her audience chamber, a lantern clutched firmly in her lap. It gave her an even more sinister aspect than usual, Veronica decided, under-lighting her substantial chin and casting her face in stark relief. Her eyes reflected the glow of the lantern and seemed to shine menacingly as she glared up at Veronica.

"You are too forgiving of his inadequacies, Miss Hobbes," she rasped. "It is a weakness. We might almost believe that you have developed *feelings* for the man." She delivered the word with such disdain that Veronica almost flinched.

Did the old witch truly have such disregard for love, friendship, companionship? Had her experiences damaged her so badly that she could not bear to even conceive of other people's happiness? Perhaps, Veronica mused, in losing someone to whom you had been so close, the only way to survive was to cauterise the wound, to shut off your emotions altogether and step back from the world. It might be this, more than anything, which had turned this woman into the grotesque entity she had now become. Perhaps she deserved pity rather than disdain. Veronica was not sure she could bring herself to do that.

"Indeed not, Your Majesty," Veronica lied. "Merely the utmost respect for his abilities."

The Queen scoffed. "Come now, Miss Hobbes. We know that Newbury has his uses. Yet he also has his flaws. *We* are not blind to them, and nor are *you*. Need we remind you that it is our concern over those flaws that keeps you so gainfully employed?"

Veronica decided not to dignify that with an answer.

She saw the Queen's jaw tighten. "We shall not tolerate excuses. Where is he? Patronising another iniquitous Chinese den, no doubt?"

"He's in the North, Your Majesty, engaged in this 'Lady Arkwell' business," said Veronica.

"Ah, yes," cackled the Queen. "The 'other woman.' No wonder you're smarting."

Veronica couldn't deny it; there was a barb of truth in that. Newbury had dedicated himself to tracking Clarissa Karswell, the ubiquitous "Lady Arkwell," to the exclusion of almost all other concerns in recent months. Ever since she'd got the better of him during the land train incident–she'd drugged and tricked him in order to escape a crash in which they were both involved–he'd been obsessed with bringing her to justice. It was almost as if he felt he had something to prove. Or, as the Queen had so pointedly suggested, he was drawn to the woman for some *other* reason. Veronica had attempted to raise the matter with him, but he'd been dismissive, arguing that Karswell was a dangerous fugitive who must be apprehended, that they were locked in a tête-à-tête that he needed to see through.

To Newbury's credit, however, he had continued to visit Amelia with impressive regularity, and she was certainly benefiting from his ministrations. Veronica had no real reason to doubt his motives, and she would defend his reputation to the Queen, even if it meant incurring her wrath.

"You will continue to work with the policeman, then," said the Queen, coming to a decision, "while Newbury seeks the Arkwell woman. Discover the agency behind this new threat. Shut it down."

"Understood," said Veronica. It wasn't as if she had been planning to do anything else. "Will that be all?"

The Queen eyed her suspiciously. "One final matter. What of this Angelchrist character?"

"I've heard mention of his name, Your Majesty," said Veronica, surprised, "but I know little else. I believe he's an acquaintance of Sir Charles. A professor."

"It is your business to know these things, Miss Hobbes," said the Queen, with a hint of menace. "I understand he is involved in establishing a new government bureau. One that we believe will put our agency at risk. Make enquiries. Find out what the policeman knows. We fear he may be involved in clandestine affairs that might prove... *inappropriate* for him."

"Sir Charles?" said Veronica. She couldn't believe it for a moment. "I've assisted him in numerous matters of late, Your Majesty, and I assure you—"

"Enough!" barked the Queen, cutting her off. "More excuses. Know your place, girl. You are an agent of the Crown. *Our* agent. You will carry out our bidding, or you, too, will discover how little we tolerate traitors."

Veronica swallowed. She bunched her fists, and then forced herself to breathe. She felt utterly trapped. This woman— this *monster*—had her cornered. Ever since the business at the Grayling Institute, when it had become clear what the Queen was pursuing there, what she'd been doing to Amelia,

Veronica had wanted nothing more than to escape. She'd yet to fathom a means to do it, however, and as the Queen had so pointedly reminded her—she didn't tolerate traitors. Veronica would have to bide her time.

The Queen undoubtedly had other agents monitoring Newbury and Bainbridge—and probably Veronica herself. This, then, was a test. The Queen was watching for her response. "Without fail, Your Majesty," she said. "I shall uncover everything there is to know about Professor Angelchrist and the aforementioned bureau."

"And Sir Charles's role in the affair."

"Indeed," said Veronica.

"Good. Then there is nothing more to be said. You may leave." The Queen placed her lantern on her knees and, with a creak of its wooden rims, wheeled her chair back into the gloom.

Burning with anger, but nevertheless relieved her interview with the abhorrent woman was over, Veronica made hastily for the door.

CHAPTER 9

❧

Breakfast in the dining car proved to be a quiet, sombre affair. While Newbury was perfectly pleasant company, passing time politely with the other passengers, he did not seem his normal self. His talk was of Veronica, of the plans he was making for her welfare and the period of recovery that she would undoubtedly need following the replacement of her heart.

Amelia listened carefully, keen to contribute, but to her it all seemed so far away, like the edges of a map that had still to be drawn. She desperately hoped their mission would prove a success—she would do everything in her power to make it so. Newbury assured her they would return from St. Petersburg with a device that would bring new life to her sister, but it still seemed so remarkable, so tenuous, that she found herself unable to properly engage in his plans. There was a part of her that wanted to wait, to avoid thinking about the future until she was sure it could become a reality. She supposed Newbury had his own way of coming to terms with the situation.

At the same time, however, it gave her a great deal of comfort to know that he *was* making such plans, that he had such faith in the future. Veronica had always maintained that if there was something you wanted enough, you could find a way to make it happen. It was certainly clear that Newbury wanted this. She wondered how he would manage–how they would *all* manage–if they failed.

Their conversation continued in this vein throughout breakfast, and they lapsed into a companionable silence as they strolled back from the dining car a short while later.

Newbury paused at the door to his cabin–the single door they had been using to gain entry to their suite. He stood there for a moment, frowning.

"What is it?" said Amelia.

"Someone's been here," replied Newbury. He stooped to examine the lock, running his fingers around the frame. "We've had a visitor."

"How can you be so sure?" said Amelia. "The door is still locked."

"It's been opened," said Newbury. "It's not how I left it. Look here, there are scratches around the lock." He glanced up at her. "We should tread carefully."

Amelia could see nothing out of sorts. Perhaps it was Newbury's trained eye, but she couldn't help wondering if the stress of the last few weeks, the pressure he was putting himself under, was starting to take its toll. Was he seeing things that weren't there? Could it be paranoia? Whatever the case, she decided to follow his instructions carefully.

Newbury withdrew the key from his pocket, slid it into the lock, and turned it slowly and deliberately. He twisted the knob and pushed gently on the door. It swung open to reveal his cabin, which was now largely in disarray.

The bedclothes had been disturbed. The doors of the small wardrobe hung open. A drawer had been upturned on the floor, its contents rifled through.

Amelia expected him to rush to his belongings, to establish what was missing, but instead Newbury stepped over the detritus on the floor and went straight through to the sitting room. Amelia followed after him, pulling the cabin door shut behind her. When she saw what was waiting for them she issued a shrill scream.

"Shhh!" said Newbury, rushing to her side and pressing his hand over her mouth. "You'll bring the guards."

"I'm all right," said Amelia, pushing him away. "It was just the shock, that's all."

"Very well," said Newbury, with a curt nod. He stepped back, giving her room. She peered hesitantly over his shoulder.

The scene was like something derived from a nightmare and brought horribly, appallingly to life. A man of around thirty years of age lay slumped in one of the chairs—the very chair Amelia had been sitting in only an hour or so earlier—his head lolling so that his chin rested upon his chest. His eyes were closed, and his mouth was twisted in a snarl of pain that looked disturbingly like a sneer of amusement. His arms tumbled over the sides of the seat, his fingertips brushing the floor. His shirt—once crisp, starched white—had been savagely torn open, and his bared chest was a bloody, lacerated mess.

It was clear from a pink, puckered wound that a blade had been slipped carefully under his ribs, puncturing his heart. Dark blood had seeped from the wound, but there was far less of it than Amelia might have expected.

Newbury fished in his pocket for a moment and handed her the key. "Go and lock the door to my cabin."

She took it and did as he said, running back through, leaving the key in the lock and sliding the bolts.

When she returned a moment later, Newbury was stooped over the body. "It's a message," he said.

"A *message*?"

"Yes. Someone's carved something here, into the flesh." He indicated the dead man's chest with his finger. Amelia didn't really want to look, but couldn't help herself. A series of blood-smeared lines and circles had been carefully cut into the pale skin.

"What is it?"

"It's a symbol," said Newbury. "A circle with two horns. The sign of the Beast."

"You're not making any sense," said Amelia, with rising panic. It was only now starting to dawn on her what had really happened here. Someone had killed a man and left the body for them to find, here, in *her* armchair, in *their* suite.

"The Cabal," said Newbury. "It's a message from the Cabal. They're here on the train. We have something they want." She watched him put his fingers to the man's throat, searching for a pulse, but they both knew it was a redundant gesture. "He's been dead for hours," he said. "He wasn't killed in here. Whoever killed this man did it elsewhere on the train, probably during the night, and then took the opportunity of us eating breakfast together to pick the lock and plant the body here." He offered her a grim smile. "It's audacious, I'll give them that."

There was a loud rap at the door. Newbury looked up, and then glanced at Amelia.

"Hello?" said a gravelly voice from the other side of the door. "Hello? This is the train guard. We've had reports of a disturbance here. Please open the door."

Amelia stared at Newbury, wide-eyed. What were they going to do? Perhaps if they could just pretend they weren't there, the guard would go away.

Newbury put a finger to his lips, urging her to remain silent.

The guard tried the handle, and then muttered something indecipherable in French. Another voice replied.

"Monsieur Newbury. We know you're inside. I demand that you open the door. Serious allegations have been made."

Newbury dashed to the window, hauling up the sash. Cold wind gusted in, billowing the curtains. The noise of the train's wheels clattering on the tracks was deafening. He ran back to the corpse.

"Help me with the body," he said, in a hoarse whisper.

"Help you *what?*" she replied, in similar fashion.

"Move it!" Newbury hooked his hands under the dead man's armpits and began to drag him from the chair.

"What? No!" said Amelia, aghast. "You're not going to…" She looked to the window.

Newbury didn't answer, but just continued to haul the body from the chair. The dead man lolled forward, his fingers trailing on the rug.

"We should let the guards in," hissed Amelia, "explain to them what's happened."

Newbury fixed her with a hard stare. "No. Trust me. It would do little good."

"But…" Amelia barely knew what to say. She couldn't believe what Newbury was considering. She glanced at the door as the guards tried the handle again. They were raising their voices now, and she knew at any moment they were going to fetch a housekeeper's key and let themselves in. "Can't you just tell them you work for the Crown, protest our innocence?"

Newbury shook his head. He looked exasperated. "We're on a French train, halfway across Europe. Indeed, if they discover I work for the Queen, it could well serve as something of a red rag to a bull." He looked pleadingly at Amelia. "And besides, it would slow us down. There'd be questions. Ceaseless questions. Veronica can't wait that long."

Amelia considered for a moment, unsure what to do. Her instinct was to trust Newbury—it always was—but this was *murder,* and he was disposing of the evidence.

"Come *on*, Amelia!" he snapped.

Her instincts took over. She ran to his side, stooped down, and gathered up the dead man's feet. His muscles had already begun to stiffen, and he was cold. She felt her stomach knot. It was horribly disconcerting, and she tried not to look down as, together, she and Newbury staggered towards the window, the body hanging like a sack of potatoes between them.

The guards were still banging noisily on the door. "We know you're in there, Sir Maurice. We're going to force the door now."

Amelia felt panic surging. If they came in and caught them like *this* it would be even worse.

She looked to Newbury. His expression was calm. There wasn't even a hint of panic in his eyes.

Newbury heaved the dead man's head and shoulders up onto the windowsill, so that the head itself was dangling over the side of the train. Amelia peered out. The rush of air was dizzying. There was a grassy verge, and wild, untamed countryside stretched away into the distance. She supposed the body wouldn't be found for many days.

The door shook in the frame as one of the guards struck it with his shoulder.

"We can do this, Amelia," said Newbury. "Come on."

Allowing the windowsill to take some of the weight, Newbury began feeding the body up and out through the window.

The door shook again, and Amelia started at the sound of splintering wood. They'd be in within seconds.

One of the dead man's arms flopped unhelpfully, jamming in the frame, and Amelia had to abandon her hold on the feet and move forward, folding the errant limb across the bloody mess of the chest. She knew there and then that this moment was going to haunt her for the rest of her life.

Newbury gave a final shove, and the balance of weight transferred. The dead man slid from the window, crashing into the verge and tumbling away like a tossed rag doll. Within seconds he was lost from sight, left far behind them.

There was a crunch as the door gave way. Amelia felt

breathless. What were they going to do? What were they going to say? How could they possibly explain?

She glanced at Newbury, standing by the open window, and then, without thinking, rushed forward and threw her arms around him. She pulled him close and kissed him fiercely and deeply on the lips.

He started to back away, protesting, but she held on to him. "Kiss me!" she insisted, and the urgency in her voice must have made her point, because he relented a moment later, taking her in his arms as the men came piling into the room.

Still she held on to Newbury, cupping his face in her hands, drawing the moment out, ensuring every one of the guards had seen them. Then, calmly, she released him and stepped back.

Newbury turned to the guards. "What *is* this?" he demanded. He still held her tightly around the waist.

One of the guards, clearly the man in charge, was staring at them, a deep frown furrowing his brow. He looked utterly confused by the scene before him. "I... ah..." He looked at Amelia. "Are you quite well, madame? Only, we had reports of a violent disturbance and a scream."

Amelia bit her bottom lip demurely. "Oh, yes. I'm quite well, Inspector. Perhaps I just got rather... carried away." She let that hang for a moment. "Please, accept my apologies if I've wasted your time. There's certainly no *disturbance* here."

The guard glanced around the room, taking in the state of disarray. "No disturbance?"

Amelia shrugged. "A row over a lost trinket," she said. "We found it, and we were... making up."

"Now, if you'd kindly leave us to our privacy?" said Newbury, sternly.

The guard's face flushed a deep crimson. "Well, I can see that we were mistaken," he said, attempting to maintain his composure. Behind him, three other men stood sniggering.

Amelia knew they'd have a good laugh at her expense later, but didn't care.

"We'll be on our way, then," said the guard. "My sincerest apologies, Sir Maurice, but I must ask that next time, you please answer the door."

Newbury nodded. "I'd like to think there won't be a *next time*. I presume you'll be sending someone to fix the lock?"

"Directly, sir," said the guard. With a quick signal to his subordinates, he left, pulling the door to behind him.

Newbury expelled a long sigh, and released Amelia from his hold.

"I'm sorry," she said. "It seemed the only thing to do."

"No need," he mumbled, clearly embarrassed. The moment stretched.

She had a sudden, unexpected urge to do it again. She buried it.

A gust from the open window stirred her hair. "The body," she said. "Who would do such a thing? And why?"

"To discredit me," said Newbury. "To get me out of the way, tie me up with questions and police officers."

"Yes, but to what end?"

Newbury crossed to the window and pulled down the sash. The room felt suddenly quiet and still again. "Now that's the real question," he said. His expression darkened. "As I explained, I have enemies." He glanced around, and she followed his gaze. She hadn't noticed during all the excitement, but the room had clearly been searched. Their belongings were strewn everywhere, drawers left open, vases overturned.

"They were looking for something," she said.

"Yes," agreed Newbury. "And I can imagine what." He didn't seem to want to discuss it any further. Amelia decided to try a different tack.

"That poor man. What about his family?" she said.

"I'll ensure his body is found," said Newbury. "From Minsk or St. Petersburg I'll leave an anonymous tip, tell them I saw something fall from the train. They'll send people to investigate. By then he'll probably have been reported missing." Amelia could see he was clenching his right fist in frustration. He clearly wasn't as calm as he would have her believe. "I'll find his killer, too. I won't let them slow us down or prevent us from helping your sister."

"You mentioned a cabal," said Amelia. "Tell me."

"It's of little importance," said Newbury, dismissively.

Amelia wasn't having that. Not after she'd helped him tip a corpse out of the window. If he had any idea what was going on, she deserved to know. "*Tell me,*" she said.

Newbury stared at her for a moment, and she was sure she saw the hint of a smile on his lips. "Very well," he said. "The Cabal of the Horned Beast, a society who believe in the ridiculous notion that humankind should be remade in the Devil's image. They accumulate artefacts of occult interest, but have no real notion of how to make use of them. They concoct silly games and rituals, and believe that in performing them, they're setting the world back on the righteous path."

"You make them sound like harmless schoolboys," said Amelia.

"Schoolboys, perhaps," replied Newbury, "but far from harmless. Those games include ritual sacrifice and the remodelling of men into grotesque beasts."

"And they're here, on this train?"

"So someone would have me believe," said Newbury. "That symbol, on the dead man's chest—that was a warning. They've been following me for some time. It looks as if they might finally have caught up with me."

"Why should they come after *you*?"

"Revenge," said Newbury levelly.

"Revenge?" Amelia was confused. "Whatever have you

done to provoke such a monstrous response?"

"I took something from them," said Newbury. "Something they would very much like back."

"It must be something very important," said Amelia, doubtfully.

"It is," replied Newbury. "I'll show you." With evident reluctance he crossed to her armchair—or rather, the armchair she had previously adopted, and the one in which the corpse had been arranged. He pulled the seat cushion free and turned it over. Amelia watched inquisitively, grimacing at the oily bloodstains she could see on the cushion cover.

Newbury unzipped the leather cover, exposing the downy material within. Wearing a frown, he inserted his hand into the cushion, rooted around for a moment, and then smiled as he clearly found what he was looking for. Unable to help herself, Amelia stepped forward, standing by his shoulder to see. He pulled his hand free. In it, he was clutching a book.

Amelia gasped. It was an all-too-familiar book. *The* book. *The Cosmology of the Spirit,* the book containing the ritual Newbury was using to heal her.

"That's it?" she said. "That's where you got it from? You stole it from that cult? You did it for *me*?"

Newbury looked at her. "I did."

"Then you must return it to them," said Amelia, with urgency. "You must give them what they want and bring an end to the matter. If they're prepared to do this to a stranger on a train, just to make a point, then think about what they're prepared to do to you—to *us*—to retrieve the book. I won't allow it. I won't allow you to put yourself in that much danger for me."

Newbury gave a humourless laugh. "I fear it's far too late for that, Amelia. Now they're out for revenge, irrespective of whether they retrieve the book or not. I slighted them. Honour demands that I pay for my crime. And besides, why should I return it to them? They don't understand what they had, what it's for. In my hands, in helping you, this book can be a force for good. They would simply try to incorporate it into their silly rituals. I won't allow *that*." He made a point of pushing the book back into the cushion, zipping up the cover, and returning it to its place. It was, Amelia supposed, as good a hiding place as any.

"They're dangerous foes, Amelia," said Newbury, in a conciliatory tone. "I'll give them that much. We must remain vigilant. Nevertheless, I will not allow myself to be intimidated. There is a purpose to our journey, and I will not stand by and allow the petty concerns of a group of squabbling fools to delay us."

"Very well," said Amelia quietly. It was obvious there was no arguing with him. "I'm going to see to my room and ensure nothing is missing."

Newbury gave a curt nod, but his expression was brooding. He remained standing over the armchair, staring at the seat cushion and the dubious treasure it contained. "I'll stop them, Amelia," he said. "I will."

CHAPTER 10

The Natural History Museum was only a short walk from Veronica's Kensington home, and so, despite the inclement weather, she struck out on foot. She huddled beneath her umbrella as she walked, her head bowed, her chin tucked into the folds of her scarf to stave off the chill breeze.

The rain had been persistent through the night, and now, in the early morning light, the pavements shone, slick and mirrored.

Veronica hadn't visited the museum properly in years. She'd come once with Newbury to meet with the man she was now on her way there to see–Dr. John Farrowdene, a zoologist–but it had been over a decade since she'd last walked its expansive halls as a tourist.

As a child, Veronica had often visited the reptile gallery with Amelia, and together the two girls had conjured stories of the great saurian beasts whose skeletons now formed the rather staid and austere exhibits. The two sisters had breathed life into those dusty old bones, imagining a time when such wild monsters had roamed the earth, scandalising one another with tall tales of dinosaurs loose in London, feasting on their nanny or their teacher. Of course, back then she hadn't known the truth–that there really *were* monsters out there in the dark corners of the world, monsters that wore many different guises. Sometimes, she longed for a return to that childhood naïvety.

She looked up to see that her destination was upon her. Even in the dull light of a rain-slicked morning, the Natural History Museum was an impressive sight. The red brick building gave every impression of being a hallowed place, a cathedral raised to the glory of science. Veronica hurried up the steps, under the recessed archway, and through the main doors.

The entrance gallery was cavernous and empty, and reminded her of the nave of a large church. Deep alcoves lining the walls on either side contained glass display cases filled with wondrous things. From just inside the door she could see very little, save for the immense form of a preserved polar bear and the fossilised shell of an enormous armadillo. At the far end, a grand flight of steps promised further treasures on the upper floor.

Farrowdene was waiting for her, perched on the end of a wooden bench, observing her quietly. He stood when he saw her looking. He crossed the gallery, his footsteps echoing loudly in the otherwise empty hall.

"Good morning, Miss Hobbes," he said, extending his hand in greeting. He was a handsome man, in his mid-forties, with a ragged mop of a dark hair shot through with tiny bolts of grey. He had a healthy, tanned complexion and thin expressive lips, which described a tight but welcoming smile.

"Thank you for agreeing to see me," she said, "particularly on such short notice."

Farrowdene shrugged. "You are most welcome. I'm only glad to be of assistance." He grinned. "Did you wish to head straight to the workshop, or did you have it in mind to take a walk around the galleries while you were here? I'd be only too happy to accompany you."

Veronica smiled. "Alas, I fear that while the idea is most

enticing, I'm all business this morning, Doctor. While there are people dying, I'd like to do all I can to get to the bottom of the matter, as swiftly as possible. We'd better press on."

Farrowdene nodded. "Your dedication does you credit. Allow me to show you the way."

He led them through an archway and along a wide corridor filled with the fossilised remains of ancient sea creatures. Veronica shuddered at the sight of them; she had always found the thought of such things unnerving.

Farrowdene's workshop was, she recalled, far away from the prying eyes in the public galleries. Indeed, his position— and therefore the reason for his acquaintance with Newbury— was to collect, categorise, and research unusual, singular or otherwise inexplicable beasts or specimens. Inevitably, this meant he tended to end up assisting Newbury in matters of a sensitive nature, and much of Farrowdene's work remained secretive and undisclosed to the wider scientific world.

"I'm surprised Sir Maurice is not accompanying you this morning," said Farrowdene as they walked, an enquiring look in his eye.

"He is, unfortunately, otherwise engaged," said Veronica, deciding it best not to give too much away. She knew Farrowdene could be trusted, but all the same, she needn't disclose anything that wasn't pertinent to the enquiry at hand.

"And Sir Charles?" ventured Farrowdene.

"Likewise," said Veronica, "although he and I are working closely on this particular matter."

Farrowdene nodded, assimilating the information. "Yes, I gathered as much from Inspector Foulkes. It's a fascinating case. Terrible, but fascinating all the same." He glanced over his shoulder at her. "It was Inspector Foulkes who brought the... um... *specimen.*"

Veronica knew exactly what he was insinuating. She couldn't deny it—it helped to think of the poor man as a specimen, at least for the duration of this exercise.

They walked in silence for a few minutes.

"I believe you hold a post at our sister institute," said Farrowdene, pointedly changing the subject. "Assisting Sir Maurice in his anthropological work."

"Quite so, although I feel I've rather been neglecting it of late. Other duties have kept me somewhat... preoccupied."

Farrowdene laughed. "No need to be coy, Miss Hobbes. I know all about Sir Maurice's work for the Queen."

Yes, thought Veronica. *But not mine.* She smiled.

"Anyway, I'd imagine that most of those fusty old objets d'art have been around long enough that they can wait a little longer for your attention. Particularly when there are pressing matters such as this one," said Farrowdene.

"My thoughts exactly," agreed Veronica.

They'd come to the end of the gallery, where the skeleton of a massive, extinct elk had been arranged on a wooden plinth. Its antlers loomed over Veronica's head. Behind the long-dead beast was an oak door bearing a nondescript little plaque that read: private.

Farrowdene produced a hoop of keys from his belt. They jangled as he sifted through them until he found the correct one. He unlocked the door and pushed it open. "Through here," he said. "You're most privileged. This is the gallery that most people never get to see." He smiled brightly.

Intrigued, Veronica did as invited and went first through the door, drinking in her surroundings. The corridor here continued for at least another two hundred feet, although it narrowed significantly, partitioned off to make way for a series of offices or workshops on the right-hand side.

There were no exhibits on the walls here, save for a series of black-and-white engravings of yet more fossilised sea creatures.

"It's the first door on the right," said Farrowdene. "Please, go in." He locked the door behind him.

The door to the workshop was propped open, and Veronica went in, stifling a gasp of amazement as she took in the view on the other side. The room was so cluttered that she barely knew where to look first.

Glass cases had been aligned along one wall, and against another stood a row of mismatched wooden filing cabinets and specimen drawers. A workbench had been set up at the far end of the room, and on top of that, another large glass case, containing what looked like a sample of the revenant bloom. A young woman in a white coat, with thick, auburn hair tied back in a tight ponytail, was standing at a bench by the window, attending to a microscope slide. She didn't look up.

What was most astonishing to Veronica, however, was not the fact that this unseen workshop existed behind a locked door at the Natural History Museum, but rather the mysterious contents of the glass cases.

To her left, an enormous squid was suspended in a bubbling tank of water, its tentacles still writhing, pressing against the glass as if attempting to push itself free. Close by, the corpse of a bipedal lizard, with a narrow, sly face, and huge curved claws, was suspended in a tank of liquid preservative. It was almost as tall as she was, and covered in colourful, downy feathers.

She walked along the row of cases, peering in. Here, the remains of a human female, naked except for a thick pelt of soft grey hair; there, a fanged monkey with alarming red eyes and a mechanically reconstructed arm. Plague revenants, butterflies, birds with two heads, phosphorescent fish, insects as big as her forearm, a homunculus the size of a small child; this was a museum of the unknowable, the unviable, the bizarre. No wonder Newbury loved it here.

She looked up, and the specimens continued, stacked in rows, crowding every available space. Hanging from the ceiling were the dried and stuffed remains of a flying reptile with an enormous wingspan and a long, spear-like beak. It reminded her of the fossils she had seen out in the museum proper, but fresh and recently preserved, its flesh still leathery.

This was, clearly, the place where those specimens unfit to be seen by the public were preserved and studied. Farrowdene must have seen so much.

"Impressive, isn't it?" said Farrowdene, coming into the room behind her and reattaching the ring of keys to his belt. "Welcome to my gallery of imagined beasts."

"What *are* these things?" said Veronica.

"These are the things that aren't supposed to exist," said Farrowdene. "The nightmare creatures, the forgotten survivors, the failed experiments. This is where they find themselves, when people such as Sir Maurice, August Warlow or the museum's field teams turn them up. I'm lucky enough to be the one who gets to study them afterwards."

August Warlow. She'd not heard that name before. She filed it away for later recollection. "Fascinating," she said. Her eyes were flitting from one specimen to another, from the mundane—organs suspended in jars—to the utterly incredible—a bat-like creature with a disturbingly human face.

The woman—clearly Farrowdene's laboratory assistant, looked up from her work, smiled knowingly at Veronica, and then returned to her preparations without a word.

"This is Angela," said Farrowdene. "I couldn't do a thing without her." He pointed to the glass case at the other end of the gallery. "Right, then. If you'd like to come this way, I've been carrying out some tests on the specimen in question."

Veronica followed him across the gallery. She circled the case. Inside were the remains of a creature that had once been a man, now utterly consumed by the strange fungal growths that she had seen in both Stoke Newington and the laboratory beneath Scotland Yard. Here they seemed even more mutated, as if there was very little left of the host now, and the growths had continued to multiply after death.

"Is that... ?" she began.

"Yes," said Farrowdene. "I rather fear this is a sample of what's left of Dr. Finnegan."

Veronica choked back an appalled sob. "Shouldn't we be wearing masks?" she said, suddenly conscious of the threat.

Farrowdene shook his head. "Oh no, do not fear, Miss Hobbes. The case is hermetically sealed. You'll come to no harm here. Besides, it's only infectious if you disturb the spore pods and it becomes airborne."

"So what have you found?" said Veronica. "Anything at all that might be of use to us?"

Farrowdene looked pained. "Well... *perhaps.* It's utterly fascinating. I can tell you that the infection is definitely fungal in nature, although of what variety or species I'm unsure." He gave a resigned shrug. "I fear I'm more at home with the fauna of this world than the flora." He rubbed his chin absentmindedly. "It's clearly not native to the British Isles, however. I can tell you that much with confidence. If I were to hazard a guess, I'd suggest the Amazon, or the rain forests of Cameroon. One of those barely explored regions that's often so profitable for a man in my line of work."

"But why plague revenants?" said Veronica. "When we first encountered it, the spores had adopted a revenant as their host. Dr. Finnegan wasn't infected until he carried out some work on the corpse in his laboratory. How could a thing like that have come into contact with an unknown species of fungus from halfway around the world?"

"Ah, you see, that's the interesting thing," said Farrowdene, suddenly animated. "The fungus appears to have a remarkable effect upon its host. The first stage of the infestation appears to be *beneficial* to the host. I've experimented with rats." Veronica shuddered at the thought. "From what I can tell from my dissections, it appears the fungal spores actually begin to regenerate the host's cells, presumably to help ensure the survival of the host into the later stages of colonisation."

"*Regenerate?*" said Veronica. "In what sense?"

"In the sense that the revenant you found actually appeared to be healing."

"Goodness," said Veronica. "Then you're telling me it might represent a cure?"

"It might seem that way," said Farrowdene. "Of course, the second stage of the infestation is something else entirely. The fungus takes over. The regeneration is simply a function of the parasite's growth. It then spreads quickly and relentlessly throughout the host's entire body. In an already healthy subject we might be talking about minutes here, rather than days. The fungus works with whatever it's got."

"Surely you're not implying it's intelligent?" said Veronica.

"No, not in any sense that you or I would recognise," confirmed Farrowdene. "Simply that it requires certain conditions in order to flourish, and it does whatever it needs to do to the host body in order to ensure them. Then, once the fungus has established itself and reached maturation, it blooms."

"Like a flower opening in spring," said Veronica.

"Precisely that," agreed Farrowdene. "Erupting from the body to scatter its spoors in search of other potential hosts. It's a simple cycle, really, and it spreads exponentially."

"But that still doesn't explain how the revenant was initially exposed to the fungus," said Veronica.

"Quite," said Farrowdene, "not unless someone was experimenting with a possible cure."

"Of course!" said Veronica. "An experiment that's gone wrong. That makes sense. It just seems so unlikely that a revenant in Stoke Newington might chance upon such an exotic strain of fungus of its own accord."

"That would be my best guess," said Farrowdene, "although as I mentioned, I'm no expert, and you can't rule anything out. I suggest you take the advice of a botanist, someone who specialises in studying previously undiscovered species of plants. I can give you a few names if that helps?"

"A great deal," said Veronica.

"Well, Gilbert Evans, William Stilwell, or Julian Wren to begin with. Hopefully, one of them might be able to shed some further light, but I'd wager that's where it started– someone with the best of intentions, unaware of quite what they were setting loose."

"Thank you, Dr. Farrowdene," said Veronica. "You've been most helpful. I'll take this news directly to Sir Charles."

"You're most welcome, Miss Hobbes. Most welcome indeed. In fact," he lowered his voice, "if I might be so bold, it would be my honour to discuss the matter further with you, perhaps over dinner?"

Veronica felt her cheeks flush, hot and embarrassed. She tried to contain her grin. "Thank you for your kind invitation, but I fear I am previously engaged."

Farrowdene laughed cheerfully, although the disappointment was evident in his eyes. "I hope Sir Maurice knows how very lucky he is, Miss Hobbes."

Veronica raised a single eyebrow, but didn't reply.

Farrowdene looked somewhat discomposed. "Well, you must feel free to stay, have a look around," he said. "I can see you're fascinated by the specimens on display here."

Veronica glanced at Angela, who was grinning knowingly to herself as she set up her slide on the microscope, and sighed. It was true; she knew she could spend hours here, poking around amongst the strange exhibits, searching out the wondrous, unknowable creatures, but the case was pressing and called for her attention. "While I would dearly love to, Dr. Farrowdene, I feel the investigation must come first. If there's a means to contain this horror," she gestured to the malformed body in the glass case beside them, "then it must be found. I shall return to Scotland Yard forthwith." She put a hand on his upper arm. "My thanks to you."

Farrowdene inclined his head in acknowledgement. "Then allow me to walk you out," he said, with a broad grin. "At least I know you do not have a previous engagement for *that.*"

Veronica laughed. "How could I possibly refuse?" She took his proffered arm and allowed herself to be led away.

CHAPTER 11

It had been over an hour and a half since the scheduled shift change, and Henry Sitton was beginning to feel rather put upon.

Everything had occurred just as it should have, up to a point—Jeffries had returned to their shared cabin, woken him and exchanged places with him on the bunk. Henry, still bleary-eyed and stumbling toward the front of the train, had passed Cornwell in the vestibule, heading off to change shifts with Clarence. This had become their routine, and Henry found a certain comfort in it. He knew where he was, and what had to be done. He'd filled the kettle and placed it on the hot plate, ready for when Clarence arrived.

But then Clarence hadn't returned, and Henry had been forced to manage by himself for the past hour or so, building up the fire for the start of the shift.

When it became clear that Clarence wasn't simply running late, but wasn't going to turn up for his shift at all, Henry had heaped extra fuel into the furnace and had marched back here to Clarence and Cornwell's cabin to find out exactly what was going on.

As he'd stalked through the passenger carriages his indignation had grown. What was the lazy blighter playing at? They had a job to do, and Henry was damned if he was going to do twice as much work as he was paid to do. It wasn't as if *any* of them got enough sleep between shifts. Why should Clarence get away with bunking off?

He rapped loudly on the cabin door. "Clarence?"

There was no response.

"Clarence! Get up, you lazy beggar! You're needed. Your shift started an hour and a half ago."

Henry waited for the panicked response, the sound of Clarence scrambling from his bunk, suddenly surprised that he'd been allowed to oversleep. Where was Cornwell, though? Why hadn't he kicked Clarence out in the first place?

Henry leaned closer to the door so that his ear was nearly touching the panel. He could hear noises from inside—the shuffling sound of someone moving about. He waited a moment longer, but still no one came to the door. He knocked again. "I know you're in there, Clarence!" He could hear the agitation in his own voice. "I tell you what, I'm finishing the shift an hour and a half early today, and you can see how you like it."

There was more shuffling, but still no response.

"Look, I'm coming in there," said Henry. "I don't know what you think you're up to."

Angrily, Henry grabbed the handle. The door was unlocked, so he shoved it open and took a step forward over the threshold.

At first, the scene that presented itself was so alarming, so disturbing and unnatural, that his mind had trouble processing it. He had to do a double take. He stood there for a second or two in the doorway, as he tried to make sense of what he was seeing.

Clarence—or rather, some *thing* that had once been Clarence—hunched over the sprawled body of Cornwell on the cabin floor. Cornwell's belly had been viciously ripped open and one of Clarence's hands was ferreting around in the dead man's guts. There was blood everywhere: dripping from the bunk, smeared on the window, and forming syrupy puddles on the floor. Cornwell's face was stricken, his eyes wide open and mercifully lifeless. His mouth was locked open in a silent scream. Beads of blood flecked his pale cheeks.

Clarence, on the other hand, looked as if he had disinterred from his grave after three weeks in the ground. His flesh had taken on a strange translucency, and in some places had begun to sag and bloat–even peeling in loose flaps behind his left ear. His eyes were yellowed and sunken, and flitted nervously like those of an animal. His fingertips were bloodied, his nails grown long to form vicious-looking talons. Worst of all, Cornwell's blood was dribbling down his chin as he chewed on a length of the man's glistening intestine. There was no trace of humanity left in the creature. Clarence had become utterly feral. A revenant.

Henry took a step back into the passageway, coughing back on the cloying tang of spilt blood, the horrifying stench of faeces. He emitted a thin stream of vomit, unable to prevent it splashing over his boots. How had this happened? They always took precautions. How had Clarence been so careless? How could he have got himself infected? And Cornwell… Good God, what the hell was he going to do?

Perhaps if he backed up carefully, closed the door, and ran for help. Yes, that was it. He had to fetch the train guards.

Slowly, Henry edged back. He clutched shakily for the door handle, but couldn't find it. He glanced back at Clarence. His former colleague was watching him, beady yellow eyes tracking every movement, like a hunter tracking prey. Henry swallowed. His throat stung.

Which way should he run? He glanced left and right. Neither direction promised much help of cover. He would go the way he came, get into the next carriage and close the door behind him, tell the passengers to stay away while he fetched the guards.

Clarence was still resting on his haunches over Cornwell's

corpse. Surely Henry could outrun him…

He turned and bolted.

There was a sound behind him. He didn't look back, but he knew, with a horrible sense of dawning certainty, that Clarence had come after him. The creature's pounding footsteps were the only sound he could hear, coming up behind him, almost upon him. It was too fast, moving with preternatural speed.

The door was in sight. He just had to make it through. He extended his arm, reaching out for the handle, but he was too late. He felt Clarence's talons rake his shoulder, tearing right through the fabric of his boiler suit, drawing blood. He flinched, turning the handle, but there was no time. The creature's breath was hot on the back of his neck.

He struck out with his elbow, trying to shake it off, trying to buy himself time. He felt one of its ribs give. But then its teeth were in his flesh, biting deep and hard into his shoulder like a wild dog.

Henry screamed, trying to wrench himself away and almost swooning with the pain. Clarence's teeth were clamped on hard, rending his flesh. Blood spurted. He could feel its warmth running down his back and chest. This was it. There was nowhere else to run, nothing else to do.

The door hung open, but the pain was too much. Blackness limned the edges of his vision. Henry sunk to his knees, and the revenant let him fall. He pitched forward onto his face. The creature raised its head and issued a sound like none that should ever come from the throat of a human being.

All of Henry's strength was gone, and he lay there on the floor in a spreading pool of his own blood, watching the revenant step over him and through the open door into the next carriage.

The last thing he heard before darkness overcame him was the scream of fifty passengers, all running for their lives.

CHAPTER 12

Veronica unfolded the slip of crisp, white notepaper and stared again at the message scrawled upon it in Bainbridge's neat copperplate:

> **MISS HOBBES**
> ONE OF THE MISSING NURSES HAS BEEN LOCATED.
> MEET ME AT 12 BROWNLOW MEWS, CAMDEN, ONE
> O'CLOCK THIS AFTERNOON. YOUR ASSISTANCE IS
> VERY MUCH APPRECIATED.

It was signed with his usual flourish.

Veronica glanced up at the property in question, and frowned. It seemed like an insalubrious sort of place, both for a meeting with Sir Charles, and for a nurse. The woman couldn't possibly live there, Veronica decided, as she took in the cobbled street slick with mud, dirty rainwater, and God-only-knew what else. The buildings on both sides of the lane were dilapidated and largely given over to industry and merchants: a sign painter, a wheelwright, a builder's office. Their frontages, once brightly painted to attract custom, were now peeling and in dire need of attention, although—judging by the thunderous noises she could hear coming from the wheelwright's shop—they were still very much in use.

Above many of these establishments were upper storeys, with tall sash windows draped with dirty nets, denoting, Veronica presumed, small flats or living accommodation for the owners. From street level, the row of mews appeared to have flat or gently sloping roofs, peppered with narrow chimneystacks and wreathed in curling smoke and soot. Two wooden carts and a police carriage were parked up ahead, outside an unmarked building on her left. There was an acrid stink about the place, of oil, burning wood, and human waste.

"Oh well," she said aloud, folding the note and slipping it back into her coat pocket. "I suppose I should be used to it by now." She had been hoping for a slightly more congenial setting for the afternoon's activities, but then, on reflection, she should have known better.

Bainbridge's note had arrived just after breakfast, delivered to her house by a young constable who gave every impression of being generally disinterested with his lot. She'd opened the door to find him kicking the stone step with the edge of his boots like a restless child, and he'd muttered only the requisite number of words as he'd asked her to verify her identity before handing over the note. He hadn't even waited around long enough for her to read it before bidding her good day and retreating down the garden path, disappearing along the high street.

With Mrs. Grant away visiting her sister for a few days, and Newbury in the North chasing after ghosts, she had to admit—the idea of some company appealed to her. It had been two days since she'd heard from Bainbridge, and aside from her brief visit to the Natural History Museum, she'd found herself with little to occupy her time. So she'd dug out a warm cardigan, wrapped herself up against the rain, and set out for the day, with the intention of grabbing a spot of lunch in Camden Town before searching out the address in the letter. And now, standing on the corner of Brownlow Mews and

Roger Street, she couldn't help but wonder if she'd have been better off staying indoors.

Veronica felt a sputter of rain on her cheek, and a quick glance up at the sky told her that another downpour was imminent. With a sigh, she stepped over a brackish puddle and crossed to the door of the unmarked building, which she assumed to be the place to which Bainbridge had summoned her for their meeting with the aforementioned nurse.

There was no number on the door, no glass insets, and no knocker. From the drab exterior of the place, she found herself doubting that the building was inhabited at all. Shrugging, she removed her glove and rapped loudly.

A moment later she heard a bolt slide on the other side of the door, and then it swung open to reveal a short, plump woman in a scarlet silk gown. The woman's hair was pinned up in an elaborate whorl, and powdered in a style that had gone out of fashion at least a hundred years earlier. Her lips were a slash of glossy red, her eyelids an unsightly blue, and her face was stark and lily-white with paint. It wasn't at all what Veronica was expecting.

"We're closed, lovey," said the woman, in a broad, Scottish brogue. "The party's over." She stepped a little closer to Veronica, looking her up and down and pulling the door to behind her, so that they were both standing out on the step. "And to be honest with you, lassie," she continued, in a sepulchral whisper, "a respectable woman like you, you'd be best hotfooting it as far away from here as possible. The Peelers are inside," she gestured back over her shoulder with a nod of her head, "and I'm sure you don't want to go getting mixed up in all that. No one likes questions, eh?" She tapped the side of her nose conspiratorially with one finger.

Veronica frowned. "Actually, Miss… ?"

"*Madame* Gloria," replied the woman, placing a hand on her hip and jutting out her chin.

"Actually, Madame Gloria, that's precisely why I'm here. I'm with the police."

"With the police?" said the woman, utterly scandalised. "*You're* with the police?"

"In an manner of speaking," said Veronica, stifling a laugh. "I'd be very much obliged if you'd allow me to come in."

"Well, I don't suppose I've got much choice in the matter, do I?" said Madame Gloria, reluctantly stepping to one side. Veronica decided it was best to consider it a rhetorical question.

She found Bainbridge and Foulkes on the first-floor landing, both wearing brooding, thoughtful expressions. Bainbridge's aspect brightened considerably when he saw Veronica coming up the stairs, Madame Gloria in tow.

"Ah, Miss Hobbes. Most excellent. Good to have you here," he said. She could tell from the tone of his voice that he was dreadfully embarrassed. He shook her hand as she arrived on the landing, and leaned close, lowering his voice. "So you found the place all right, then?"

"Evidently," said Veronica, amused.

"It's a house of ill-repute," said Bainbridge, as if expecting Veronica to be at a complete loss. "A *lushery*." He was quite red in the face, as if the very notion of explaining this to a woman represented a terrible contravention to the natural order of things.

"I gathered," said Veronica.

"You did?" Bainbridge looked almost affronted. Veronica caught Foulkes's eye. He was grinning.

"Quite so, Sir Charles. It's not the first brothel I've visited in the course of my duties, and I dare say it won't be the last."

Bainbridge opened his mouth to speak, but no words were forthcoming.

"Well?" said Veronica. "Aren't you going to introduce me to this 'missing' nurse?"

"Ah," replied Bainbridge, his brow creasing. "You see,

Miss Hobbes, when I wrote that she'd been located... well, I fear..."

"She's dead," finished Veronica, with a resigned shrug. "I feared as much."

Bainbridge nodded. "Quite."

"She's in there, Miss Hobbes," said Foulkes, indicating the open door they'd been clustered around when she arrived.

"But for God's sake, cover your face," said Bainbridge, catching her arm, "and don't touch anything. I refuse to be responsible for any one of us succumbing to that blasted disease, whatever it might be."

Veronica nodded, and pulled a cotton handkerchief from her jacket pocket. The thing had probably seen as many crime scenes as she had, she mused, or at least as many corpses. She held it firmly over her nose and mouth with her left hand, and Bainbridge stepped aside to allow her to pass.

The scene inside the room was both heartbreaking and strangely beautiful. The room itself was nothing to speak of— the sort of small, dilapidated box room found in such places: peeling wallpaper, damp patches, a dark claret-coloured carpet to hide stains, dim lighting, and a double bed. There was a distinct lack of personal effects.

Upon the bed, however, was something else entirely. Two figures were locked in a passionate embrace, their limbs intertwined, their faces turned to one another, lips almost touching. Both of them had bloomed, their bodies twisting and altering into weird organic shapes. Vines had sprouted from fingertips and follicles, arms and legs twisting and growing, wrapping themselves ever more intricately around the other person. A sweeping cascade of foliage and button-like fungus cups had displaced hair. All over the flesh had puckered and shifted, taking on new forms, melding with the other host. This had occurred to such an extent that it was now nearly impossible to decipher where one person started and the other stopped. They'd become locked in an eternal lovers' embrace; quite literally, they had grown together.

There was a thick, floral scent in the air, very different from the stench of decay that had been so evident at the police laboratory. She wondered whether that had as much to do with the revenant as it did the disease. She walked around the bottom of the bed, noticing as she did that the vines had tangled themselves amongst the brass spokes of the bed frame.

It was all quite ghastly, of course, but at the same time, Veronica found the whole scene deeply moving. At least these unfortunates had died together, and would remain together, whoever they were. She supposed it might only have been a casual acquaintance, given the venue, but something about the intimacy of the episode was different from the scores of other death scenes she had witnessed in her time working alongside Newbury and Bainbridge.

Veronica left the room, pulling the door to behind her. The others were still waiting on the landing. She lowered the handkerchief from her face. "So, the first of our missing nurses," she said.

"Yes, but what was she doing here?" said Bainbridge. "Did she work here?" He seemed doubtful. "Surely she wasn't a dollymop?" He was frowning, as if attempting to fathom what a young female nurse might be doing frequenting a place such as this.

"Och, no," replied Madame Gloria, with a flutter of her gaudily painted eyelids.

Foulkes gave an uncomfortable cough. "I think she was a client here, Sir Charles. A *customer,* if you catch my drift."

"But... but..." stammered Bainbridge. "She's a *woman.* And that—" He waved his hand in the direction of the open door. "That's two women. *Together.*"

Veronica shook her head, exasperated. "And what of it, Sir Charles? How two women choose to express their carnal desires is no business of ours. Women have sought each other's company in such fashion since history began. Whether they come together out of love, or merely passion, what right have we to pass judgement upon them?"

Bainbridge looked suitably admonished. "I'm not nearly as unworldly as you would care to believe, Miss Hobbes. I understand what goes on behind locked doors. It's simply that I'm rather surprised a woman should lower herself to visiting a place such as *this*."

Veronica smiled. "Women have appetites, too, Sir Charles."

"Well, quite. And some clearly more than others." He waved in the direction of the entwined corpses with the end of his cane. "Now, what's to be done? I mean, we need some way of properly identifying these unfortunates."

"Their clothes, Sir Charles," said Foulkes. He reached for a pile of neatly folded garments, which he had evidently placed upon a chair on the landing earlier. He handed them to Bainbridge who, fumbling with his cane and looking slightly uncomfortable with the idea of handling them, passed them straight on to Veronica.

Veronica accepted them with an amused sigh. She draped them over the banister behind her and took them each in turn, unfolding them and holding them up so that she might examine them properly.

The clothes of the prostitute were just as she might have expected; a pale silk gown decorated with frills and lace that had once been grand but was now worn and mended. The nurse, however, had clearly come here in her uniform, and amongst her articles was a white, starched smock, spattered with chemical stains. Veronica checked the front pocket. Inside was a small slip of yellow paper. She held it up for the others to see.

"What is it?" said Foulkes.

"A wage slip," replied Bainbridge. He held out his hand

and Veronica allowed him to take it. He examined it for a moment. "Made out in the name of Molly Wright, and issued by the St. Giles Hospice, Percy Street." He paused for a moment, a broad smile growing on his lips. "Oh, well done, Miss Hobbes. Well done indeed!"

"I'm sorry, sir, but I'm not quite with you," said Foulkes.

"Keep up, Foulkes," said Bainbridge. "Miss Hobbes here has just found the address of our missing hospital." He folded the slip of paper and secured it in his breast pocket. He turned to Madame Gloria. "Keep that door shut. Under no circumstances may you allow any of your other... *lodgers*... to visit that room. I will send people to remove the bodies within the hour. Have I made myself clear?"

Madame Gloria nodded enthusiastically. "Thank you, Inspector." She put her hand upon his jacket sleeve, her fingertips fondling the button. "If there's ever anything I can do in return..."

Bainbridge, flushed, snatched his arm away, and Foulkes stifled a laugh. "I think not. The most helpful thing you can do is to ensure that people are safe. Turn away any visitors until this has blown over." Veronica noted that Madame Gloria was careful not to make any promises, despite her encouraging nods.

"Foulkes," said Bainbridge, "make the necessary arrangements." He hooked his arm through Veronica's and led her to the top of the stairs. "Miss Hobbes and I have an appointment in St. Giles."

CHAPTER 13

Newbury dreamed of leaves.

They smothered him, crowding him, their damp, cloying scent thick in his nostrils. Vines writhed around his arms and legs, pinning him to the bed. They crawled across his chest, slipping around his throat, constricting, questing for his mouth. He screamed, gasping for breath, fighting desperately against his bonds, but still they came at him, a grasping emerald tide. They tightened around his throat, throttling the life from him. He scratched at them with fingers that were raw and bloody, but they had wrapped themselves around his wrists, too, dragging his hands away.

He couldn't breathe. Panic swelled. This was it–the vines were taking over, consuming him…

And then they were gone, and he was lying on the floor in his Chelsea study, surrounded by familiar, comforting objects. Still gasping for breath, he sat up, rubbing at his throat. It had seemed so real. So…

He felt something warm spreading across his chest, and then pain blossomed. He glanced down to see crimson blood soaking through the white cotton of his shirtfront. Panicked, he scrambled to his feet, ripping at the garment and scattering buttons across the floorboards. Frantically, he searched for the wound. There was something there—a shape—carved into his milky-white flesh. Appalled, desperate, he tore the remains of his shirt free, and, bare-chested and dripping with blood, he ran for the stairs. He took them two at a time, hurrying along the landing to his bathroom. He flung open the door and staggered in, leaving a trail of stark blood spots on the white tiles behind him.

Tentatively, he examined himself in the looking glass. How had this happened? Someone had taken a knife to his chest, roughly scoring an image in his flesh. It was partly obscured now by seeping, dribbling blood, but their intention was obvious; it was a witch mark, a symbol of occult significance, a hand held palm out inside a ragged pentagram. Only, something was wrong. Most witch marks he'd seen before were of six-fingered hands—the sign of the witch—but this one only had four. Four fingers. He had no idea what it could mean.

Newbury stared at the raw and bloody wound in the looking glass, clenching his jaw at the stinging pain. He turned at the sound of someone shouting his name from the hallway below.

"Maurice? Maurice?"

Newbury opened his eyes to find himself in the familiar surroundings of the train carriage. He was in the drawing room, laid out on the floor, head cradled in Amelia's lap. She was brushing his hair back from his forehead and dabbing his face with a cool, damp cloth. She was looking down at him, her face creased in concern. "Oh, Maurice," she said, with visible relief. "You did give me a fright."

Newbury sucked greedily at the air. His throat was dry and sore. He felt hot, sweaty, uncomfortable. "What happened?" he asked, his voice a croak. It was a dutiful question; he already knew.

"You had a seizure," said Amelia. "A seizure just like mine. Like…" She hesitated. "Like the ones I *used* to have. You were thrashing about like you were under attack, and murmuring something about witches."

Newbury expelled a long, deep sigh. "It was just a dream, Amelia. Nothing to worry about."

She frowned. "Just a dream? How can you say that? You know as well as I do what's just occurred. How dare you dismiss it all as 'just a dream'? Remember who you're talking to."

"I'm not you, Amelia," he said, propping himself up on one elbow. He sipped at the glass of water she held to his lips. "I can't see the future."

She looked skeptical. "Don't you think I know the signs? Don't you imagine that if there were one other person who'd *know,* it would be me? You won't pull the wool over my eyes that easily, Sir Maurice Newbury."

Newbury didn't have the strength to argue with her. The truth was, he didn't *want* to believe, to admit to himself that what he'd seen had been a precognitive vision of the future. To be choked to death by writhing vines, or to have his body mutilated in such barbaric fashion—well, it didn't bear thinking about. Perhaps it was more that they were warnings, he considered, symbols that his mind was attempting to interpret or construct a story from, a sequence of images from which he might be able to discern meaning.

Then again, perhaps they were simply the random output of a feverish mind. Such episodes were far from unknown to him; he'd consumed enough opium in his time, after all.

He closed his eyes. Whatever the case, these seizures were coming upon him more and more frequently, and after each one, it took him longer to recover. They could no longer be ignored. For the time being, though, he needed to be strong for Veronica.

He raised himself up, meaning to get to his feet, but Amelia put her hand on his shoulder to stop him. "You're still feverish. Here, let me help you."

He didn't argue as she wrapped his arm around her shoulders and hauled him up, staggering a few feet to the nearest armchair. He collapsed back into the soft embrace of the seat, resting his head against the winged back. The leather felt cool against his cheek. "I need a drink," he said.

He watched Amelia through half-closed eyes as she disappeared into his cabin. He could see she was already dressed for dinner in a pretty green frock, her dark hair loose around her shoulders.

She reappeared a moment later carrying a small brown bottle with a peeling label. She crossed to the sideboard, searched out a wineglass and decanter, and poured a small measure of red, before adding a few droplets of laudanum. She carried it over to him, and he took it, gulping it down gratefully.

"Thank you," he said. He knew Veronica would never have administered the drug in such a casual fashion. Amelia, though, seemed to understand his relationship with the narcotic, how he *needed* it, how it calmed him. Besides which, she was right; she *was* the only one who could understand what he'd been through–the after-effects of the seizure, the strange lambency that made everything seem vibrant and hyper-real, the crippling muscle pain from the spasms, and the exhaustion.

She took the seat opposite him, watching him closely. He regarded her through hooded eyes. Her concern seemed so genuine that he was touched. She must have suspected the truth of what was going on, of course–that the healing ritual he was performing on her was not, in truth, a healing ritual at all, but one of transference. He was taking upon himself her symptoms, her condition, in the vain hope that he might perhaps be stronger than her, able to survive it for longer.

"Tell me," she said. "Tell me what you saw."

"Creeping vines," said Newbury. "Curling around my throat, choking me."

"Creeping vines?" she echoed.

"Don't read too much into it," said Newbury. "I'm sure it's nothing."

Again, the look. He sighed. "It's as if the plant had somehow become animate, and the more I fought it, the more it overcame me, smothering, binding me, strangling the life from me."

"I wonder what it means," said Amelia. She glanced at the window, as if seeing the corpse of the dead man still hanging there, watching them. "I wonder what's to come."

"The only thing to come," said Newbury, "is dinner. For you, at least. I couldn't eat a thing."

She shook her head. "I'll stay with you. You need me here, to ensure you're well."

"No, I need rest. You should go to the dining car." He waved at the door. "Lock the door behind you, and keep your wits about you and your eyes open. Remember, there's danger on this train. Perhaps by mingling with the other passengers you might help to identify our enemy."

"Well, if you're sure… " she started.

"I'm sure," said Newbury. "Go. I'll sleep. I'll be here, in this chair, when you return. Trust me. One of us needs to keep our strength up."

Amelia gave a curt nod, and got to her feet.

He heard the door to his cabin shut behind her, and the key turn in the lock. He heaved another deep sigh, and embraced the circling threat of unconsciousness.

CHAPTER 14

♛

She didn't feel quite right about leaving Newbury alone, having suffered such a violent episode, but Amelia knew all too well the desire to be granted solitude after such an occurrence. For many years the seizures had plagued her, imparting their often-harrowing glimpses into the future. Sometimes they were stark and clear, like recent memories; other times they were opaque and impressionistic, near impossible to interpret, and easily forgotten, like gossamer dreams.

Now, because of his rituals, Newbury had begun to suffer while she, herself, had remained undisturbed for many months. She carried the guilt of that like a tightly wound knot in her stomach, ever-present. She knew it could not last forever. It was unfair of her to allow Newbury to take it on. He might be stronger than her, yes—more resilient, even—but it was *her* burden. Each and every time she broached this subject, however, Newbury would simply smile and offer her assurances, explaining that if they could just continue for a little longer, then the treatment would be complete. They would only have to suffer this indignity until she was fully recovered. He was sure of it.

She found these avoidances terribly infuriating, and if she was honest with herself, she suspected him of bending the truth, or at least sugaring it for her benefit; she did not dare believe that she might one day be fully healed, and that there would be no consequences for Newbury as a result. She could see it in his eyes; the stoic manner in which he pressed on, despite the fact the process was slowly eroding him, draining the vitality from him.

No. It had to stop. She resolved to act as soon as they returned to London and she was certain that Veronica would be well. Doing anything now, on the train, particularly while they were facing the very real threat of this strange cabal, would be madness. Back in London, though, she would force the issue, preferably with Veronica there to lend her strength.

"Excuse me?"

Amelia started and looked round to see a gentleman in an evening suit waiting to pass. She realised she was now standing in the doorway of the dining car, and had wandered here, oblivious, her mind on other matters. She stepped aside to allow the man to pass. He inclined his head in thanks, tugging unconsciously at one end of his walrus-like moustache. Painting a smile on her face—one that she did not entirely feel—she entered the car behind him.

It was an opulent sort of place, a separate carriage given over to two distinct rooms. The main, and largest, was a dining room, reminiscent of the grandest London or Parisian restaurants. A crystal chandelier hung from the roof, glittering in the warm reflected light of the gas lamps and table candles. Mahogany dining tables, each designed to seat four, were situated in two rows along either side of the carriage, each providing a splendid view of the rolling countryside beyond the windows.

The light was beginning to fade outside, the sun low and watery on the horizon. It was beautiful, and Amelia hovered just inside the doorway for a moment, watching the landscape whizz by framed by the pale, swollen orb.

Waiters dressed in immaculate uniforms dashed from table to table like flapping penguins, murmuring pleasantries in expressive French. They were coming and going from the other small room in the carriage, an area that Amelia presumed to be a kitchen or serving room. The smells wafting from the doorway were rich and glorious, and she realised just how hungry she really was, and how welcome a hearty meal would be.

She crossed to an empty table and pulled out a chair, choosing a seat closest to the window. Immediately a waiter was by her side, smiling down at her expectantly.

"Oh, good evening," she said, feeling a little embarrassed that she wasn't confident enough to use the man's native tongue.

"Good evening, mademoiselle," replied the waiter, in smooth, fluid tones. "Dinner for one?"

"Yes, please," she said, with slight reluctance.

"Very good. Today we have a tomato consommé, followed by duck confit and lemon torte."

"How lovely," said Amelia.

The waiter gave a short, polite bow, and then hurried away to see to her order. Recalling what Newbury had said about keeping her eyes peeled for any useful information, she took a moment to survey the other passengers.

There were ten others taking dinner, including the whiskered man who had passed her in the doorway earlier, who was now sitting at the other end of the dining room, his back to her, discussing something in hushed tones with his disinterested wife.

She took the rest of them in, one at a time. None of them looked particularly *dangerous*. Bored, perhaps—tired; inebriated, even—but not likely to murder anyone and carve bloody sigils into their flesh. But then, she supposed, she had no idea what a real murderer might look like.

Finding the corpse in their cabin, pushing it out of the

window—it all seemed like a distant dream to her now, so outlandish, so *awful,* that it couldn't possibly have happened. Nevertheless, there was *someone* on this train with murderous intent. The problem was identifying who that person might be. They were hardly going to be carrying a placard.

She decided to take things a little more seriously, and to pay closer attention to what everyone was saying and doing. At the table closest to her was an elderly couple. He was busily forking mouthfuls of duck into his gap-toothed mouth, while she picked at hers like a disinterested bird, stirring the food around and sighing with abject disappointment. They were in no way likely candidates for the murder, although Amelia wouldn't have been surprised to learn the woman had murderous intentions towards her spouse; the glower of hatred she had fixed upon him as he merrily chewed away at his food could have withered a spring bloom.

Everyone else appeared to be engaged in pleasant, meaningless conversation with his or her dining partners. The young couple she had seen earlier in the observation lounge; two middle-aged men, laughing; an older lady and her younger travelling companion, perhaps a niece or a granddaughter. She listened to snippets of their conversations:

"Miraculous contraption, what?"

"Think how much fuel it must consume."

"*I've* heard they burn plague corpses."

"Don't be ridiculous, Mildred."

"Look, you've dropped *another* stitch!"

"I really think they could have tried harder with this duck."

". . . And then he said, 'what she doesn't know can't hurt her!' Can you believe it, Jones?"

"What, *plague* corpses?"

Amelia almost wanted to laugh at the mundanity of it all.

"Oh, it's *all* going on in here," said a familiar voice. Amelia looked up to see Petunia Wren standing over her table, smiling down at her. "All of life in this carriage." The woman pulled out a chair and dropped into it, opposite Amelia. "You don't mind if I join you, do you?" The question was clearly rhetorical; she was already removing her hat.

Amelia noticed Petunia was smoking a cigarette with her left hand, waving it around expressively as she talked. She took a long draw on it, expelling the smoke from the corner of her mouth. Amelia hoped she didn't plan to smoke through the entirety of their dinner.

Petunia shrugged off a small fur jacket she'd been wearing, and hung it tidily on the back of her chair. She brushed her hair from her face and settled a napkin on her lap, making herself comfortable. Peculiarly, she kept her dainty teal gloves on. "So, Constance—I imagine you're brimming with gossip. I hope you're going to share it with me."

Amelia shrugged. "Well, not really. I've rather been keeping myself to myself." *Aside from throwing corpses from windows, of course,* she thought.

Petunia raised an eyebrow, as if indicating that she understood Amelia's response to have some deeper, undisclosed meaning. "In the company of your travelling companion, hmmm?"

Amelia flushed. The waiter, who had spotted Petunia's arrival and made a beeline for the table, saved her any further embarrassment. "Good evening. Will you be joining mademoiselle for dinner this evening?"

Petunia nodded. "Why yes, of course. I couldn't very well allow her to eat alone, could I?"

"Indeed not," said the waiter, with the briefest of glances at Amelia.

"Just bring me whatever my dear Constance is having," said Petunia. "I'm sure it's perfect."

"Very good, mademoiselle," said the waiter. He turned away and made for the kitchen.

Amelia wished *she* could be quite so confident. She'd grown up without a great deal of experience of the outside world, spending her formative years moving from institution to institution, always under the watchful care of doctors who would treat her like something fragile, to be protected. Even recently, hidden away in the small village of Malbury Cross, pretending to the world that she was dead, her interactions with others had been limited. Consequently, she sometimes struggled with social conventions. She admired Petunia, however, for the blatant manner in which she disregarded them.

"So, as you were saying," said Petunia.

"I wasn't saying anything," protested Amelia.

"Well, at least tell me a little about this man you have squirreled away. Nobody's seen him yet. A knight of the realm, I hear? You're keeping him locked up so no one else can get to him, is that it? It's terribly unkind of you." Petunia placed the tip of her cigarette holder between her lips and took another long, deep draw. "Although I can't say I blame you," she added, smoke pluming from her nostrils.

"It's not like that at all," said Amelia, embarrassed.

"I understand he's terribly dashing."

"Where did you hear that?" said Amelia.

"Oh, you know, from the girls." Petunia waved her cigarette around theatrically, taking in the entire carriage. "I understand he caused quite a stir at the Gare du Nord." She pronounced the last three words with an impeccable French accent. Inwardly, Amelia groaned. "And what about all of this business with the guards being called to your cabin?"

Amelia was beginning to feel very uncomfortable. Her cheeks were now burning. Was this really what people on the train were discussing? How did people know about that? She supposed the guards must have been gossiping. She couldn't blame them, really. She had given them quite a show.

Petunia laughed. "Don't worry, my dear," she said, reaching across the table and patting Amelia's hand, in what

Amelia supposed was intended as a reassuring gesture. "I quite understand. If I had a man like that, I'd want to keep him hidden away from all of these excitable ladies, too."

Amelia sighed, relaxing a little. "It's not that," she said. "More that he's a trifle unwell, and he's using the journey to recuperate."

"Ah, now *that* I can understand. My husband, Julian–he's a sickly sort, too."

"I hope he's recovering well," said Amelia.

Petunia smiled and nodded, but for a moment there was a flash of something in her eyes, a momentary look that told a different story. Perhaps, Amelia considered, her husband was more seriously ill than she was letting on. She decided against prying; the woman would volunteer the information if she wanted to.

"Well, look at the two of us. Leaving our men to their own devices and getting on with things." Petunia stubbed the end of her cigarette in the ashtray as she spoke, and Amelia felt a wash of relief. "Still, it offers us an excellent opportunity to gossip, does it not?"

"I suppose it does," said Amelia, "but as I explained, I have very little to gossip *about.*"

Petunia gave her a sly look. She placed both of her hands on the table, palms down, and leaned closer. "Surely you must have noticed there's *something* going on?"

Amelia swallowed. Her throat was dry. "Whatever do you mean?" she said.

"Things aren't quite right on this train. People are sneaking about. The guards are whispering to one another in the passageways." She grinned conspiratorially. "There's something in the air. Can't you feel it?"

Amelia shrugged. "I'm not sure I know what you mean," she said, affecting her best air of nonchalance. "What is it that you suppose is going on?"

Petunia was about to respond when the waiter arrived with

their consommé. She paused until he was once again out of earshot. "I believe the staff know something that we do not," she said. "Things aren't quite adding up. They look nervous. We missed our last scheduled stop."

"We did?"

"Yes. Sailed on straight through. No explanation." Petunia picked up her spoon.

"Might it just be that there were no passengers intending to alight or join the train there?" said Amelia.

"No," said Petunia. "This isn't one of those provincial little railways we get in England. A scheduled stop is a scheduled stop. They'll have been planning to exchange mailbags and refuel. Mark my words–either there's a scandal brewing, or an important passenger who hasn't been announced."

Amelia smiled indulgently. These were just the wild imaginings of a woman who'd spent too long reading the gutter press, or gossiping in the tearooms of London. She took a mouthful of her consommé. "Surely if that were the case, they'd warn us?" she said. "If we were in any danger whatsoever, wouldn't they want us to know, to prepare us?"

"Not if they thought they could contain it," said Petunia, "or they were considering their reputation. It wouldn't look good for them, a blot on their record. Heaven forbid they had to issue refunds. This is the finest transcontinental engine there is, patronised by the wealthy elite of Europe. Reputation is everything."

"Yes, I suppose you're right," said Amelia. She eyed Petunia over the top of her spoon. "So how have you heard all of this?"

"My husband and I are in the first carriage," said Petunia, as if this explained everything.

"The first carriage, indeed?" said Amelia. She'd noticed this when she had boarded the train in Paris, and had assumed the rather grandiose-looking suite on the other side of the dining car would be reserved for royalty or travelling dignitaries. Then again, she wasn't entirely sure that Petunia and her husband were not.

"Is it terribly impressive?" said Amelia.

Petunia laughed, perhaps a little unkindly. "It cost an arm and a leg," she said, "but then, you only make trips like this once in a lifetime. You must come and visit us for tea, so you can see it for yourself."

"I'd like that very mu–" started Amelia, but stopped short when she saw the startled expression on Petunia's face. She sensed a quiet murmur ripple through the other diners as they set their cutlery down and all turned to look toward the carriage door.

"Here you are, you see," whispered Petunia. "I *knew* there was trouble brewing."

With a mounting sense of trepidation, Amelia twisted around in her seat.

A small woman, in her late twenties or early thirties, had stumbled into the dining car. She looked stricken, like a pale ghost, one hand held over her mouth, the other bunched into a tight fist by her side. Her eyes were wide and glistened with tears. Her dark hair, which had previously been tied back from her face, had begun to come loose, falling in strands around her shoulders. She looked pleadingly from face to face, as if searching for someone.

"Florence?" A young man from two tables away got slowly to his feet, his brow creased in concern. "Are you quite well?"

The woman gave a stifled sob when she saw him, and he rushed to her as she collapsed into his arms.

"What is it?" he demanded. "Whatever's wrong?"

"Blood," said the woman. "I saw blood."

There was another murmur throughout the carriage as the possible implications of this registered.

"Blood, you say?" said the young man levelly.

The woman, Florence, gave a short, sharp nod. "In our carriage. It was pooling under the door of our neighbour's cabin. There were guards, and talk of murder..." At this she burst into fitful sobs, burying her face in the young man's arm.

Amelia's mind was whirling. *A murder. Pooling blood.* Might this be related to the body she and Newbury had found dumped in their rooms? Or could it be a second, related death, enacted by the same killer? She had to get back to Newbury and tell him immediately. If this was related to the Cabal, then he had to intervene before anyone else was killed.

She turned back to Petunia, who was staring at her, agog. "A murder!" Petunia said. "How thrilling."

"I fear there's very little thrilling about it," said Amelia, testily. "What about the poor victim?"

"Who's to say they didn't deserve it?" said Petunia.

"I don't believe anyone deserves *that*," said Amelia. She retrieved her napkin from her lap, dabbed the corners of her mouth with it, and stood. "Excuse me."

"Where are you off to?" said Petunia. "Don't tell me you're running away just as things are starting to get interesting?"

"I must talk to Sir Maurice," said Amelia. "Make him aware of what has occurred."

Petunia leapt to her feet, almost spilling the remains of her consommé over the table. She grabbed Amelia's arm. "In that case, I'm coming with you. We can explain it together. Besides, I'm eager to meet this secretive man of yours."

Amelia sighed. She could see that Petunia was not to be dissuaded, and she wasn't prepared to expend any more energy fighting the woman off. She seemed harmless enough, although Amelia was already beginning to find her overbearing attitude a little wearing. Newbury wouldn't be pleased, either. Still, she didn't want to delay getting word to him.

"Come along, then," she said, resignedly. "This way."

CHAPTER 15

"God, I detest this place," muttered Bainbridge. "I've never been able to understand how human beings can tolerate living in such squalor."

"I don't suppose they have a great deal of choice," said Veronica, attempting to rein in her exasperation.

After quitting Madam Gloria's insalubrious establishment, they'd come directly to the rookery of St. Giles, a foetid, labyrinthine warren of slums, close to the heart of London. Here, deprivation was simply a way of life; two, sometimes three families living on top of one another in the same room, children quite literally dressed in nothing but threads. No running water, no sewers. It was demoralising, to say the least, to see people living like rats—a debasement of all that was human and civilised. Veronica knew that these people had no other option, of course. This is what they were born into, without the means of escape—no money, no jobs, no purpose. Her disgust was not with the people themselves, but with those in government who should allow such a place to exist.

"I understood there was a program to clear these streets," said Veronica, as they walked along side by side, avoiding the filthy puddles. "To move these poor people into more sanitary facilities."

The streets here were narrow, a maze of soot-blackened houses. The stench was near overwhelming, causing Veronica to hack and splutter. But what else were people to do but empty their chamber pots into the street and hope the rainwater would carry it away? She cringed at the sight of a dead cat lying in the gutter a few feet from her. Its fur was matted and wet; its body mangy. It had probably died from eating rancid scraps, or worse. Now its carcass would continue to feed the cycle of death and decay.

"It takes time, Miss Hobbes," said Bainbridge, "to deconstruct a place such as this. I know that work has begun, but I wish they'd get a damn move on. The city is hard enough to police as it is, without warrens like this. Once we lose the trail of someone in one of these streets, we're done for. The place shuts up, closes ranks. Here, they look after their own."

Veronica raised her umbrella a little, and glanced from side to side at the dilapidated houses. People of all ages crowded in doorways, or peered suspiciously from behind broken windowpanes, watching them, sometimes nervously, sometimes with outright aggression, as they traipsed along in search of the address they'd taken from the nurse's pocket.

"You really expect us to find a *hospital* in a place like this?" said Veronica. It seemed to her like the last place one would expect to look.

"I admit to having my doubts," said Bainbridge. "Although I'm not altogether dissuaded. I've seen such things before–charitable projects, missionaries, that sort of thing." His voice was tinted with scepticism. "You know, someone trying to do their civic duty."

"Surely that's laudable," said Veronica. "Think of the difference it could make to these people."

Bainbridge sighed. "I used to think like you, Miss Hobbes, but perhaps, to my discredit, I've grown too weary and cynical in my old age. A single hospital–it couldn't make a difference to a place like this. These people need more than a two-bit doctor operating in his spare time. They need hope, and reform."

"And who's going to offer them that?" said Veronica.

"Precisely," said Bainbridge. "Someone needs to ring the bells of change. I have a notion that time is coming. Ah, here we are." He raised his cane, indicating a filthy street sign on the corner of a nearby building. "Percy Street. That's what it said on the slip, isn't it?"

"Yes," said Veronica. She retrieved the note from her jacket pocket and unfolded it, smoothing it out. "Percy Street, that's right."

"Come along then," said Bainbridge. "Let's get this over with." He started down the narrow lane. Veronica hastily stuffed the slip of paper back into her pocket, hoisted her umbrella, and followed after him.

Here, in similar fashion to the surrounding streets, the houses were arranged in narrow terraces, although the brick shells had now been complemented by ramshackle wooden outbuildings and lean-tos, in an effort to create more shelter.

Veronica and Bainbridge picked their way through the detritus. She was beginning to think they'd made a terrible mistake; that their efforts amounted to nothing but a wild-goose chase—when Bainbridge called to her from a few yards ahead. "Here, this looks like the place."

Veronica wandered over to join him. At the far end of the lane was a civic building that had once, she surmised, been a community hall or theatre. It had originally been grand, but time hadn't been kind, and now it was as dilapidated as the rest of the rookery, its windows streaked with brown grime, its brickwork filthy and stained.

There was no sign above the peeling door, but Bainbridge was right—it had to be the place. It was the only building large enough on Percy Street to house the sort of establishment they were looking for. Although, judging by the look of the place, Veronica didn't hold out much hope. She'd seen plenty of hospitals in her time; this did *not* look like one of them.

"It looks rather abandoned," she said. "Perhaps your philanthropist has given up."

"Perhaps," said Bainbridge. He crossed the street and tried the door. It was locked. He rapped loudly three times with his cane. "Hello?"

There was no sound or movement, other than a startled pigeon, fluttering away from an upper-storey window ledge. He rapped again. "Hello? I say, is there anybody there?"

The moment stretched. Still no answer. "Well, I suppose that's that, then," said Veronica morosely. The trail, it seemed, had grown cold again. She wanted nothing more now than to return home for a soak in a hot bath.

"I'll be damned," said Bainbridge. He took a step back from the door, turned his body slightly, and launched himself forward, ramming it with his shoulder. The rotten wood gave almost instantly, and the door burst open, swinging back on its hinges and overturning something on the other side, which clattered noisily to the floor.

"Right then," he said, dusting flecks of peeling paint from his jacket. "After you?"

"How kind," said Veronica, with the sweetest of sarcastic smiles.

Inside, it was clear the building had seen recent use. There were signs of industry in the reception hall—heaps of paper files and empty teacups littered the oak desk, and a trolley bearing medical implements and kidney bowls had been abandoned in a doorway. The immediate impression was that whomever had recently occupied the place had simply upped and left, leaving everything just lying in situ.

"Looks like the right place, then," said Bainbridge, indicating the trolley.

"It's a miserable sort of hospital," said Veronica. "I can't say I'd want to be treated here." It had clearly never been an affluent establishment. The filthy windows allowed only a thin, watery light to filter in from outside. There was a thick reek of effluvia, but additionally, the hint of something sweet and floral, like perfume. To Veronica, who had grown accustomed to the interiors of sanatoriums, hospitals, and morgues, it seemed oddly out of place. Veronica wondered what sort of treatments they'd been carrying out here.

"Hello?" called Bainbridge again. "Is there anybody here?" His voice echoed through the dark, tiled corridors, but provoked no response. He crossed to the desk on the other side of the lobby. Veronica watched him rifling through papers. "Patient records," he said, holding aloft a sheaf of files. "Some light reading for later this evening. But where the hell is everybody?"

"Something's very wrong," said Veronica. "It's as if everyone was in a hurry to go. Can you feel it?"

Bainbridge nodded. "Yes. I most certainly can. The hairs on the nape of my neck are standing on end. You know I don't go in for all that mumbo-jumbo that Newbury's so fond of, but something here feels out of sorts." He placed the files back on the desk. "Keep your wits about you, Miss Hobbes."

"We'd best take a look around," she said.

Bainbridge nodded. "But let's stick together for once, eh?"

"Very well," Veronica didn't require much encouragement. "We should check the wards. I'd wager they're over here." She indicated the set of heavy wooden doors to the left of the reception desk.

The floral perfume she'd noted was even more potent on the other side of the doors, which opened into a small ward, lined with empty beds. Again, it was clear that they had not been abandoned for long; they were neatly made, with clean white linen, the corners folded down as if ready to receive incoming patients. The porcelain tiles that covered the floor and ceiling had been washed down with disinfectant. Further trolleys topped with kidney bowls, bottles, bandages, and scalpels stood at the ready. At the far end, another set of double doors led on to what Veronica supposed would be a second ward.

"Do you suppose they encountered financial difficulties?" she said, glancing at Bainbridge. "They couldn't keep up the rent, perhaps?"

"A possibility," said Bainbridge, with a shrug. "I can't imagine they were frequented by many patients with the means to pay. Perhaps we should find the offices, see if there's any other paperwork that might give us a clue."

"Yes, you're right," said Veronica. "Allow me to just check through here." She approached the other set of double doors and pushed one of them open, then recoiled in horror, stumbling back and almost falling over a nearby bedstead.

Bainbridge was at her side immediately. "What is it? Are you hurt?"

Veronica hardly knew what to say. "It's… full of corpses."

"*Corpses?*" said Bainbridge.

"So *many* of them," said Veronica. She righted herself, smoothing her jacket and gently removing Bainbridge's hand from her arm.

Bainbridge crossed to the door. He started to push it open.

"No!" she called after him, her composure now fully regained. "Be careful. Cover your face." She took her handkerchief from her coat pocket and held it over her mouth and nose. "Don't touch anything." Her voice sounded muffled; her breath hot through the thin linen.

Bainbridge, startled by her sudden outburst, released the door and followed suit, clamping a red kerchief against his face. "More spores?" he said.

Veronica nodded. "Like nothing you could imagine."

She saw his brow furrow, the concern in his eyes. "Are you ready?"

"Yes, I'm ready," she said, steeling herself. Together, they opened the double doors and stepped through into the adjoining ward.

Here, just as in the previous room, utilitarian beds were arranged in neat rows along the left-hand and right-hand walls. These ones, however, were far from empty.

It was difficult to tell if the sorry things that lay upon them were even human; the host bodies had warped so dramatically from the ministrations of the infection that they were close to unidentifiable.

Vines sprouted and snaked in a thousand directions at once, the protrusions from one body becoming entangled with those of another, and another, scaling the walls and forming a dense canopy across the ceiling. They quivered, questing for the upper windows and the weak light they provided.

Fat spore pods hung like bulbous fruit amongst the vines, ripe and ready to burst. Some, she could see, had already given up their deadly payload, and had cracked open, showering their spores into the atmosphere.

Veronica pressed the handkerchief tighter over her face and took a few steps further into the room. Amongst the melange of growths and vines she caught a glimpse of a distorted face, thick, ropey vines bursting from its ruined eye socket. Elsewhere, woven into the bizarre web work, was an errant hand, a few toes, and an elbow.

"Good Lord," said Bainbridge. "There must be a dozen of them here."

"At least," said Veronica. The only way to be certain was to count the beds. She couldn't bring herself to do it.

This, she realised, was the source of the sickly-sweet perfume she had smelled upon entering the hospital; a vast breeding ground for the fungus. The dead hosts were now nothing but fertiliser, being steadily consumed. "What do you think happened here?" she said. "Were they trying to help them?"

Bainbridge shrugged. "I hope that's what they were doing, Miss Hobbes," he said. He crossed to her and took her gently by the upper arm. "Come along. Let's get out of here. It's not safe. We'll send the experts in."

"Experts?" she said. "Dr. Finnegan was an expert. Look at what happened to *him*. I don't believe there's anyone whose experience will be enough to help them attend to *this*."

"Nevertheless," said Bainbridge, "you and I are neither trained nor appropriately attired for such work. We cannot risk any further exposure. I won't be responsible for you contracting this abysmal condition."

Veronica nodded her assent. She had no desire to remain in the ward any longer than necessary.

They left in silence, returning to the main lobby before removing the handkerchiefs from their faces.

"What now?" she said.

"Now? Now we post guards on the door," said Bainbridge, "and send medical men in to handle the remains. The whole place will have to be incinerated." He offered her a meaningful look. "And the sooner the better."

"What about the offices?" she said. "We still need to establish who owns this place, who's responsible. If they were trying to treat those poor patients, they might be able to tell us more about the disease."

Bainbridge crossed to the reception desk and scooped up an armful of files. "Everything we need should be here, in the paperwork," he said. "How about we split it, and meet again tomorrow to compare notes? In the meantime, I'll have the others clear the place out properly and have it all taken back to the Yard."

"Very well," said Veronica. She extended her hand, meaning for Bainbridge to pass her a sheaf of files, but he shook his head.

"No. We'll take a carriage back to the Yard first; make all of the necessary arrangements. Then I'll see to it that you're returned to your home. I intend to see you safely out of St. Giles, Miss Hobbes, and I'll be hearing no words of dissent."

Veronica sighed. She knew it was well intended, but Bainbridge's old-fashioned chivalry could be somewhat stifling. "As you wish," she said, not wanting to hurt his feelings. This way, at least, she'd probably get home quicker than on foot. "Lead on, lead on."

CHAPTER 16

It was with some trepidation that Amelia led Petunia Wren back to her cabin. She was blatantly disregarding Newbury's earlier instruction, but Petunia was not about to be given the slip, at least without arousing her suspicion. It was paramount that Newbury receive word of the murder as swiftly as possible, though, and so Amelia had decided to allow Petunia to tag along. She seemed harmless enough, if a little trying. Amelia only hoped Newbury would see it that way, too.

With a dry mouth, she turned the handle and ushered Petunia through Newbury's cabin and into their suite. Newbury was sitting in his armchair, reading from a folio of papers. He looked up, about to welcome her back, but then caught sight of her visitor and gave Amelia a quizzical—and somewhat accusatory—look.

"Oh, hello," he said, quietly. "Constance, you've brought a guest." She could tell from his clipped tone that he was not impressed. Nevertheless, he leapt up from his chair, straightened his shirtfront and approached Petunia with his arm outstretched. "Sir Maurice Newbury," he said. "A pleasure to meet you."

"Oh, Constance, my dear. No wonder you were keeping

him locked away. Quite the handsome devil." Petunia took his hand, clutching it in both of hers.

"This is Mrs. Petunia Wren," said Amelia. "She's travelling with us as far as St. Petersburg. She has a suite in the first carriage."

"The first carriage, indeed?" said Newbury. "We *are* honoured. I was under the impression they reserved that carriage for royalty."

Petunia smiled. "Well, it's a once in a lifetime trip, so I thought I'd push the boat out a little. Anyway," she said, positively fawning over Newbury in a way that made Amelia feel quite nauseous, "I'm so delighted to meet you. Constance here hasn't stopped talking about you since we met."

Amelia felt her cheeks redden. "No... well... that's not *strictly* true."

"Oh, as good as," said Petunia, dismissively.

Newbury smiled, but Amelia could see there was something wrong; the way he'd reacted when Petunia had taken his hand, the slight tightening of his jaw. She knew him well enough now to read his mood, and this wasn't simply consternation at an unwanted intruder. She'd have to talk to him about it later, when they'd managed to shake the woman off.

"So," said Newbury. "To what do I owe the pleasure?"

"Oh," said Amelia. "Petunia and I have just overheard something in the dining car, and I thought you should hear of it immediately."

"A *murder*," interjected Petunia, in scandalised tones. "Right here on the train."

"A murder?" said Newbury. He glanced at Amelia, and a moment of understanding passed between them.

"Yes, it's a terrible business," said Amelia. "A young woman came stumbling into the dining car, all in pieces. She claimed she'd seen blood seeping out from beneath the door of the neighbouring cabin. She was as white as a sheet."

"Just think of the scandal," said Petunia. "I wonder what happened. A lover's tiff, perhaps? A terrible tale of revenge?"

"I think, Mrs. Wren, that perhaps you've indulged in one too many romance novels," said Newbury. "I fear murder is rarely as exciting as you seem to think. You can take my word for it. I've witnessed enough of it in my time."

"Oh, come now, Sir Maurice. You must admit, a spot of intrigue to help us while away the long hours—it's not entirely unwelcome, is it?"

Newbury frowned. "Murder is *never* welcome, no matter the circumstances."

"I wondered if you might wish to intercede," ventured Amelia. "Perhaps offer your advice and experience?" She looked at Newbury pointedly, and saw that he had already reached the same conclusion—that the woman in the dining car might have discovered the aftermath of the ritual killing they were already aware of. If the cabin in question marked the site of the original murder, it might provide Newbury with evidence of the Cabal and their whereabouts on the train, or at least the opportunity to prevent either himself or Amelia from being further implicated in the death.

"Yes," said Newbury. "I think you're right. I should go and take a look, see if I can't lend a hand."

"Oh, excellent!" said Petunia. "Our very own sleuth. You're just like the hero in one of those romantic novels I'm so terribly fond of." She shot Newbury a sideways glance, but he seemed too preoccupied to notice.

"I would suggest, ladies," said Newbury, "that you both return to your cabins and lock the doors. At least until we're clear who's responsible for this unfortunate business. If there *is* a killer aboard the train, then I'd advise you to remain out of harm's way until he's been apprehended."

He put his hand on Amelia's shoulder. She could see that he wasn't comfortable leaving her like this, with a stranger, but she'd given him little choice. He couldn't ignore the opportunity to get to the bottom of what was going on, and perhaps even nullify any further threat. Besides, she could look after herself. These days, she was probably stronger than he was.

"You *understand,* don't you, Constance?" he said.

"Of course. That's why I came to find you," she replied.

"Very well. Remember what I said. Return to your cabin and lock the door. As soon as I know that it's safe, I'll be back." He stepped into his cabin, and with one final glance back at the two women, pulled the door shut behind him. A moment later, they heard his footsteps in the passage outside.

"He's very gallant," said Petunia. She crossed to the chair in which Newbury had been sitting, shifted his folio of papers, and dropped down into it. "So, what have you got to drink?"

Amelia frowned. "Didn't you hear what he said? We're to return to our cabins and lock the doors for safety."

Petunia waved her hand airily. "Oh, where's the fun in that? He'll be back soon enough, with news of scandal and intrigue. I'm not missing out on *that.*" She smiled, and Amelia thought she caught a glimpse of something else in the woman's expression: a hint of desperation, perhaps? Fear?

"Come on, fetch us both a drink and pull up a seat. I'm dying to know how this thing plays out."

With a sigh, Amelia turned the key in the lock and set about pouring them both a large brandy. She had a feeling she was going to need it.

CHAPTER 17

They met mid-morning in a tearoom just off Piccadilly Circus, a place called Rosalie's, familiar to her from her younger years, and still a place of comfort and charm. She liked it there: the heady aroma of baking cakes, the whoosh of steam from the kettle, the chitter-chatter of so many ladies gossiping raucously about the latest scandals.

She arrived a full half hour early, so that she might soak up the atmosphere while she finished leafing through her share of the files. Even their dire contents couldn't quite shake her buoyant mood as she relaxed, untroubled, in the corner. She kept half an eye on the door as she read.

Bainbridge arrived punctually, as expected, bustling through the door in his big overcoat and hat, and looking somewhat out of place in such a dainty establishment. He glanced around, looking a little crestfallen as he took in the other clientele. Veronica noted how he drew the attention of these other women; this curious fellow who'd barged into their world like a sudden gust of wind, ruffling all of their feathers. She laughed.

He spotted Veronica in the corner and made a beeline for her table. She stood, greeting him warmly.

"Good morning, Miss Hobbes," he said, removing his coat and hat and handing them to the waitress.

"Morning, Sir Charles," said Veronica. "You found it all right, then?"

"Oh, I'm well aware of the place," he said. "Isobel was a frequent patron." His expression lightened for a moment at the mention of his late wife. "Very fond of the coffee cake, she was."

"She must have had excellent taste," said Veronica. She beckoned to the waitress. "Let's organise you some tea." The waitress approached, and she gave a short order. She considered scones, but decided against it. Bainbridge was looking rather well fed of late. Too many trips to his club, she decided.

Bainbridge sat back in his chair, folding his hands on the table before him.

"No files?" she said, when she realised he hadn't brought anything with him.

"No, left them back at the Yard," he replied. "All except for one." He patted his jacket pocket. "I'll come to that." He eyed the heap of files on the table. "I see you're making good headway."

"You could say that," said Veronica. "Although I fear it's the same story, repeated over and over again. It's a ghastly business. It seems whomever is behind this—and he was very careful to keep his name off the paperwork—was carrying out experiments on the poor individuals named in these notes."

"Go on," urged Bainbridge. "I'm interested to hear what you've deduced."

"It seems many of them were wounded soldiers, returned from Africa. There are a high proportion of amputees. The doctor—if that's what he is—seems to have claimed to be able to regenerate their missing limbs, and used that promise to lure them in." She stopped as the waitress approached with Bainbridge's tea. The woman set it out before him on the table, and then retreated with an apologetic smile.

Veronica lowered her voice. "From what I can gather, he was infecting them with the revenant plague, first allowing that to take hold, and then treating them with a compound derived from a rare fungus. Whatever he was doing, though, it didn't work. Not judging by the records here. And you saw as well as I did what became of the men in that ward."

Bainbridge smiled as he poured himself some tea, and Veronica knew that he was holding something back. He'd found a lead, and was waiting to hear what she had to say before springing it on her. She'd seen him do this to Newbury, too, and she found it endearing, rather than frustrating—a sign that he took great pleasure in being good at his work.

"Yes," he said. "I concur. The patients' notes all tell the same story. It seems clear to me that the man's true purpose, however, was to search for a cure for the revenant plague itself. Nothing to do with the excised limbs."

"Then why didn't he simply experiment on existing revenants?" said Veronica. "There are plenty of them wandering the slums."

"Too dangerous, I'd imagine," said Bainbridge. "Risk of exposure. You've seen what the brutes can do. This way he could keep them tied up, monitor their transformation, study them."

"How awful," said Veronica. "Those poor men. As if they hadn't already given enough. To be taken in like that, tricked into giving their lives..." She took a sip of her tea. "It makes sense, though."

"What, experimenting on soldiers?"

"No," said Veronica, with a wave of her hand. "What you said about trying to cure the revenant plague. That first corpse we found—Dr. Finnegan said it had been a revenant. Perhaps it had escaped from the hospital. And it fits with what Dr. Farrowdene told me, too. That the fungus first of all seemed to have rejuvenated the dying cells, healing its victim while it festered parasitically within."

"Quite appalling," said Bainbridge, with a grimace.

"Just imagine if it had worked," she said. "Think of the

difference it could make. A cure for the revenant plague."

"It did," said Bainbridge. "At least in a manner of speaking." He pulled a folded piece of paper from the jacket pocket he had indicated earlier. "Throughout the notes he keeps making a reference to another case. A patient with the initials E.P."

"Yes, I'd noticed that," said Veronica. "As if he's likening the other cases to that one."

Bainbridge grinned. "I managed to locate E.P.'s notes in the file. Ernest Pargeter. A soldier just like the others. Lost the use of his arm from a bullet wound in the Boer conflict."

"And?" said Veronica.

"He underwent the same treatment at the hospice, the one you've just described. Only in Pargeter's case, it appears to have proved successful."

"What?" said Veronica. She took the piece of paper from Bainbridge. It was a discharge note.

"The regenerative process appears to have worked," Bainbridge went on. "Not only does he appear to have recovered from the dose of revenant plague administered to him by our mysterious doctor, he also regained partial use of his arm."

Veronica set the paper down. "That's *remarkable*," she said.

"Not only is it remarkable, Miss Hobbes," said Bainbridge, "but it's also the breakthrough we've been searching for. I looked him up before leaving the Yard. Ernest Pargeter rents a property in Limehouse."

"If it's true, if he's still alive," said Veronica, "then he should be able to point us to the man responsible."

"Precisely," said Bainbridge. "The noose is tightening."

"Then we should leave for Limehouse immediately," said Veronica. She pushed her chair back to get up.

Bainbridge shook his head. "It'll keep, Miss Hobbes," he said, waving her back to her seat, a broad smile on his face. "At least until I've finished my cup of tea."

CHAPTER 18

It was with a deep sense of disquiet that Newbury set out to locate the scene of the disturbance. This, he reflected, was due in part to his uncertainty regarding what he might find—more evidence of the Cabal's appalling practises and their continued presence on the train, or perhaps even the original site of the dead man's murder and a clue to his identity. Yet there was something else, too, worrying away at the back of his mind: Amelia's surprise visitor, Petunia Wren.

She'd seemed harmless enough—utterly odious, in her overbearing, ingratiating manner—but innocuous, nevertheless. The sort of self-obsessed braggart that were ten a penny in places such as this, intent on lording it over those less fortunate than themselves. Yet when he'd greeted her, he'd been startled to discover she was missing a digit on her right hand. The mercurial finger of her glove had been soft and padded, hollow.

This, in and of itself, was so insignificant as to be meaningless—the result of an accident or childhood trauma—and would have been easily dismissed if it hadn't been for the dream.

He'd attempted to rationalise it as a harmless coincidence, reasoning that the vision he'd experienced during his seizure was most likely a hallucination akin to those he'd succumbed to before, on account of his laudanum habit. Nevertheless, he couldn't shake the notion that something was wrong, that the symbol he'd seen carved into his chest in the dream was a warning of some kind.

But a warning of what? It seemed unlikely that the woman had any connection to the Cabal. Ludicrous in fact–she simply didn't have the temperament. Yet there was something nagging at him, and over the years he had learned to trust his intuition. It had saved his life on more than one occasion.

Not that he was able to do anything about it now. Amelia had been right; the most important thing was to establish what had happened back here on the train, and whether it was going to present any difficulties for them. If that also meant he was able to uncover more about the Cabal's activities or intentions, all the better. Indeed, it might mean he'd find the opportunity to intervene without needing to alert the authorities, and therefore risking the outcome of his mission. Nothing could get in the way of procuring Veronica's new heart.

Newbury had passed through three full carriages before he encountered any further signs of life, assuming that, with news of the murder spreading, people had begun to confine themselves to their cabins to wait out the investigation. Or until they got bored or hungry; in his experience, people's stomachs often took precedence over concerns for their safety.

As he opened the door to the next carriage, however, he heard rapid footsteps heading toward him, and had to throw himself back against the wall as someone came barreling straight into him.

She was a slight woman, no taller than five feet, with long blond hair and a slender figure. Her face was somewhat angular, with exceptionally high cheekbones, accentuated even further by the misapplication of rouge. He caught her as she tumbled into him, grasping her by the arms. The woman let out a whimper and looked up at him, frightened, as if expecting him to suddenly lash out.

Concerned by her reaction, he released her and she backed away from him nervously, refusing to meet his gaze. He could see that she'd been crying.

"Are you quite well, madam?" he said, fully in the knowledge that she was not. "Can I assist you in any way?" The woman shook her head. She tried to speak, but all that came out was another whimper. She was clearly scared out of her wits. "All right, try to breathe. Take a moment to compose yourself. You're quite safe."

"M... m... m..." she mumbled.

"Take your time."

"Monster!" she blurted. "There's a monster on the train. Back there. I saw it... it... it *ate* that poor man." It came as a sudden deluge, almost impossible to decipher.

Newbury frowned. This was not at all what he'd been expecting. He wondered for a moment if the woman was delusional. "It ate him?"

The woman nodded frantically. "Bit him. Right in his neck. Blood everywhe–" She swooned suddenly, and he stepped forward and caught her again. He lowered her to the floor in the vestibule, propping her into a sitting position with her back against the wall.

A monster, biting people? The thought wasn't entirely encouraging. He'd expected to hear word of murder, of a ritual killing or a missing passenger whose cabin had been discovered doused in blood. But this–this sounded disturbingly like something else. Perhaps it was one of the Cabal's weird creations, an animalistic hybrid of man and machine. He'd fought them before, back in London, and they were utterly deadly. But how on earth had they managed to bring one onto the train?

"What did it look like?" he said. He was crouching low, facing the woman. She still had her eyes closed. "Can you hear me? Hello?"

The woman groaned, but didn't respond. It was no use questioning her further—she was clearly suffering from shock. She'd evidently witnessed something horrific, and it had temporarily rendered her delirious.

Newbury stood, considering his next move. Really, he should seek some assistance, but that would be a further distraction, and she seemed safe enough here. If there really *was* something loose on the train, then he might be able to help stop it. At the very least, he'd be in a position to make an informed decision about whether or not to get involved.

"I'm sorry," he said. "I'm going to leave you here while I find out what's going on. Stay exactly where you are, and I'll come back for you shortly. Do you understand?"

The woman said nothing. Feeling torn, he left her in the vestibule and continued on his way, rocking from side to side with the steady motion of the train.

It wasn't long before the source of the disturbance became evident. Train guards were ushering back a press of rowdy onlookers, who had gathered in the vestibule area of the offending coach and were shouting questions in a variety of colourful languages.

Newbury muscled his way through the crowd, causing a bearded man in a grey suit to round on him angrily. Newbury mumbled an apology and pushed on through the morass of limbs.

It was growing close and increasingly uncomfortable in the carriage, as people shuffled shoulder-to-shoulder, each of them vying to see. Newbury decided his only option was to disregard politeness and began manhandling, forcing his way through the crowd and bellowing "Out of the way! Police!" as he started to push the other passengers aside.

To his surprise, people began to make way, forming a central aisle to allow him through. As he got closer to the front of the crowd, he realised why: the rich, coppery scent in the air; the revulsion on the faces of the train guards; the spatter marks halfway up the wall; and the ragged, half-shredded corpse on the ground.

Newbury's lip curled in disgust. This was no ritual murder. The man *had* been eaten alive. Rend marks parted the pudgy, buttery flesh of his belly and chest, and fat gobbets had been gouged free by claws and teeth. He'd been opened up like a tin of sardines, peeled back to reveal his glistening innards. The man's face was so smeared in his own blood as to appear indistinguishable. One of his eyes had been pushed back so far into the socket that it had burst.

The dead man was lying in the passageway just outside his cabin, in a puddle of thickening blood. A quick glance at the interior of the small room told Newbury it was undoubtedly the scene of death; unlike the dead man he had found in his own cabin earlier, this one had not been moved. The cotton sheets on the lower bunk were stained with splashes of crimson blood, which had spread like blotches of ink on blotting paper. The floor was slick with arterial fluid, along with scattered hunks of gristle and an errant human tooth.

Hanging on the wardrobe door was the heavy boiler suit, thick leather gloves, and the sooty cap of a fireman. This, then, had happened between shifts at the furnace.

Newbury felt a cold knot tightening in his stomach. He'd seen corpses like this before, eaten by wild, unnatural things—things that should be nowhere near a passenger train hurtling across the Continent. He could feel the eyes of the crowd on his back, the weight of expectation upon him. He'd told these people he was with the police; now they expected him to make sense of what they were seeing. He wasn't sure *anyone* could make sense of such a mess, however.

He looked up to see one of the guards staring at him. The man had obviously asked him a question and was waiting for his response.

"I'm sorry?" said Newbury.

The guard narrowed his eyes, sighed, and then repeated his question. Newbury's French was rusty at best, but he gathered from the man's outstretched hand that he wished to inspect Newbury's papers. He'd obviously heard him telling the other passengers he was a policeman.

Newbury gave up his most charming smile. "I represent the interests of Her Royal Britannic Majesty, Queen Victoria," he said. "I've come to offer my assistance."

The guard glanced at his companion, and then offered Newbury an indulgent smile. "Your Queen has no jurisdiction here," he said, in broken English. "We do not require your assistance. Please step aside, before my men are forced to return you to your cabin."

I'd like to see them try, thought Newbury. He swallowed and moistened his lips. It wasn't worth engaging with this man any further, he decided. He'd seen what he needed to see. The death here was not the result of some grotesque ritual. Nor was it the design of the Cabal or its agents, but something far worse.

"Very well," he said, backing away. "Good day." He turned and slipped into the crowd again, heading back toward the vestibule where he'd left the woman.

When he got there, he discovered she had already gone. He hoped she'd plucked up the courage to flee for the relative safety of her own cabin. Or perhaps some other concerned citizen had come by to assist her. He supposed it mattered little at this juncture. If he was right, if what he feared were true, then every one of them, every single person on the train, was at risk.

He weighed his options. As he saw it, he had a choice: retreat to his cabin with Amelia, bolt the doors, and attempt to sit out the rest of the journey; or attempt to unpick what had happened here, and protect as many people on the train as he could. He knew, though, that there was really no choice at all. Turning a blind eye wouldn't get him back to Veronica any faster, and, indeed, might jeopardise his mission even further, if a revenant was left to roam free, wreaking havoc and infecting further passengers or members of the crew.

He'd have to avoid the guards, however. They certainly didn't seem to want the help of an Englishman, irrespective of his position or experience with the creatures. Then, of course, there was the Cabal, still at large and no doubt planning to make the most of the chaos. He had to expect them to make another move soon.

Nevertheless, he couldn't stand by. Decision made, he quit the vestibule, and cautiously set out the way he had come, heading toward the front of the train. He would pay a quick visit to the engine room, to speak, if he could, with the other firemen, and try to get a measure of what had happened to their colleague.

CHAPTER 19

❦

From amidst the crowd, the Keeper observed Newbury's brief confrontation with the train guards, before watching him peel away into the shadows. He smiled inwardly. This, he knew, would be his best chance yet. Newbury was distracted, more concerned with the imminent threat of the revenants than with protecting the girl or the book.

The Keeper straightened his tie, and took one last look at the bloody ruins of the fireman on the carriage floor. The guards had begun to usher everyone back while they brought in a stretcher to remove the corpse. Soon enough, the whole mess would have been tidied away as if nothing had occurred, as they attempted to restore some semblance of order and normality upon the train. Within a few hours it would be nothing but a rumour, tittle-tattle spoken in hushed tones amongst the rich wives in the observation lounge. At least, it was clear that's what the train guards were hoping. Like Newbury, however, the Keeper knew better. If a revenant were loose on the train, the likelihood was that it had already passed on the infection, and there would be glorious chaos and bloodshed to follow. It was a ticking bomb, and they were all trapped aboard, hurtling through the countryside.

The Keeper suppressed a laugh. It was everything he could

have hoped for. The revenants would provide the perfect distraction, so that he might seek his revenge and claim another trophy for his treasured necklace. All he had to do now was find the book while Newbury was indisposed. The girl would be no trouble. His blade would drink its fill as it parted her soft, yielding flesh.

He watched Newbury quit the carriage, pausing at the door to allow a plump, moustachioed buffoon with a gin-soaked complexion to waddle through before him. Newbury's demeanour had changed, however—there was intent in his eyes. He planned to investigate, or find some means to contain the revenant threat, to save these little people from their fate. He was a compassionate fool, concerned with the lives of these rich wastrels. It was this, more than anything else, that would be key to his downfall. The Keeper would ensure it.

Quietly and calmly, so as not to draw attention, the Keeper slipped through the crowd, trailing a few feet behind Newbury and leaving the hubbub of the still-gaping crowd behind him.

In the vestibule, he paused at the sound of a drawn breath and a scuff of movement, and for a moment found himself wondering whether he had underestimated Newbury; that the man had not been quite so distracted as he seemed, and was lying here in wait, ready for a confrontation. As it was, he discovered upon turning his head, the situation was considerably worse.

It was not Newbury whom he saw lurking in the recess by the train door, half-shrouded in shadow, but a wretched creature, ravaged by the infection burning through its bloodstream: a revenant.

The Keeper almost laughed. Hadn't he wished this chaos upon himself, only moments earlier?

The revenant lurched forward, talons gleaming. He caught a glimpse of its face. It had once been a man, but now its flesh was bloated and puckered with open sores. Its lips were curled back in an animal snarl, teeth bared and flecked with the gore of a recent kill.

The Keeper fell back, smoothly reaching into his jacket and withdrawing his blade. His heart was hammering, his temples throbbing. He'd been trained for moments such as this, but he'd always anticipated *living* enemies, not the ravenous half-dead. He'd never fought one of the creatures before, but he knew it would not die easily or well. If he engaged it, the likelihood was that he, too, would die, or himself become infected by the diabolical plague.

He risked a glance at the door. There was no running for it. A single graze is all it would take to transmit the infection, and he had no doubt the creature would reach him before he made the door, even if he were to make it through without having his innards ripped out.

He considered screaming for help, which might afford him a momentary reprieve. Perhaps even Newbury might come running. But time was not on his side. The creature had his scent now, and he represented the closest, easiest kill. It was no good. He would have to engage it, attempt to stun it before making a play to escape.

He had no idea if it were even possible, and recognised his chances were slim at best.

He took another step back, and the revenant lurched forward again, closing the distance between them. He could see now that its left cheek had been raked by its previous victim, the flesh torn in weeping, necrotic strips, which now hung loose across its lower jaw. Its left eye, too, was red and bloodied, unseeing. It hardly mattered—he could see from the way it was preparing to spring that it meant to overpower him.

"Good Lord!" The sudden voice almost startled the Keeper into taking his eyes off the snarling revenant in front of him. "What is that thing? It's *monstrous*!"

The Keeper issued a nervous, quiet laugh. It was the moustachioed buffoon he'd seen entering the carriage earlier.

"I say! The situation looks a bit tricky, what? Are you in need of some assistance?"

The revenant turned its head to regard the newcomer, clearly weighing its options.

"Quickly now," said the Keeper. "I'm armed. Move behind me."

"Well, yes, all right," said the man. He kept his back to the vestibule wall as he shuffled around behind the Keeper. He stank of cheap cologne and brandy.

"Now, come closer. Stand just behind my left shoulder." The man did as he was told. This, in the Keeper's experience, was typical of such idiotic gentry—so concerned with saving their own skin that they were only too happy to let someone else tell them what to do.

The revenant issued a low, rumbling growl.

This was it. This was his one chance. With a single, deft movement, the Keeper reached behind him, grasped the man's collar in his bunched fist, and flung himself backwards, shoving the buffoon in front of him like a shield.

The revenant saw its opportunity, and struck.

"Now hold on a mo—" The man broke off into a strangled wail as the creature surged forward with surprising agility, burying its teeth in the man's throat. For a moment, his eyes met those of the Keeper—betrayed, imploring, shocked—and then, as the revenant began to feast, they were filled with only horror, panic, and pain. The man's lifeless body slumped to the floor, and the revenant fell upon it, shredding clothes with its talons to get at the milky-white flesh beneath. It buried its face in his belly, tearing gobbets of fat, bloody flesh.

The Keeper did not take his eyes off the creature as he slid carefully towards the door, opened it, and stepped through. He didn't draw another breath until the door was shut and he was already entering the next carriage.

Outside of Newbury's cabin, the Keeper paused, his ear to the door. He could hear the sound of voices—women's voices—squabbling inside the room, followed by the crash of a smashing vase. A struggle, he decided. This was an unexpected development, but not an unwelcome one. He'd thought to dispose of the girl, slitting her throat before searching the cabin—again—for his prize, but there was an inherent risk in such an endeavour, that she might escape or raise the alarm before he'd finished. With Newbury absent, it sounded as if someone else was seeing to the problem for him, however.

Mercifully, this section of the train appeared—so far—to be free of revenants. He would bide his time for a short while, catch his breath and wait to see what transpired. Then, when the moment was right, he would make his move.

His mission would soon be over, and he would return triumphant to London. The book would be restored to its rightful place at the heart of the Cabal, and with it, proof positive of Newbury's death. The Cabal's revenge would have been enacted. The Keeper's sense of certainty was almost palpable. One way or another, Newbury was not getting off this train alive.

CHAPTER 20

Things had evidently returned to normal in the dining carriage. The heady scent of roasting meat and spices, along with the general hubbub of scandalised gossip, was sign enough that despite the events transpiring elsewhere on the train, the passengers here were relatively unconcerned. Or perhaps less unconcerned, and more exhilarated, Newbury considered, judging by the snatches of conversation he overheard as he passed through, sidestepping buzzing waiters.

"Oh, haven't you heard? There's been a *murder* onboard!"

"How *terribly* alarming."

". . . I hear she was covered in blood, from head to toe. She came right in here before she collapsed in shock."

"In *here*?"

Newbury left them to their salacious chatter, and ducked out the far side of the dining car, through the vestibule, and into the next carriage. Here, just like his own carriage, a narrow passageway traversed the length of the car, but unlike the suite he shared with Amelia, the cabins were far bigger. From what he could tell, there were only two of them, comprising a number of linked rooms. This was the first carriage, where Petunia Wren had taken a suite—typically the domain of the excessively rich. He chose not to loiter, in fear of disturbing the woman and inadvertently announcing his presence.

The door at the end of this carriage led to another small vestibule area, which in turn opened out onto the rear platform of the engine itself. Here, the brisk force of the wind buffeted him, and he was forced to catch hold of the railing to steady himself as the train sped through the velvet night.

The best of the light had long since gone, but on the horizon he could see the jagged slopes of mountains capped in snow, shimmering in the reflected twilight. A ragged patchwork of farmland spread out at their feet, demarked by a web of dry stone walls. The scent of soot and smoke was cloying and familiar.

The engine's tender was of an unfamiliar design. Unlike typical load-bearing cars, which would be piled high with heaps of dusty coal and pulled along behind the engine, this tender was a smaller, enclosed unit that formed part of the engine housing itself, accessible, he presumed, from somewhere close to the furnace.

Newbury inched along the narrow walkway, feeling exhilarated by the sense of motion. The wind whipped through his hair, blowing away the last vestiges of his dreariness. He reached the covered housing of the furnace a moment later.

He ducked his head inside, aware immediately of the hot glow of the fire. There was something else, too: an acrid, rotten stench that caught in the back of his throat. He spluttered, drawing the attention of the fireman on duty, who until that point had been gainfully stoking the fire with a long, iron shovel.

He was a thickset man with a stocky, angular profile. He was balding, in his late forties, but looked fitter than many men half his age. He was dressed in similar navy overalls to the ones Newbury had seen hanging in the other fireman's cabin, and wore thick, padded leather gloves. He was covered in a patina of black soot, all the way up to his elbows. Newbury saw his grip tighten on the haft of the shovel as he slowly turned to regard him.

"Good day," called Newbury, over the roar of the engine. "May I come in?"

"Looks to me like you already have," said the fireman. He narrowed his eyes. "Who are you?" His voice was low, his tone measured. He spoke good English, with a thick, Gallic accent.

"My name is Maurice Newbury. You might say that I'm an inspector, investigating the death of your colleague."

Newbury saw the other man swallow. "Might I, now?"

"Look, I'm not here to cause any trouble." Newbury showed his hands, holding them both palm out, as he stepped forward, ducking fully under the cover of the engine room. "I'm just trying to get to the bottom of..." He trailed off as his eyes caught sight of the open door to the tender and what lay beyond. "Good Lord." He took a step closer, and the fireman tensed, but Newbury was beyond offering platitudes.

There was an arm on the floor.

It was limp and pallid, the fingertips ending in vicious protrusions. It had once been clothed, but now all that remained were the ragged remnants of a cuff and shirtsleeve. He took another step forward, peering around the door, holding his breath in horrified anticipation of what he was about to see.

The arm was still attached to a torso, although that torso was no longer attached to its head or legs. Similarly, there was a leg, another arm, a head, and an almost complete corpse. The room was filled with pile, upon pile, upon pile of human bodies. It was a charnel house, a repository of desiccated plague corpses. There were hundreds of them, thousands, even, crushed into the small interior of the tender, their sallow expressions eerie in the partial light of the furnace.

Newbury felt bile rise in his gullet and choked it back, raising his hand to his mouth. So many abandoned souls.

He took a step backwards, reaching for a handhold as the engine shook. After a moment, when he had regained his composure, he looked again at the fireman, who met his gaze, eyes defiant.

"You're burning them for fuel," said Newbury. "Revenant corpses."

The man made a minute gesture with his shoulders that might have been a shrug. "What else are we to do with them?" he said.

"They were *people* once," said Newbury. "Men, women, *children*."

"They were monsters," said the fireman. "And damn their souls to Hell."

Newbury watched as the other man scooped an appendage from the floor and cast it into the hungry mouth of the furnace, as if to underline his point. A shower of sparks blossomed where it disturbed the embers. He could see it now–the chain of events that must have led to the bloody mess he'd seen on the floor of the other fireman's cabin. The padded leather gloves–they weren't designed to protect the men from the heat, but from wounds, scratches, infections. All it would take to spread the terrible blight was a single cut, an open sore.

He backed away towards the gangway, stepping out onto the platform. The fireman eyed him suspiciously for a moment longer before returning to his work, stirring the embers with his shovel, seemingly oblivious to the horror right before him.

Newbury gulped at the rush of cool air, hoping to cleanse himself of the cloying stench. This was all the confirmation he needed. Now he was in no doubt: A revenant was loose upon the train.

CHAPTER 21

The salty stench of the river permeated everything here, suppressed only by the rancid stink of the gutters, and the human effluvia swimming in them. It had been some months since Veronica had last had cause to visit Limehouse, and she was not pleased to be back. The place had a lawless, frontier sort of atmosphere, and although on one hand she could appreciate the heady mix of ethnicity and cultures, the depravity, homelessness, and general disdain for the law made it an unwelcoming district, for both a woman and an agent of the Crown.

She could tell Bainbridge was having similar thoughts, judging by his sour expression and wrinkled nose.

"It's like a warren," she said. "People could disappear here, and no one would ever know."

"In my experience, that happens all too often, my dear Miss Hobbes," said Bainbridge. "The gangs here harbour wanted criminals in exchange for payment, or favours. It can be near impossible to ferret someone out of this maze once they go to ground. It's worse than that damn rookery. We could do with Newbury here. He has a remarkable working knowledge of these streets."

"Yes," said Veronica, "but only because he has a penchant for a particular type of establishment."

Bainbridge shrugged. "Nevertheless, it would be useful now."

"Oh, I don't think we're that incapable," said Veronica. "Look, down here." She led him into a narrow lane on their right, sandwiched between a warehouse and a small, run-down mews. These were tenement buildings consisting of three floors, largely given over to the workers and their families, or those too poor to afford anything better. "This looks like the place," she said, indicating a doorway.

Unlike the others surrounding it, the navy blue paint was not peeling, but looked as if it had recently received a fresh coat. The steps were clean and, despite everything, there appeared to be a certain aura of respectability about the place.

Bainbridge cleared his throat and rapped on the door. Within moments, a young woman had opened it and was peering out, her expression concerned. "Yes? How may I help you?" she said.

Bainbridge smiled. "Good afternoon, Miss… ?" He let the question hang for a moment, but the woman, unfazed, simply put her hand on her hip and cocked her head, waiting for him to go on. "Um… my name is Sir Charles Bainbridge, of Scotland Yard, and this is my associate, Miss Hobbes. We're looking for a man whom we understand may lodge here, by the name of Mr. Ernest Pargeter. Perhaps we could speak to the landlord?"

The woman's eyes narrowed. "I *am* the landlord," she said. "Miss Carstairs." She looked from Bainbridge to Veronica, and then held out her hand. "Look, I'm going to need to see some identification."

With a sigh, Bainbridge reached into his jacket and withdrew his papers. He handed them to the woman, who unfurled them, studied them for a moment, and then handed them back with a brief nod.

"Very well, you'd better come in," she said, opening the door a little wider to permit them.

Inside, the place was nicely kept, and although the furnishings were all a little worn or cheap imitations of the sort Veronica might see in some of the grander homes she visited, it was homely and welcoming.

"So, Miss Carstairs, you're the landlady of this establishment?" said Bainbridge.

"Yes," said the woman. "I thought we'd established that. I've managed the house ever since my father passed away. I try to keep it as he would have wished me to."

"I'm sure he'd be very proud," said Veronica. She looked young to be running an establishment like this, in a *place* like this. Veronica felt herself warming to the woman. She clearly had some mettle.

"And Ernest Pargeter?" prompted Bainbridge.

"Yes," said the woman. "Yes, of course. He keeps a room here, just down the hall."

"He lives alone?" said Veronica.

Miss Carstairs nodded. "Yes, ever since... well, I'll let him tell you."

"He's at home?"

"I'll show you his room. This way." She led them along the hallway, past a silent grandfather clock, to a door that, Veronica considered, had probably once served as a dining room. It was now given over as living quarters.

"Do you have many lodgers?" said Veronica.

"Another four," said Miss Carstairs. "I don't mind telling you that I'm a little choosy over whom I welcome into my home. Mr. Pargeter is a good soul. I can't imagine what Scotland Yard might have to do with him."

"Just a few questions," said Bainbridge. "In here?" He indicated the door.

Miss Carstairs nodded, then rapped three times. "Ernest? It's Jane. You have some visitors."

The floorboards creaked on the other side of the door.

"Tell them to go away," came a brusque voice. "I have no need of visitors."

"Well, Ernest, I think that might be a little ou–"

"Sir Charles Bainbridge, Scotland Yard," said Bainbridge, over the top of Miss Carstairs. "Open up."

"Subtle," said Veronica, under her breath.

More footsteps, and the door creaked open.

Pargeter was a strapping young man in his early twenties: tall, slim, fair-haired, and handsome. He was dressed in black trousers and shirtsleeves, and his left arm was held in a sling. He was unshaven, but alert and interested. "Scotland Yard?" he said, with a hint of incredulity.

"Yes," said Bainbridge. "We'd like to ask you some questions."

Pargeter frowned. "I can't imagine what you'd have to ask me. I keep my head down and my business to myself."

"Quite," said Bainbridge. "We simply want to ask you about your hospital treatment since returning from the war. Nothing sinister, I assure you. All part of an ongoing investigation."

"Very well," said Pargeter. "You'd better come in." He smiled at Miss Carstairs who, Veronica noted, was watching him most attentively.

"I'll put a kettle on the stove," she said.

"No," said Pargeter, firmly. "I'm sure our guests won't be staying long."

Miss Carstairs appeared a little crestfallen at the rebuke, but nodded all the same. "Well, then I'll leave you to it." She turned to Bainbridge. "I'll be just down the hall in the kitchen if you need anything," she said, before making a swift exit, her cheeks reddening with embarrassment.

Veronica eyed Pargeter with interest. That was no way to speak to a woman who so clearly doted on him.

He must have seen the disdain on her face, as his demeanour softened as he ushered them into his compact little room. It was far from the squalid hole that Veronica might have expected in this part of the city. Inside, the sparse furniture was neatly arranged, with Pargeter's scant belongings precisely ordered upon a chest of drawers. There was a small table with two chairs by the window, and he beckoned for Bainbridge and Veronica to accept them, taking a seat himself on his low bunk in the corner.

"Please forgive me," he said, "if I seem a little brittle in my dealings with Miss Carstairs. She's a remarkable woman, and I know she means well, but I fear she sees me as a project, a thing to be fixed, and I am not that."

"No, I can see that," said Veronica.

"The Boers?" said Bainbridge, nodding in the direction of Pargeter's damaged arm.

"Yes. It damn nearly put me out of action completely," said Pargeter. "The bullet tore through my arm and lodged in my chest. The arm was near useless, and I would have bled out on the battlefield if it hadn't been for one of the other men, who dragged me to safety. Took a bullet in the thigh for his trouble, too."

"I can't even begin to imagine the horror," said Veronica. She'd seen so much in her time as an agent—more so again since she'd fallen in with Newbury—but conflict on that scale, the sheer bloodshed... she was grateful she had never had to face it.

"The trouble is," said Pargeter, "no one has much time for an invalid." He hung his head while he talked, refusing to make eye contact. "I'm an educated man. I fought for my country, but now I am reduced to this"—he gestured at the walls, as if they were somehow closing in on him—"eking out an existence like a pauper. Pitied by my landlady." He looked up, catching Veronica's eye. "Fate can be a cruel mistress."

Veronica could see that he was clenching his jaw. He was clearly a proud, honourable man, and she decided that perhaps she had misjudged him, despite his obvious mistreatment of Miss Carstairs. Nevertheless, she refused to feel sorry for him. He wouldn't want that.

"So, what is it?" he said, after a moment. "What do you want to know?"

"Information is all, Mr. Pargeter," said Bainbridge. "We were hoping you could answer some questions regarding your recent hospital stay?"

Pargeter looked bemused. "Well, I don't suppose it could do any harm."

"Excellent," said Bainbridge. "Then tell me—your treatment took place at an institution in St. Giles?"

"That's right," said Pargeter. "A private hospital, created with the specific goal of helping returned soldiers like myself. The work they do there is quite remarkable. The doctor said he could repair my arm."

"And earn some money into the bargain?" said Bainbridge.

Pargeter shrugged. "The treatment was experimental. I suppose he needed willing test subjects. I didn't have much to lose—the arm was already useless."

"Tell us," said Veronica. "What did it involve?"

Pargeter sighed. "If I'm honest, I don't recall a great deal of it. I was down on my luck when I checked into that place, with barely a penny to my name, and nowhere to go. I needed money, and one of the other lads, a chap I'd known out in Africa, told me about the place. He said they paid well for soldiers willing to take part in an experimental treatment."

Veronica glanced at Bainbridge, who was studying Pargeter intently.

"Well, the whole place appeared to have been hastily put together, but I didn't have any other choice. I agreed to undergo the treatment. I was administered a series of injections and given a bed. That's really all I can remember. I think I must have suffered a bout of fever, a reaction to the medicine. I have vague recollections of strange dreams, of the other men on the ward raving, chained to their beds, sprouting strange growths from their mouths, chests, and fingertips, when in truth, they were nothing but the fevered imaginings of my mind. When I came round, the other patients were all fine, and I'd been moved to a side ward to recover."

"And you did? Recover, I mean," said Bainbridge.

"Of course," said Pargeter. "I felt rejuvenated. Reinvigorated. It was quite remarkable, as if the weariness had been scrubbed from my bones. I even regained partial use of my arm." He wriggled the fingers of the hand in the sling to underline his point. "They paid me, and I left."

"And that was all?"

Pargeter nodded. "It may not seem a lot to people like you, miss, but I don't mind telling you that it changed my life. The money was enough to take on this place, to set myself up with a reasonable suit and a clerk's position at a local accounting firm. It's not much, I grant you, but if it wasn't for that hospital I should think I'd be dead on the street by now, or in the workhouse, which might as well amount to the same thing for a cripple."

"Did you remain in touch with the doctor who treated you?" said Veronica. "The man who established this hospital."

"No," said Pargeter. "He called on me a few times in the weeks following my discharge, but I've not been back there, and I've not heard from him for months." He rubbed absently at his bristly chin. "Why? Is he in trouble? Is that what this is about?"

Bainbridge shook his head. "At the moment, Mr. Pargeter, just like you, all we want is to ask him a few questions. Do you recall his name?"

"Yes. Of course," said Pargeter. "Dr. Julian Wren. One of the most remarkable men I've ever met. He changed my life, and for that, Sir Charles, I owe him everything. I'm sure whatever it is you need from him, he'll be only too glad to give it."

"Do you have an address for Dr. Wren?" said Veronica.

"Only the hospital," said Pargeter. He started to get to his feet. "I can look it out for you."

"Oh, no. No need," said Bainbridge. "We're aware of the establishment already."

"Yes, of course," said Pargeter. "Then I'm sure Dr. Wren won't be too difficult to find."

"You've been most helpful," said Bainbridge, getting to his feet. "Thank you for your time." He extended his hand, and Pargeter shook it.

Miss Carstairs was waiting for them in the hallway, pretending to dust a vase, and clearly anxious to know more of what had gone on. Veronica smiled warmly as they passed. "My thanks to you, Miss Carstairs."

"Was Mr. Pargeter able to assist you as you'd hoped?"

"Oh yes," said Veronica. "And I'm sure he would be most grateful of that cup of tea now."

Miss Carstairs smiled. "Thank you, Miss Hobbes."

Outside, Veronica looped arms with Bainbridge, drawing an uncomfortable cough from him, as they hastily made for their carriage.

"Poor devil," said Bainbridge. "To be reduced to that."

"Do not pity him," said Veronica. "He's a strong man, and when he realises that she's a strong woman, too, he'll be right enough."

"Miss Carstairs, you mean?" said Bainbridge, surprised.

"Oh, Sir Charles," said Veronica. "How can someone so intelligent be so blind?"

Bainbridge sighed. "I never was able to fathom the mysterious ways of women," he said.

"It's not the women you need to understand," said Veronica, "but yourself."

"You see?" said Bainbridge, as they approached their waiting carriage. "It's comments like that which I'm talking about. You're not making any sense at all!" He laughed as he hopped up onto the footplate and opened the door. "Now, to Scotland Yard, where we can set to work finding out where this 'Dr. Wren' is hiding, and see about paying him a visit."

CHAPTER 22

Newbury quit the engine room with a heavy heart. He wanted to rail against the stupidity—admonish the fireman and go directly to the train conductor and berate him for his foolishness. Couldn't they see the inherent danger in burning revenant corpses for fuel on a passenger train? Couldn't they see the *horror* in it?

Instead, he fought the urge, suppressing his instincts to intervene. Newbury had never been able to stand by and witness injustice or imperilment, but this time—despite every fibre of his being screaming at him to act—he stood down. He could not become embroiled in the whys and wherefores of official business here on the train. That would lead to questions, investigations, and the one thing Veronica didn't have: time. Besides, the situation had already escalated. It was no longer a hypothetical danger. He had no doubt now that a revenant was loose on the train—perhaps more than one. Everyone aboard was trapped, like beasts in an abattoir, awaiting slaughter.

He hurried past Mrs. Wren's cabin, and through into the dining car, resolute. Things aboard were getting a little too hot, what with the Cabal, and now this. He'd head back to their cabin, tell Amelia to pack her things. They would find a way off the train before the situation deteriorated any further, and take an alternate route to St. Petersburg. He couldn't afford any further setbacks or distractions.

The dining carriage was still full, although some of the faces had changed, as new passengers had arrived to take the place of others. Waitstaff flitted from table to table, and the sight of a freshly cooked steak made his stomach growl. He briefly considered stopping to collect something to eat, but dissuaded himself, choosing to focus on more pressing matters. There'd be time for food at the next station as they awaited an alternative train.

Newbury navigated around the buzzing waiters and out the other side of the dining car. People were milling about in the lobby of the adjoining carriage, traipsing back and forth from the observation lounge—people with little to occupy their time other than idle chitchat and salacious gossip. He tried not to listen to their conversations lest they infuriate him. He wanted to scream at them that they were all blundering into danger, but they'd either mark him down as a madman, or he'd risk starting a riot.

Minutes later, he was standing outside of the cabin he shared with Amelia. He'd already drawn his key, confident that she would have followed his instructions and locked all of the doors behind her. To his dismay, however, as he inserted the key into the lock, the door to his cabin swung open. Nervously, he examined the frame. There were splinters of wood where the lock had been forced. Someone had gained entrance, and then pushed the door to so as not to arouse suspicion.

Newbury cursed himself for not carrying a weapon, and then, steeling himself for what might lay beyond, he stepped into the cabin; jaw set, alert for any signs of an intruder.

He knew immediately that something was wrong. He could sense it, like a sense of stillness in the air. Cautiously he crossed the room, balling his hands into fists and peering into the shadowy recess behind his bunk. There was no one there. Again, though, the door to the adjoining drawing room stood slightly ajar.

He wanted to call out to Amelia, but dared not risk it in case he inadvertently gave warning to the intruder—although it was likely they'd already moved on.

Carefully, he pushed open the door, his palm slick and sweaty against the wood. The drawing room was in disarray. Everything had been overturned; drawers emptied, vases smashed, a curtain pulled free of its rail, now resting crumpled upon the floor. There'd clearly been a struggle, and a systematic search, too, and with dismay he saw that Amelia's armchair had been overturned, the seat fabric shredded, and the book removed. This, then, was clearly the work of the cult, and not the train guards, or an errant revenant that had forced its way in.

Newbury swallowed. His mouth was dry. The missing book was one thing, but what about Amelia? What had they done to her? Terrible images spiralled through his mind, of the corpse laid out in the chair, the icon of the horned beast carved into its dead, pale chest. He thought, too, of the monstrous things he'd encountered in London—the men who had once been human, but had been *adapted,* mechanised, and otherwise transformed through ugly science into slavering beasts.

He closed his eyes for a moment, drawing a deep breath, but all he could see was Amelia's screaming, bloodied face in his mind's eye, silently mouthing his name. And then Veronica, too, pale and on her deathbed, as her ailing heart finally gave in. How had he failed these women so completely? How had it come to this?

With a curse, he crossed the drawing room and kicked angrily at the door to Amelia's cabin, in the vain hope that she might still be locked inside. It rattled noisily in the frame.

"Amelia?"

The door flew open with a bang.

"Amelia? Amelia? Are you there?"

He knew she would have followed his advice, given the opportunity. She would have locked herself away in here until he returned. Something had stopped her. The cultists had obviously been lying in wait, looking for the opportunity to strike, and he had allowed himself to be distracted by the revenant murder.

"Damn it!"

Amelia's bunk had not been disturbed.

He retraced his steps, circling the devastated drawing room, searching for any clues. There was certainly no sign of spilled blood. That had to suggest she'd been taken hostage, rather than murdered outright. Perhaps they intended to use her to draw him out, to lure him into a trap? If so, there was no clue, no sign of where they might have taken her. The room didn't appear to have been staged in any way.

He glanced at his pocket watch. He hadn't been gone for long, certainly no more than an hour. And what of Petunia Wren? She must have parted company with Amelia shortly after he had, if she'd paid any heed to his instructions. Was there a chance, then, that Amelia had gone against his wishes and left with the other woman, taking refuge elsewhere? He hoped so.

He knew now that he had no choice. If she were still alive, he would find her and get her to safety. They had to find a way off this train.

The first carriage was as good a place to start as any. If Amelia was not with Petunia Wren there was at least the chance the woman might have seen something useful, some clue that could point him in the right direction. That was what he would do.

Hurriedly, Newbury ran to the door, pulled it aside, and dashed out, straight into the waiting arms of a revenant.

CHAPTER 23

Amelia woke with a start. Her eyes were gummy and the back of her head was throbbing—a deep, thundering pain, like the beat of horses' hooves against her skull. She took a breath, and tried to move, but her ankles and wrists were bound with what felt like lengths of rough twine. There was something soft pressing against her cheek. She blinked and tried to focus—she was lying on a plush red carpet. Beneath it, like the rumble of distant thunder, she could hear the wheels of the train against the tracks; feel the steady, rhythmic motion of the carriage.

She moistened her lips with her tongue, fighting panic. The last thing she remembered was going to fetch a drink for Petunia. What had happened? There were no stuttering images, no half-recalled scenes—just a horrifying void in her memory. One minute she'd been in the cabin she shared with Newbury, the next she was here—wherever *here* was.

Wincing at the pounding it set off inside her skull, she turned her head, craning her neck to try to get a sense of her surroundings. The room was lit with gas lamps, and in many ways was similar to the drawing room of her cabin. Only this one was far more sumptuously appointed. A grandfather clock ticked ominously in the corner, and paintings hung on the walls between the windows. The ceiling had been painstakingly decorated with a rococo design, and what she could see of the furniture was of an exceptional quality, the woodwork gilded to suggest luxury.

Much of the furniture had been pushed back, however, to create a large space in the centre of the room. In it, a wooden coffin had been propped upright on a mahogany frame to form a macabre centrepiece. There was no lid, and to Amelia's dismay the grim, desiccated corpse of a man stared out at her with a fleshless smile.

She stifled a scream. This was no ordinary corpse. Although the body had been dressed in a smart, black suit, she could see that the torso beneath was grossly misshapen, and what was more, strange, fibrous tendrils had erupted from it, like questing vines, poking their way through the flaking muscles and sinews, worrying holes in the fabric and erupting up and out of the coffin, spreading outwards like the uppermost branches of a tree. They curled across the carpet, burrowed into the nooks and crevices of the walls and ceiling. The vines were everywhere, quivering with what she hoped to be the steady movement of the train. Amongst them nestled strange, grey sacs, like bulbous fruit, ripe and ready to be plucked.

Amelia had no idea what had become of this man, how his body had become host to such horrendous growths, and why he was here, on the train, propped inside an open coffin inside a luxurious cabin.

She sensed movement behind her and twisted to try to see, but couldn't strain far enough because of her bonds. She wondered if it were the cult, if they'd come for her after Newbury had left, slipped into her cabin and struck her from behind. Were they about to do the same to her as that poor man they'd found earlier, carving detestable runes into her flesh before slitting her throat? She gritted her teeth. She hadn't come this far to die like that.

And then she heard the woman's voice, and she knew

that she had made the gravest of errors.

"Oh, Miss Hobbes, the look on your face is a picture. If only you could see it." It was Petunia Wren.

"Petunia? What's happening?" said Amelia. A thousand thoughts flickered through her head, like grains of sand stirred by the wind. Had the cult got them both? Was Petunia tied up behind her? And then it registered–the malign tone in the woman's voice, and the fact she had called Amelia by her real name.

Petunia was still laughing, finding amusement in Amelia's predicament.

"How do you know my real name?" said Amelia, trying to keep the tremor from her voice.

"It wasn't a difficult deduction, my dear," said Petunia. She was moving. Amelia could sense it. A moment later she'd circled around to stand before the prone Amelia, who looked up at her, trying to discern the expression on the woman's face.

"Why? What could I have possibly done to you to warrant this?"

"You really don't know?" said Petunia, with venom. "You really don't remember? Perhaps you don't recognise him with all his... enhancements." With a grunt, she pulled back and loosed a running kick into Amelia's stomach. Amelia buckled, howling in pain, bringing her knees up in defence against any further assault. She knew it was useless however–she was entirely at the mercy of the other woman, a woman who, for some as yet undisclosed slight, had befriended her, before abducting her and taking her hostage.

"Listen, Petunia, I don't know what's going on here. I really don't." Amelia drew a breath, her stomach muscles aching from the sudden assault. "But it's not too late to stop this. Untie me, and tell me what's wrong. If I can help, I will. There's no need for all this."

Petunia dropped into a crouch, reaching out with her gloved

hand and taking hold of Amelia's face. Amelia struggled ineffectively, as Petunia turned her head, squeezing her jaw. She tasted blood as her teeth bit into her cheek.

Petunia brought her own face closer, peering directly into Amelia's eyes. The malice in her expression was unnerving. She wasn't thinking straight. "Come now, Veronica, let us be honest with one another." She released her grip on Amelia's face.

Amelia's eyes widened. "*Veronica?* No, you've got it wrong. I'm not Veronica. I'm her *sister,* Amelia Hobbes."

Petunia lashed out, striking Amelia hard across the face, so that her head rebounded painfully against the floor. "Lies! All of it lies." She was scowling now, and Amelia knew that it wouldn't take much to provoke her to further violence. "Don't you think that I've done my research, that I've planned every stage of this encounter; turned it over and over in my mind? No, this has been *months* in the making. I know that your sister is dead, Veronica. Amelia died during the raid on the Grayling Institute last year. So you can stop it with the pretence, and start facing up to what you've done. You can start taking responsibility for your actions."

"No," said Amelia, quietly. "That's not what happened. I didn't die there. That's what we wanted everyone to believe. It was a cover story, and it's the reason I'm travelling under an assumed name. I've been living incognito in a little English village. You must believe me, Petunia. Whatever Veronica might have done to you, they were not *my* actions."

"It matters little," said Petunia, with a resigned smile. "Whether you admit it or not, the result will be the same. I *know* that it's you. Always by the side of the dashing Sir Maurice, always 'assisting' him with his investigations. You're quite the little agent, aren't you?"

"No!" protested Amelia, tears prickling her eyes. She didn't know what else she could do. Whatever Veronica had done, she must have had her reasons. Yet now this crazed woman was about to enact her revenge on Amelia in Veronica's stead.

It was not the first time Amelia had faced peril, and she would willingly put herself in danger to save her sister—but if she died here and now, on this train, then there was every chance that Veronica would die, too, back in London. It couldn't end like this. Not here, halfway across the continent, with no opportunity to say goodbye to those she cared for, no chance of seeing Veronica restored to health.

Nor, though, could she rely on Newbury to assist her. He was most likely embroiled in the machinations of the cult elsewhere on the train. He wouldn't even know she was missing until it was too late.

No, she had to get out of this one alone.

Carefully, so as not to draw Petunia's attention, she tested the strength of the twine around her wrists. It bit painfully into her flesh. She curled her fingers around, feeling the edges of the knot, picking at it with the bitten-off ends of her fingernails. Her only hope was to keep the woman talking, keep her gloating, while she worked at the knot to free herself.

"Supposing for a moment that you're right," said Amelia. "That I am, indeed, Veronica Hobbes." She swallowed. "You're going to have to remind me what it is that I'm supposed to have done."

Petunia narrowed her eyes. "Very well, Miss Hobbes. If you're going to die, I suppose you should at least know why. Let me tell you a little story…"

CHAPTER 24

Doctor Wren's house was in Tottenham, a melancholy island in a sea of change. Here, the district was swelling with new modern homes designed to house the workers from the railways, and what had once been a pretty suburban landscape was now built-up and overcrowded.

The address that Bainbridge had managed to extract from the records at Scotland Yard was a small detached home, built some time during the previous century, with mature, overgrown gardens and strands of hungry ivy clinging to the porous brickwork. Veronica felt apprehensive as they trudged up the gravel pathway and stood before the peeling front door.

"It doesn't seem particularly well kept," she said to Bainbridge, pitching her voice low in case anyone might overhear and interpret her comment as a slight.

"Indeed not," said Bainbridge. "This is the home of someone who has had money, and has lost it. I've seen the signs too many times before." He raised his cane and rapped loudly on the door, leaving indentations in the flaking blue paintwork. "Let's see if he's at home."

Veronica raised an eyebrow, but didn't comment.

After a moment, she heard a key turn in the lock, and the door swung open to reveal a young maid. She couldn't have been more than sixteen or seventeen, and she looked decidedly nervous at the sight of the two visitors standing on her doorstep.

"Hello?" she said, warily.

"Afternoon," said Bainbridge. "I am Sir Charles Bainbridge of Scotland Yard, and this is my associate, Miss Veronica Hobbes. We're here to see Doctor Wren."

The girl chewed thoughtfully on her bottom lip for a moment, glanced over her shoulder, and then shook her head. It was a short, sharp, decisive gesture. "No," she said. "That is, I'm afraid not."

Bainbridge narrowed his eyes. "No? You mean to say he's not at home?"

The maid looked stricken, but didn't respond.

"Then when will he be back? We'll wait."

The girl shifted her weight from one foot to the other. "It's not that, sir," she said. "It's just... I'm under strict instructions, you see."

"Well, go on," said Bainbridge, impatiently.

"Doctor Wren is working in his study, and when he's working, I'm to permit no visitors. He can't be disturbed, you see? It's delicate work."

"Delicate work, my foot!" said Bainbridge. "Didn't you hear me, girl? We're from Scotland Yard!"

"Well, yes, sir," said the maid. She looked as if she were about to burst into tears. "But nevertheless, I'm under orders. I might lose my position. He'll have me for a hiding if I let you in."

"And I'll have you for a hiding if you don't!" said Bainbridge, his cheeks reddening in anger.

"Sir Charles!" admonished Veronica. She put her hand on his arm. "I think perhaps what the young lady means to say is that she might need us to explain to Doctor Wren that she did everything she could to prevent us from disturbing him, but that you were most forthright about an urgent matter."

"Hmmm. Yes," said Bainbridge. "I see what you mean. In that case," he took a step forward, carefully manoeuvring the maid to one side with his cane. There was no force in the gesture—Veronica knew he would do nothing to harm the girl. Regardless, she moved aside without protest, smiling weakly at Veronica as she followed Bainbridge into the hall.

"Where is he, then?" said Bainbridge.

The maid, seemingly regaining her senses, closed the door behind them, and then made a dash for the stairs.

"Upstairs, is he?" said Bainbridge. "Right then, lead on!"

"Now, Sir Charles," said Veronica, as he thundered up the stairs behind the maid. "You're not going to go in there like a bull in a china shop?"

"I'll go in there as I damn well please," said Bainbridge. "I've been given enough of a runaround already. I want answers."

Veronica sighed. It was times like this she wished Newbury were with them, to help temper Bainbridge's somewhat bombastic nature.

"Doctor Wren? Doctor Wren?" The maid had made it to the first-floor landing ahead of Bainbridge, and was knocking hurriedly on one of the bedroom doors. "Doctor Wren? I'm afraid I really must speak with you. Some visitors have arrived and are quite insistent on seeing you immediately."

Veronica rounded the top of the stairs just as the door opened, and a man—whom she took to be Doctor Wren—appeared in the doorway. He was dressed in a shabby black suit that was covered in streaks of a powdery substance, which Veronica took to be chemical stains. He was wearing a white handkerchief tied over his lower face, and his darting blue eyes were looking past the frantic maid and down the landing towards Bainbridge and Veronica. She saw him frown, stiffen, as if he were about to scold the maid for the interruption, but then he appeared to think twice, and instead gave a shrug of resignation.

"I couldn't stop them, sir. He says he's from Scotland Yard. Just pushed his way in, like. Said he needed to speak with you urgently."

"It's all right, Martha," said Wren. "You go and put the kettle on the stove and leave our visitors to me."

Martha gave an almost comical sigh of relief, nodded in understanding, and then hurried back down the landing, past Bainbridge and Veronica and down the stairs two at a time, evidently anxious to get as far away from proceedings as possible.

"Doctor Julian Wren?" said Bainbridge, marching forward to stand before the man in the open doorway.

"Yes, that's right," said Wren. "Just bear with me a moment, will you, and I'll be able to give you my full attention." He took a step backwards, and then disappeared into the bedroom.

Veronica joined Bainbridge in the doorway. She peered in. It was no ordinary bedroom. The room had been given over to become one of the strangest laboratories she had ever seen. The small space was crammed full of workbenches and bookcases, each of them covered in jars, bottles, and bubbling chemical flasks, but the thing that drew her attention was the fact the room was bristling with vines. They covered the walls and ceiling in a near impenetrable web, quivering green limbs that formed a canopy above their heads. These were, in many ways, identical to the vines she had seen sprouting from the corpses in Stoke Newington, in St Giles, and in the house of ill repute. Only here, they weren't growing wild, but had been trained, clinging to strips of fine trellis that had been nailed to a series of wooden frames. Ripe, bulbous spore sacs dangled like plump lemons, ready for harvesting, and amongst the thick clumps of vines, she was appalled to see the half-rotten corpses of monkeys, nailed to the frames and partially subsumed by the foul fungal growths. This, she realised, was a hothouse, a farm—the place where Wren was cultivating the mysterious fungus that had caused so many deaths.

Veronica glanced at Bainbridge and saw that he, too, had drawn the same conclusion. Wren, across the other side of the room, appeared to be ignoring them, and with a small paring knife was carefully removing one of the spore sacs. She watched as he teased it free of the vine, handling it gingerly so as not to break its delicate membrane. Reverently, he placed the sac in an open bell jar on the workbench beside him, laid the paring knife down beside it, and unhooked the handkerchief that had been covering his lower face.

"There, now," he said. "I'd like to apologise for Martha. She's an excitable young woman. If my wife, Petunia, had been here, I'm sure she would have been dismayed to find such prestigious visitors treated in such a fashion."

"No matter," said Bainbridge, his voice level. "We're here now, and we didn't come to exchange pleasantries."

"No," said Wren. "Indeed not. So tell me, Inspector—what can I do for you?"

"We've been talking with a Mr. Ernest Pargeter," said Bainbridge, clearly testing the water.

Veronica studied Wren's reaction. He narrowed his eyes, as if considering how to respond. "I'm sorry, I… ?" he started.

"A soldier," said Bainbridge. "Returned from the Boer conflict having lost the use of one arm. He said you'd carried out some miraculous procedure on him, restored partial feeling in the damaged limb."

"Ah, yes," said Wren, unable to procrastinate any longer. "I recall the case. He was in a rather sorry state when I found him, but we soon got him back on his feet. I'm glad to hear he's doing well."

"Hmmm," said Bainbridge. "Better than the man we found in Stoke Newington, half eaten by the revenant plague, and half by a strange breed of tropical fungus. Or one of your former nurses, whose body, along with that of her lover, had become infested with the stuff. Or, indeed, all of the dead soldiers in your hospital ward in St. Giles." Bainbridge took a step forward. "Your experiments don't always seem to have quite the desired result, do they, Doctor Wren?"

Veronica saw Wren swallow. His cheeks had flushed, and his lips had grown thin as he tried to maintain his smile. "I… I'm not sure I understand what you're talking about," he said. "A hospital? Experiments?" He stumbled over his words. He was growing increasingly nervous. "I think you must be mistaken."

"So you're saying you *didn't* treat Ernest Pargeter, then?"

"Well… no… that's not what I'm saying."

"So then *he's* mistaken, in the fact that he visited you at the hospital and underwent your treatment programme there?"

It was excruciating to watch—like a worm caught on a hook, and yet still attempting to escape. "Well, like I say, he wasn't in a good way when we found him. He must be misremembering," said Wren.

"I think we both know, Doctor Wren, that he is not," said Veronica.

Wren's shoulders dropped. His expression altered, taking on a hint of defiance. His eyes flicked from Veronica to Bainbridge. "Listen, I have all the relevant paperwork. Every one of my patients signed their consent. They knew exactly what the risks were. I'm pioneering a radical new treatment here, and it's had results. You've seen what it can do. You've seen the impact it had on Pargeter. If only I could re-create that, think of the possibilities, the application. Think how many people I could help."

"Think of how many people you've already killed," said Bainbridge. "Think of *that.*"

"I told you, they knew the risks."

"Really?" said Veronica. "They were fully aware that you were administering doses of the revenant plague to really test the veracity of your miracle cure?"

Wren glowered at Veronica, as if accusing her for bringing such upset into his home. "I…" he faltered. He had no answer.

"It's over, Wren," said Bainbridge. "I've known people like you before. You think you're doing good work, think you're trying to help people, but you've lost sight of what's right and wrong. You've wandered so far off the track that you've become the villain. Don't you see that? You've become the very thing you're trying to prevent. A killer."

Veronica watched Wren chew on his bottom lip. His hands opened and closed nervously.

"Your experiments end here," said Bainbridge. He took another step forward, his hand outstretched, ready to take Wren by the arm. "You're going to come down to the Yard with us, now."

Veronica saw the change in Wren's eyes too late—the look of sudden panic, the frantic search for an escape route—a look she'd seen a hundred times before. "Charles!" she began, in warning, but Wren had already swept up the paring knife in his hand. He brought his arm down in an arc, burying the blade deep in Bainbridge's right shoulder.

Bainbridge howled in shock and pain, staggering back, the knife still buried in the muscle and sinew of his upper arm. Wren twisted, reaching for a glass demijohn, clearly intending to try to finish Bainbridge off with the heavy vessel. He didn't get the chance.

With a roar of anger, Veronica charged across the room, slamming into Wren as he raised the demijohn above his head, and causing him to overbalance, stumbling backwards and sending the glass jar smashing to the floor.

Wren wheeled his arms, but the sudden blow had sent him reeling, and he tumbled back into the nest of vines covering the wall behind him. They seemed to clutch at him like living things, welcoming him into their embrace, just as their many swollen sacs detonated, spilling forth a cloud of deadly spores.

It billowed around Wren like a cloud of buzzing flies, and he gasped, choking back as he inhaled the dreaded substance into his lungs.

"Quickly! Get back, and cover your face," said Bainbridge, grabbing Veronica by the arm and dragging her towards the door. She did as he said, burying her nose and mouth in the crook of her arm, trying not to breathe until they were both safely out on the landing.

Inside the room, Wren wasn't moving. He just hung there amongst the vines; arms splayed wide like a crucifixion. There was a look of abject terror on his pale face.

The spores had begun to settle over his head, his shoulders– the front of his suit: a fine dusting of certain death.

Slowly, Wren reached for his throat, and his body jerked as he made a spasmodic, spluttering motion. He hacked, bringing both hands up to his mouth. His eyes were squeezed tightly shut, as if he couldn't bear to take in the reality of his situation. He seemed wracked in sudden pain. He issued another deep, spluttering cough, and then his eyes flickered open in sudden shock, and something spilled from between his lips. At first she thought it was his tongue, but then she saw, with a dawning sense of horror, that it was the end of a vine.

Wren shuddered, his whole body shaking. His face was beginning to turn purple as the blockage in his throat continued to swell and grow, spilling down his chin like the writhing limbs of a squid. He flung his arms wide again as more vines burst from his chest, burrowing out through his flesh and clothes, smothering him, caressing him, wrapping him in their indecent embrace.

Veronica heard a clatter of dropped china from behind her, and turned to see Martha at the top of the stairs, teacups, spoons, and hot liquid all in disarray by her feet. She screamed–a shrill, piercing shriek–and made to rush forward into the room, but Veronica interceded, sweeping her up, pinning her by her arms and holding her back as she doubled over, weeping. "Oh God, oh God," she was saying, over and over again.

Veronica looked at Bainbridge. He grunted as he yanked the paring knife from his shoulder and tossed it into the room, where Wren's corpse was still blooming, growths unfurling from within him, slowly turning him inside out.

"There's nothing you can do for him now," said Bainbridge.

Martha turned to him, her eyes imploring. "What am I going to say?" she said. "What am I going to tell her?" She slumped to the floor, burying her face in her hands.

Silently, Veronica shut the door to the study and began gathering up the broken china at the top of the stairs, while Bainbridge guided Martha to the drawing room and sent word for assistance.

It wasn't until an hour later, when they were clear of the house and halfway across London, that she finally allowed herself to take a deep, relieved breath.

CHAPTER 25

At first the revenant seemed startled by Newbury's sudden appearance in the passageway. It turned its head back and forth as if conflicted by the choice it had suddenly been presented with—to carry on to the dining car, from where it had evidently caught the scent of roasting meat, or to set upon this fresh delight that had stumbled into its path.

Its indecision was fleeting; it fixed him with its gimlet stare and bared its teeth in a menacing, mindless, grin. Evidence of its previous gruesome meal was all too apparent, flecked upon its teeth and lower lip. The stench of it made Newbury balk.

The creature was dressed in the shredded uniform of a train driver; now barely distinguishable due to the sheer amount blood it had spilled down its front during its recent cannibalistic baptism; Newbury could tell from the rosy pallor of its flesh that the man had not long succumbed to the infection.

He kept pace with it as it shambled closer; raising its arm for the attack, tongue lolling.

His foot encountered the wood-panelled wall. He braced himself, raising his fists. He wasn't carrying a weapon, and here, in the passageway, there was little he could use to improvise. The creature swung at him and he sidestepped, jabbing hard and fast, striking it in the throat. It reeled back for a second, confused, and then lurched forward again, hissing ominously, like an animal backed into a corner.

Newbury twisted and launched himself forward, throwing all of his weight behind the move. He collided with the revenant, grabbing the side of its head and slamming it hard against the window, trying to daze it. The glass panel shook, but didn't shatter, and the creature seemed to barely notice the impact. It shoved him aside, tossing him easily across the narrow passage, so that he slammed into the wall of his cabin, the wooden panels breaking with a rending crack.

He shook his head to clear the grogginess, and then hurriedly twisted out of the way as the revenant's fist struck the wall where he'd had been standing, further splintering the wood. He kicked up and out, impacting with its chest and forcing it to stagger back, providing himself with a little room to manoeuvre. He wiped blood from his burst lower lip, streaking it across his chin.

Newbury had been exposed to the revenant virus once before, during his time in India, and it meant he'd developed a certain level of natural resistance to the infection. He could afford to get scratched without fear of becoming one of them.

Nevertheless, that did nothing to deaden the impact of their talons or arrest their savagery, and he was at just as much risk as anyone else of being disembowelled and eaten. The prospect was not particularly attractive.

It came at him again, and he ducked out of the way, jabbing at its kidneys with two short, sharp punches, to no visible effect. There was no way he was going to beat it in this confined space, especially just with his fists. He would tire long before the creature, and all it would take was one mistake, one misplaced step, and it would all be over. He had to lead it somewhere he could find a weapon.

The dining car was the obvious choice, or rather the

adjoining kitchen, presumably with its stock of knives, cleavers, and other implements.

Newbury treated the creature to another forceful kick in the chest, this time managing to narrowly avoid having his leg mauled by its grasping talons. It fell back against the window, and he bolted, darting past while the thing was off guard. He staggered out into the foyer area, gasping for breath, to realise people were screaming, hurriedly clambering up the spiral steps to the observation deck, or retreating to one of the nearby cabins and bolting the doors. Newbury hoped that meant the other passengers throughout the train were finally waking from their privileged torpor and realising the nature of the threat now manifest all around them.

The revenant, as predicted, came lumbering into the foyer in pursuit, and Newbury waved his arms at it, drawing its attention while the last of the civilians scattered. This particular specimen had yet to develop the preternatural speed that made many of the infected so dangerous, but it nevertheless moved with surprising agility, and a few lurching steps brought it almost within reach again. Newbury backed away, leading it on.

Of course, there was every chance the dining car was still inhabited by passengers intent on their supper, and Newbury knew that he risked exposing them to the creature, but he had little choice; if he died attempting to take it on out here, in the open, then they'd be just as likely to encounter it regardless, when it was done with him.

He felt behind him as he walked, until his hand encountered the door that would lead them through to the dining car. He shoved it open, almost tumbling inside.

Here, four sets of diners were still engaged in their evening meals, merrily sipping from wineglasses, leaning across the table to touch hands, or in the case of one portly chap, helping himself to his wife's leftovers.

"Well, we wouldn't want such delicious food to go to waste now, would we?"

Newbury staggered back as the revenant thrashed in the doorway, caught momentarily in the frame.

"Get out! Everybody get out, *now*!"

The portly man turned to look up at Newbury, dabbing his moustache delicately with a serviette. "Now look here, my man. You can't just come bursting in here deman–"

Newbury cut him off by unceremoniously grabbing the man's head and twisting it around so he could see the revenant.

"Ah. Yes, right. Well, sorry about that," he muttered.

Behind him, one of the other men started to scream.

"I'm going to lead it into the kitchen," said Newbury. "The rest of you get out. Get back to your cabins as quickly as you can, bolt the doors, and stay inside until someone tells you otherwise. Understand?"

The round of murmured affirmatives was cut short when the revenant stumbled three steps further into the carriage, and lurched across at the dinner plate of one of the women, grasping a fistful of roast beef and forcing it into its mouth. It chewed on it with obvious pleasure, juices running down its chin. The woman, whimpering, seemed frozen bolt upright in her seat, her hands on her lap, her eyes flitting from side to side in terrified fashion. The revenant watched her with interest.

Newbury reached across the portly man's place setting and grabbed a discarded fish slice. It wasn't going to do much harm to a revenant, but it should be enough to give the woman chance to flee.

Newbury dropped his shoulder and ran, leaping into the air with his right hand raised above his head, and then, as he came down upon the revenant, bringing his fist down as if thrusting with a spear. The fish slice parted the creature's flesh, and Newbury buried it deep in the thing's exposed throat.

It was a blow that would have killed a man, but the

revenant, sustained by the unnatural virus coursing through its bloodstream, simply staggered back, blood spurting from its severed carotid artery. It doused the walls, showering the table and floor in a fine, red mist.

Newbury grabbed the woman, hauling her from her seat and shoving her at the door. Her white dress and milky skin were speckled with stark crimson drops. Her eyes were wide with shock.

"Go! All of you!" He turned, beckoning to the others, just as the revenant lashed out, catching him square on the shoulder and sending him spinning across one of the tables. Glasses, pots, and plates of food crashed to the floor as Newbury sought to right himself, throwing himself into one of the chairs as the revenant's claws raked the tabletop, its talons scoring runnels in the dark wood.

His shoulder burned where those same talons had punctured the skin, and he could feel warm blood trickling down his arm inside his shirtsleeve.

Newbury dropped to the floor and rolled, before jumping back to his feet, fists ready. The other passengers had fled. In the doorway, beyond the lumbering form of the revenant, stood the portly man, wearing a pained expression, as if he somehow felt he couldn't simply abandon this man who had saved his life, and was considering joining the fray.

"Go!" bellowed Newbury. "While you have the chance!" Their eyes met, and then the man ducked away into the foyer beyond.

Newbury heard voices behind him; the kitchen workers and waitstaff, he presumed. He backed up the central aisle, and the revenant watched him with malign interest, like a hawk studying the short, sharp movements of its prey.

One step... two steps... Newbury turned and bolted for the door to the small kitchen. He heard the revenant growl as it started after him. He shouldered the door, nearly lifting it from its paltry hinges as he crashed through, right into the midst of the hustle and bustle. A waiter was berating one of the cooking staff in clipped French, while the others, standing at their workstations chopping and stirring, pretended not to be listening. They all looked up as Newbury burst in, and the waiter spun on his heel, ready to issue another tirade.

"Revenant," huffed Newbury, as the thing smashed its way through the doorway behind him. Almost instantaneously, the kitchen staff dropped their implements and ran out through the back into what Newbury presumed to be a storage area.

He glanced at the counters: a chopping knife, a potato peeler... and a meat cleaver. He grabbed the handle and swung it around with a cry as the revenant fell upon him.

The blade sunk into the creature's neck with the satisfying crunch of bone. Its talons scratched feebly at the front of his jacket as its head, now only partially attached, lolled slowly to one side, oily blood welling up at the site of the wound, streaming down over Newbury's hand and wrist. He released his hold on the cleaver and the revenant, its body still twitching, slid backwards, and thudded to the floor.

Newbury stood in silence for a moment, his breath ragged, blood dripping from his hand, his shoulder burning with pain. All he could hear was the sound of his own inhalations, and the steady creaking of the train.

How many more of them were there? If they were lucky, the infected still numbered in the single figures. On a train such as this, though, they could multiply exponentially, or worse, maim, kill, and devour their way through the entire passenger list.

The outbreak stemmed from one wound, received in the engine room. The fireman's quarters were further back on the train. That was the origin point. This one had obviously been drawn here by the scent of roasting meat from the dining car. If he were going to attempt to contain them, it would be towards the rear of the train, and he needed something to draw them in. Bait. Something that would call to them even more than warm, living bodies.

Blood.

Cringing, Newbury stooped over the corpse of the revenant. The foetid smell of the corpse turned his stomach, and he fought back a wave of nausea. Despite the obvious signs that the body had been ravaged by the infection—the pallid flesh, the talons, the yellowed eyes—the body, as he had previously assumed, was still relatively fresh. That meant the blood was still close to human.

Newbury took a deep breath, and then rubbed his hands in the gaping wound at the creature's throat, covering them with blood. Then, standing, he smeared the blood across the front of his jacket. It felt slick and gritty, and was already beginning to clot. Scarbright would never forgive him for ruining such a good suit.

He'd sworn he wasn't going to get involved. Amelia was missing, Veronica was dying, and for all he knew, he'd just killed the thing that had once been the train's driver, meaning they were hurtling across the Continent with no one watching the controls. And now he was covered in blood.

He grinned, and swept up the meat cleaver in his fist. Hopefully, this wouldn't take long.

CHAPTER 26

The alarm had clearly been raised throughout the rest of the train; people had scattered, abandoning the communal areas and retreating to their cabins to wait out the emergency.

As Newbury marched through the carriages he encountered only a handful of stragglers, and each of them gave him a decidedly wide berth—doused in revenant blood and carrying a meat cleaver, he must have looked a fearsome sight as he strode through each of the carriages in search of the infected.

Here and there he saw evidence of the creatures' passing—a spray of dark blood upon a wall, a damaged cabin door, an errant shoe—but even the train guards were noticeably absent. They, too, must have retreated to the relative safety of their rooms. He hoped they were making preparations for a rescue, or at least a plan to deal with the situation somehow.

He was in no doubt now that they faced serious delays— the train would have to be stopped, the surviving passengers and staff checked for signs of infection—but anything he could do to minimise that delay would be of service to Veronica. Finding a means to confine the revenants to one area of the train would hasten proceedings, and prevent any further innocents falling victim to the diabolical creatures.

He only hoped that wherever Amelia was, that she, too,

was safe. She was strong—and growing stronger almost daily—but she hadn't been exposed to the world like Veronica; she hadn't yet learned to handle herself in a fight, or to readily identify those who might mean her harm. He supposed in many ways that was a good thing—the life of an agent was not an admirable existence, dedicated to subterfuge, violence, and mistrust. Perhaps it was better that Amelia didn't become hardened to the world like he and Veronica had. But then... he supposed that wasn't his choice to make.

He pushed through another set of doors, passing from one carriage into another. Here, a lone train guard was coming in the other direction—a cadaverous-looking man with a neat moustache and a heavy brow, which seemed to jut out from beneath his peaked cap. He started to say something in French—Newbury didn't catch the entire gist of it, but it seemed to be a warning about returning to his cabin—but then stopped short when Newbury's dishevelled appearance finally registered. His eyes widened, and he fumbled for his truncheon as Newbury strode towards him.

"Out of my way," said Newbury. "You don't want to do that. I'm trying to help."

The man mumbled something, unsure of how to respond, and then Newbury was in front of him, shoving him aside as he pushed past and onwards down the passageway.

"You might want to think about finding somewhere else to stand," he called, over his shoulder. "The revenants will be along in a moment."

He knew for certain that one of the creatures had already picked up his trail—he'd heard it shambling behind him in the previous carriage. It had yet to make its move, and he hoped that if he were swift enough, he might be able to avoid any direct conflict with the creature or its brethren. His plan was to lure them to the end of the train—the last carriage in the line—and entrap them there. He had no idea yet if it would work, or whether he was simply going to get himself torn to pieces, but it seemed to him like the only option.

He passed through into another carriage. Here, someone had clearly fared badly during an encounter with one of the creatures; a man's legs protruded from the open door of a cabin, and glossy streams of blood were flowing into the passage. Newbury slowed, conscious of the other revenant coming up behind him.

Cautiously, his back to the wall, he edged around the man's legs, gripping the handle of the cleaver tightly in his fist. The inside of the cabin hove into view.

A revenant was hunched over the carcass of the man, its hands buried deep in the hole that had once been his chest. The revenant was female—a former passenger, judging by her flower-print dress—and had its back to him as it gorged itself on the bloody remains.

Newbury took another step along the passageway, and the revenant stopped, suddenly aware of his presence. It raised its head, sniffing the air and listening. Newbury swallowed. He heard the door swing open further up the passage—the other revenant, the one that had been following him, had entered the carriage, too.

The revenant in the room twisted around to look at him. Its yellow eyes seemed to burn right through him. Blood dripped from its chin, and the fatty remnants of the man's flesh were still stuck in its teeth. From further up the passageway, the shambling footsteps of the other one were growing louder, closer.

Newbury steadied himself. He couldn't take on two of them. Not here, like this. His only recourse was to outrun them, and hope the others picked up on his trail in the process. He was more than halfway to the rear of the train now—assuming he didn't find his way blocked, there was still a chance he could beat them there.

Decision made, he turned and ran. A thud from behind told him that the revenant from the cabin had set out in pursuit. He felt his heart quicken. Up ahead, the door to the next carriage loomed. He slammed into it, fumbling for the handle, and threw it open, stumbling through. The passage beyond was empty. Hurriedly, he slammed it shut behind him and ran.

The door didn't hold the thing for long, as it thundered through, splintering the wood in its haste to reach him. Newbury, though, was already at the next door, dragging it open and slipping past, drawing ragged breath as he moved into the next carriage.

This one, too, was empty. He was through it in seconds, bursting into the vestibule of the adjoining car—only to find his path interrupted by the hulking form of a third revenant. He sighed, beginning to think his plan had been somewhat lacking.

The creature was holding a dismembered human arm, still swaddled in rags, and it raised it like a club, baring its teeth in a vicious snarl. Newbury didn't have time to stop. He charged it, swinging the meat cleaver in a wide arc.

The revenant, caught off guard, fell back as the weapon bit deep into its chest. He felt it crunch through bone and wedge amongst the splintered rib cage. He yanked on the haft, but the weapon was stuck fast. Grimacing in frustration, he abandoned it just in time to avoid a swipe from the creature's talons, which narrowly missed his cheek as he twisted past, darting for the door. Within seconds he was through and into the next carriage.

He was starting to fear his plan was not going to work— the revenants were too strong, forcing their way through the doors. Even if he managed to succeed in trapping them, it wouldn't be for long; he'd have to find a way to barricade them in, or else destroy them somehow.

There were at least three of them now, probably more, in pursuit. He hurried through the next carriage, rebounding off the walls as he ran, shaken by the stuttering movement of the train.

He rushed through another vestibule, and into another carriage. This was it—the final carriage of the long, snaking train. Rather than cabins, it was set out as another observation lounge, with rows of faded armchairs flanking the windows, small card tables and potted plants, and a rear door leading to a small viewing platform surrounded by a high metal rail.

He heard a noise from behind and spun around on the spot, fearing the presence of another revenant. Instead, he felt a human fist smash into his jaw, knocking him sideways and causing him to topple over the back of an armchair and sprawl across the floor.

Smarting, he picked himself up, pulling himself around behind the chair for cover while he got a measure of his opponent.

It was a man in a smart black suit. He was clean-shaven, with two thin scars upon his face—silvery white lines from ritual cuttings, rather than accidental trauma. He was grinning manically as he watched Newbury get to his feet, and was brandishing a long, curved, bone dagger in his right fist. It was etched with a series of elaborate channels and engravings.

This, then, was a representative of the Cabal; the man who'd left the corpse in his cabin; who had taken the book, and was most likely responsible for Amelia's abduction.

"Sir Maurice. How good to finally make your acquaintance. My masters send their regards."

"You fool!" said Newbury. "They're coming."

The cultist smiled. He took a step forward, raising his blade. "No one's coming. No friends from Scotland Yard, no *assistants*. You're all alone now, Sir Maurice, and it is time to pay for what you took from us."

"No, you don't understa—" started Newbury, but was forced to duck to one side as the cultist lashed out suddenly with his blade, nicking Newbury's ear and drawing a stream of blood.

Newbury wished he'd hung on to his cleaver—the revenants would be on them any second, and he was woefully unarmed. He feinted left, then right, sweeping up a small table lamp and swinging it up and around. The heavy iron base caught the cultist under the chin, causing him to stagger back, shaking his head. He grabbed for a nearby table, righting himself, and spat a gobbet of blood.

"I was hoping you'd put up a fight," he said.

"It's not me you need to be worried about," said Newbury.

The cultist turned at the sound of a low growl from the doorway. One of the revenants—a hulking male in the tatters of a fireman's uniform, ribbons of flesh peeling from its face—loomed in the opening, its eyes flicking from one of them to the other, as if sizing up its next meal. Behind it, others were clamouring to get through the doorway. Newbury counted at least five pairs of limbs, scratching and tearing at one another as they fought for dominance.

The cultist backed away, his dagger held aloft. He glanced at Newbury, accusation in his eyes. "You led them here?"

Newbury didn't deign to answer. He hefted the table lamp. It wasn't going to protect him for long, but he might be able to brain a couple of them before he went down.

The revenant in the doorway lurched for the cultist, covering the ground between them in less time than it took to draw breath. The cultist was quick to react, slashing with the blade and opening the creature's throat. It gargled and lashed out with its talons, and Newbury saw the cultist parry the blow with another swipe of his blade. He didn't have time to ponder on it, however, as the others had now spilled into the carriage and were circling him, teeth and talons bared.

The female he'd seen in the cabin earlier was the first to move. It darted forward, slashing with its right hand, and Newbury kicked the armchair forward with as much force as he could muster, catching it in the midriff and taking its legs out from beneath it. It went down in front of him and he smashed the table lamp across the back of its skull, feeling it crack like an eggshell beneath the force of the blow.

He came up swinging the lamp before him, striking another across the side of the head, so that it fell into the path of a third, which gouged at it furiously, tearing out its throat and tossing its corpse aside.

Newbury could see more of the creatures lurching in through the doorway behind it.

He risked a glance at the cultist, to see that he was still valiantly defending himself, his porcelain-coloured blade flashing back and forth. One revenant was already dead by his feet; another was clutching at its throat, blood spurting through its fingers.

"Make for the rear door," bellowed Newbury, edging around behind another armchair, attempting to keep another of the creatures at bay. "If we work together we can hold them off long enough to get free."

The cultist laughed. "What delicious irony. The enemy of thine enemy."

Newbury battered aside another swipe. His entire body was aching, his arms and legs like dead weights. The blood he had smeared upon himself earlier seemed to have seeped into every pore: a sticky, gritty film that coated his skin, leaving him feeling as if he were fighting through treacle. He knew he was on the verge of nervous collapse; the treatments he'd been performing on Amelia had sapped much of his stamina. Yet he could think only of Veronica, her lily-white face upon her pillow, fading slowly towards oblivion.

The thought gave him strength, and he lashed out again, catching another revenant across the side of the head. It stumbled, disorientated, and then came on again. Newbury kicked a card table into its path as he backed away, heading incrementally towards the door.

He was standing almost shoulder-to-shoulder with the cultist now, and as the two of them swung and slashed, he wondered what would happen when they finally made it to the door. There was no doubt the cultist would resume his efforts to kill him, if Newbury didn't take the opportunity to strike first. Nevertheless, he had to find out what had happened to Amelia: where the man had taken her, and what he had done.

The cultist's blade flashed before Newbury's face, and he flinched, stumbling back, thinking for a moment that the man had decided to cut him down now. Instead, though, he felt the splash of warm blood, as a revenant fell back, its face parted from jaw to forehead, its left eye blinded and dribbling out across its pale cheek.

He sensed the rear wall behind him. The carriage was packed with revenants now—at least a dozen of them, including those that had been recently put down. The cultist had proved useful in keeping the creatures at bay, but had disrupted his plan—the door to the carriage was still open. He needed to find a way to close it from the other side, trapping the revenants within. There was no going through them, though—he'd have to find a way to go round, or worse, to go *over*. Preferably before they began to disperse.

"Are you ready?" he said, risking a glance at the cultist, who had his foot up on a revenant's chest as he worked to free his blade from its lolling head.

"Whatever you're going to do, do it *now*," said the cultist.

Newbury took a final swing with the table lamp, launching it at another of the lumbering creatures, and then turned and grabbed the door handle. He shoved the door open and stepped through, then, in one fluid motion, pivoted on the spot, grabbed the cultist by the back of his collar and hauled him out onto the viewing platform, before slamming the door shut behind him.

CHAPTER 27

"So you see, Miss Hobbes, the maid told me everything. I know *exactly* what happened." Petunia had been pacing back and forth across the cabin while she recited her tale, and now she had stopped beside her late husband's coffin and was slowly caressing his malformed face, cupping his cheek in her palm as if he were simply asleep. "I know what she did to you, my love."

"Where is the maid now?" said Amelia, desperate to keep the woman talking for as long as possible. Whatever form of revenge she had in mind, she was planning to enact it here, on the train. There wasn't much time.

Petunia looked over, and smiled. It was a wicked sort of smile. "Oh, *she's* feeding the vines back in Tottenham. The police cleared out Julian's laboratory, of course, but they missed the stuff in the garden. She made quite a display, opening up like a flower in the potting shed. She'll be ripening nicely by now." She shrugged. "It was the least she could do, keeping his legacy alive like that. She might have stopped you, you see? She should never have let you in. She was under express orders to keep people away. So I had to teach her about responsibility. She had to pay for her part in things."

Amelia worried her bonds. They were finally starting to

work loose around her left wrist. It was clear to her now that the woman was completely unhinged. This was more than a simple desire for revenge–the death of her husband had unleashed something monstrous in this woman; had broken her in ways Amelia could not understand. Over the years, Amelia had seen others like her, abandoned to the institutions, slowly retreating inside cocoons of their own carefully constructed realities. She needed help.

"I'm sure Veronica didn't mean for things to end that way," said Amelia, trying to keep her tone as reasonable as possible. "How could she have known what would happen?" She twisted her wrists again, and winced as the twine bit into her skin. She could feel blood trickling down into her palm, making it harder for her fingers to find purchase on the knot.

"And *still* you persist with this ridiculous fallacy," said Petunia, scowling. "Can't you see that I know the truth? I know everything about you, Veronica." She left her husband's side and crossed the cabin to stand over Amelia. "It matters little. I should have expected such lies. A woman such as you, lurching from one deceit to another–you've probably forgotten *how* to tell the truth. Whether you go to your death protesting your innocence, or finally admitting the truth, justice will still be served, and Julian's legacy will go on."

"I thought you said the police cleared out his laboratory?" said Amelia.

Petunia frowned. "What of it?"

"Then how is he here, on the train? Didn't the police impound his body? I should have thought they would mark it for incineration."

Petunia grinned. "They incinerated *something*," she said. "Or rather, some*one*."

"One of those poor soldiers," said Amelia. "You had someone switch the remains."

"It's surprising what lonely young men can be coerced to

do, isn't it, Miss Hobbes? It wasn't difficult to arrange. There was a policeman." She paused, suddenly serious. "I couldn't allow them to *burn* him."

There was *a policeman.* Amelia didn't like her use of the past tense. Just how many people had this woman already killed? "And what next? You kill me, and then continue with your little crusade? When is it going to end?"

"You still don't understand, do you?" said Petunia. Her manner, as always, was smug and superior.

"I'm sure you're going to tell me regardless," said Amelia.

"*This* is where it ends. Here and now. This is the moment I've been waiting for. I've crafted a perfect ending. Julian and I, we'd always wanted to take a trip across the Continent, but his work… it was so important. It's going to change the world. Now, though, we've finally made the time. We're seeing the world together."

"He's *dead,*" said Amelia.

Petunia drew back her foot and kicked her, hard, in the stomach. Amelia spluttered as she gasped for air. The pain was excruciating, and she brought her knees up defensively in case Petunia hadn't finished.

She'd started pacing again, however, lost in her own make-believe world. "How can he be dead? Look at him! Look at the *life* he's creating. He's changed. *Transformed.* But not *dead.* He's just… moved on to better things. His work is more important now than it ever was. And soon we're going to be properly reunited."

The wild look in the woman's eyes told Amelia everything she needed to know. "You're going to kill us both, aren't you?" she said. "You're going to open up one of those spore sacs and turn us into something monstrous, like *that.*" She indicated the corpse in the coffin with a nod of her head. The thought of it appalled her. Worse, she wondered what would become of Newbury when he found her, whether the spores might infect him, too. And what would that mean for Veronica? There would be no one left to help her, and she'd die back there in London, with no one coming home to save her.

Amelia redoubled her efforts to free her wrists, biting down on her lip as the twine slipped and slid across her flesh, slicing agonising furrows.

"'Do unto others as you would have them do unto you.' That's how it goes, isn't it?" Petunia was laughing now. "From the moment I discovered Sir Maurice had bought tickets for the train, I knew this was how it would end. You were so easily taken in, Miss Hobbes. Almost like a child. It was as if you wanted to believe the world was still the innocent place you'd always dreamed it to be. You really should know better by now. All the things you've seen. The things you've *done.*"

"I've told you. I am *not* Veronica."

Petunia wheeled around on the spot, intending to administer another blow, but this time Amelia was ready for her. She'd carefully manoeuvred her bound legs into position, and she propelled herself forward with a sudden kick. Her arms—now free of the twine—encircled Petunia's calves, and the momentum carried them both over.

Petunia howled in shock and consternation, throwing out her arms to save herself. The tackle was sound, however, and she fell hard, striking her face and rolling onto her side.

Amelia rolled, too, but her bound legs were too much of a hindrance, and she was unable to hold on to Petunia's legs as the woman kicked and thrashed, catching Amelia in the face with her boot.

Amelia released her, falling to one side and bringing her knees up again, this time feeling for the knot that would release her ankles. As she scrabbled, Petunia dragged herself up onto her knees, twisting about and aiming a blow at the side of Amelia's head. She ducked, but was too slow, and the cuff knocked her sideways. She hit the carpet, her thoughts sluggish. She blinked, trying desperately to bring herself round, expecting another blow at any moment.

Petunia, however, had other plans. She was on her feet by her husband's coffin, reaching out for one of the bulbous spore sacs with her gloved hand.

"No! Don't do it. *Please,* Petunia. You don't have to do this."

Petunia turned to look at her, and their eyes met. Then she closed her fist, and the spore sac exploded.

Dust plumed all around her, like the discharge of a deadly perfume bottle. The air filled with a musty scent, and Amelia clamped her mouth shut, trying desperately not to inhale as her fingers worked at the knotted twine.

Petunia was laughing. "It's too late, Veronica. It's done. There's nothing either of us can do." She reached over and burst another spore sac, then a third, hacking as she took the stuff deep into her lungs.

Amelia could feel her cheeks reddening as she fought against the desperate urge to breathe. Her fingers were slipping on the knot, unable to find purchase. Panic flared.

She glanced over at Petunia, whose eyes had grown suddenly wide, and was clutching at her chest, hugging herself, her mouth hanging open in a silent scream.

Tears pricked Amelia's eyes. The knot was stuck fast. There was no time. She threw herself onto her stomach and began dragging herself across the carpet, grabbing fistfuls of it as she made for the door. Her lungs were on fire now, and her vision was growing hazy, as if the world was slowly closing in on her from all directions. She wasn't going to be able to hold out for much longer.

She heard a wet retching sound from behind her, and turned to see a thick bundle of vines bursting from Petunia's mouth, spilling out like curling green tentacles. Three plump vines had erupted from her stomach, too, and shoots were beginning to emerge from her fingertips, blood dripping upon the floor as they forced their way out beneath the fingernails. These fresh vines were interlacing with those of her dead husband, forming an intricate web, finally returning the two lovers to the embrace for which Petunia had been longing. The woman was already dead—her head was hanging limp, her eyes staring and unseeing. It had taken only moments for her to be utterly subsumed.

Amelia was close to the door. She shuffled forward, pushed herself up into a sitting position, reached for the handle... and then fell back, teetering on the brink of unconsciousness. Her vision swam. Her body was protesting from the lack of oxygen. She tried to keep her mouth clamped shut, but the act was involuntary, and, unable to stop herself, she parted her lips and took a short, gasping breath.

Immediately she tasted the spores on her tongue—the dry, fusty flavour of something stale or rotten—and she knew that it was over. Within moments they'd be in her bloodstream, coursing through her body, *altering* her from the inside out. She was going to die here, halfway across the Continent, apart from her friends and family.

Her head felt fuzzy, and she noticed a sudden chill, starting deep in her stomach and spreading up through her abdomen and lower back. She closed her eyes, and willed it to be over quickly.

CHAPTER 28

"What did you do to her?"

Newbury shoved the cultist back against the door, one hand around the man's throat, the other pinning his knife arm to the wall. The revenants inside the carriage were scratching at the glass with their talons—it would be a matter of moments before they broke through and the two men found themselves hemmed in, with nowhere left to go. The iron railings out here were shoulder high, designed to prevent unwary passengers from stumbling off the end of the train as they took in the view. If the revenants got loose, they were both dead.

It was dark now, the only light coming from the distant, gibbous moon and the paraffin lamp dangling from an overhead hook. It swung with the motion of the train, causing the cultist's face to flicker with shadow. The cool breeze was revitalising, whipping at the two men as the train sped through the velvet night, stirring their clothes and hair.

"Oh, now *this* is interesting," said the cultist, struggling to catch his breath as Newbury's thumb pressed against his windpipe. "You think *I* took her."

"You're the only one on this train with good reason to," said Newbury. "Now tell me what you've done to her."

The cultist laughed, and Newbury squeezed a little harder. "Tell me."

"I didn't take her," gasped the cultist. "But I know who did." He twitched at the sound of breaking glass, as one of the revenants' fists burst through a window, clawing for them.

Newbury forcibly turned the man's head, until he could see the revenant's talons only inches from the end of his nose. "*Tell* me."

The cultist grinned again. "It was a woman. I heard them squabbling inside your cabin and waited until they emerged. She dragged the girl off while no one was looking, and I seized my chance to take another look inside. As pretty as she is, I'm not here for the girl... only you."

Newbury released his grip on the man's throat. So it had been Petunia Wren. There was no reason for the cultist to be lying.

Newbury cursed himself. He should have trusted his instincts about the woman. But what business did she have abducting Amelia like that? It made no sense.

"Drop the knife and I'll let you live," said Newbury.

"It's a little too late for that," said the cultist. He dipped his head to indicate the wound on his chest. The fabric of his suit had been torn, and there were three long welts across the man's scarred chest. The flesh had puckered around the wounds, and blood oozed from the scratches. One of the revenants had caught him during the fight inside the carriage. He was already dead. He had nothing to lose.

The cultist's knee came up and collided painfully with Newbury's groin.

Newbury staggered back, bringing his fists up, as the cultist swung at him with his blade. Newbury was too slow to avoid it, and the knife slashed his forearm, parting fabric, flesh, and muscle. He grimaced in pain, punching low and striking the cultist in the gut, and then again on the side of the head. The man staggered groggily, and then came up and at him again in a smooth stabbing motion. Newbury was expecting it, however, and dived out of the way as the blade whistled past his midriff. He threw another wide punch at the man's head, trying to keep him down.

The cultist shook it off, flexing his shoulders. "You might consider me the villain," he rasped, "but think on this, Sir Maurice: It was *you* who stole from *us.*"

"I did what I had to do," said Newbury.

"As do I," said the cultist. He roared, throwing himself forward, aiming his weapon at Newbury's throat. Newbury dropped to one knee and punched upwards, striking the cultist hard in the chest and causing him to overcompensate, falling back against the railings.

Newbury heard more glass shattering behind him. He was running out of time. All that the cultist had to do now was keep Newbury fighting long enough for the revenants to break free. His own life was already forfeit, yet he was clearly intent on taking Newbury down with him.

The train shuddered, and the paraffin lamp swung wildly on its hook, momentarily bathing them in light, and then sudden darkness. Newbury glanced at it, calculating the distance. Three steps. He moved, and the cultist circled, knife at the ready. Newbury took another step, and the cultist shifted, closing the distance between them.

Over the cultist's shoulder, the revenants were attempting to clamber through the broken windows.

It was now or never. He reached up for the paraffin lamp as the cultist swept forward, dragging it off its hook and swinging it down against the man's head. He felt the cultist's blade slide into his upper arm as the lamp shattered, dousing the man in oily paraffin, which—exposed to the flame—ignited almost immediately.

The cultist screamed as his head and shoulders were

consumed by the sudden conflagration, and Newbury shoved him away, yanking the knife from his shoulder and tossing it through the railings to the tracks below.

The cultist staggered back, attempting to smother the flames with his hands, but succeeding only in spreading the fire up his arms, and across his chest. Blindly, he stumbled back from Newbury towards the grasping arms of the revenants.

They grappled for him, and he screamed again as their talons punctured his flesh, pulling him closer. They lifted him from his feet, dragging him bodily through the broken window and into the carriage. Newbury watched as the flames spread hungrily, first igniting the blinds, then the carpet, then the two revenants who had set about trying to consume the roasting man.

Within seconds the entire carriage was ablaze.

Newbury felt the heat of the fire against his face, even from the viewing platform outside. He flexed his damaged arm, testing his strength. He had nowhere left to go, but up. With the fire spreading, he had to get word to the driver, to stop the train. Worse, Amelia was on the other side of that burning carriage, held captive—if not already dead—at the hands of the mysterious Petunia Wren.

Sighing, he cast around for anything he could use as a foothold, but there was nothing. He'd have to pull himself up on the railings and jump across. He didn't fancy his chances, but neither could he see any choice. If he stayed where he was, he was likely to burn to death within the hour, regardless.

Gritting his teeth, he grabbed hold of the railing and hauled himself up, twisting into a sitting position. He balanced precariously on the top of the railing, holding on for dear life as the train shook, rumbling over the metal tracks below. One false move now, and he'd be over the side, and dead.

He scanned the roof of the carriage, looking for possible handholds. There was a slight camber, with a thin lip running around the edges of the carriage roof. If he could throw himself across and catch hold of that, he could pull himself up from there. Then it was a short crawl across the rooftop to the next carriage, where he'd have to kick out one of the windows and swing himself in.

He knew it was lunacy, particularly in his present condition. But then, he supposed it had never stopped him before. Tentatively, he raised himself up, lifting one foot onto the top of the railing. He tested his footing. The railing was strong enough and wasn't going to give way. He remained in a crouching position for a moment, breathing steadily, before raising his other foot, still clinging onto the railing with one hand.

For a moment he rocked back and forth with the steady movement of the train, and then, with an almighty roar, he launched himself through the air towards the roof of the flaming carriage.

CHAPTER 29

As the roof of the carriage swam up to meet him, Newbury realised he'd overshot. Instead of catching hold of the rim, he was sailing right over it, and he flung out his arms, his fingers grasping for purchase as he came down.

He struck the roof with an almighty thud, and for a moment he thought it was about to give way and send him tumbling into the hellish pit of burning revenants below. It held, buckling slightly beneath his weight, and instead he found himself sliding dangerously off to one side, dragged by the momentum of the train and with nothing to grab hold of to prevent him from falling. He pressed himself flat and allowed himself to career over to the camber, then swung his legs around at the last minute, jamming the tip of his boots against the rail, his palms flat against the thin metal roof. Slowly, he slid to a halt.

He lay there for a moment, forcing himself to breathe. Beneath him, the tin roof was hot from the blaze, searing his hands. He wouldn't be able to hold on for very long.

The train was still hurtling through the gloaming, and showed no signs of slowing. To either side there was nothing but rolling fields of corn, punctuated by occasional farmhouses, distant and shrouded in shadow, like slumbering dragons, smoke curling from their chimneys.

Up here, the force of the forward motion threatened to sweep him off every time he lifted his head. He was going to have to keep low and slide across on his belly like a snake, keeping one foot jammed against the rim to prevent him from slipping off.

Cautiously he dragged himself along, inching over the smooth metal surface, clinging to each available rivet. His arms ached, and the stab wound throbbed dully, his shirt soaked through with blood. It felt cold and damp against his skin now—a constant reminder. He'd need to get it seen to as soon as he'd found Amelia.

He laughed at himself, clinging to the roof of a moving train, barely holding on to to his life by a thread, and yet still making plans regarding the medical treatment he would need when it was all over. Perhaps he was more of an optimist than he'd ever realised.

The train bucked as the carriage rolled over a section of uneven track, and his foot slipped, causing him to thrash frantically, almost skittering over the side before his other foot found purchase and he was able to halt his sudden, alarming descent.

He dragged at the air, taking deep breaths and forcing himself to remain calm.

Below, he could hear the sounds of the revenants howling grotesquely as they burned, thundering around inside the carriage. Smoke curled from numerous broken windows, inky and pungent, spiralling away into the night like broiling storm clouds.

Soon the creatures would spread the flames to the adjoining carriages, if he weren't able to close the remaining door and seal them in. Not that the door would hold the fire or the revenants for long—the only real hope was to stop the train and decouple the burning carriage entirely. If he made it off the damn roof alive, he'd make sure that's what happened.

Newbury resumed his crawl across the rooftop. It was painstaking work, shifting his weight carefully, creeping no more than a few inches at a time. His palms were beginning to blister from the heat, and he could sense the revenants below, their arms grasping through the windows beneath him, as if, even now, they could still recognise his scent.

He risked a glance along the rooftop. He was close now. Another few yards and he'd be able to start planning his descent. He shifted his foot, prising it from the rim as he edged another few inches. And then the train hit a sharp bend in the rail, and he was suddenly sliding over the edge, his hands scrabbling at the roof, unable to find anything to grasp onto. He dropped, his legs swinging out as his fingers sought the rim, clutching desperately.

They caught, smashing painfully into the metal runnel. He fought to cling on, his feet scrabbling at the window frames below, searching for anything that might help to prop him up. He had no more than a few feet to go, now, before he reached the vestibule area at the end of the carriage and could attempt to find a way back inside.

Something growled, and he glanced down to see a revenant's hand shooting out through a hole in a shattered pane, grappling for his ankle. He kicked at it wildly, swinging out of the way and nearly losing his handhold in the process. His fingertips burned. He tried to peer into the carriage, but the smoke obscured everything but the hulking silhouettes of the creatures. He choked back on it, trying to ignore the horrific scent of roasting flesh.

The revenant's hand was still blindly searching for him, its talons scratching at the paintwork around the window. He was going to have to go past it.

He cursed himself for setting out on this path in the first instance. What was it about, this self-appointed need to help in a crisis? Why couldn't he just sit back like everyone else and allow the authorities to do their work?

He eyed the revenant's talons. He had two choices: Try to go around it, or use it as a foothold to boost him over to the end of the carriage. It was a risk—if it got hold of him, he didn't know if he'd have the strength to fight it off and still maintain his grip on the roof.

He sighed. He supposed one more risk wasn't going to make much difference now. Working himself into position, he began to swing back and forth like a pendulum, using the motion of the train to his advantage. His fingers were growing numb, threatening to seize, but he clenched his jaw and forced himself to continue, working up a good momentum.

One more swing...

Newbury let go of the roof with his left hand and allowed the momentum to take him. He reached out with his foot, planting it as firmly as possible on the revenant's forearm, and then propelled himself forward, releasing his other handhold for a split second as he sailed through the air, parallel to the train.

He heard the revenant issue a growl, and the arm twisted, grasping for him, but he was already past it, clutching hold of the roof again and pulling himself along. His feet flapped in ungainly fashion as he dangled, his arms about to give out... and then he was there, at the vestibule, beyond the worst of the flaming carriage.

Getting inside was another matter entirely. There was a window here, probably big enough for him to wriggle through—but it was closed from the inside. He was going to have to break it.

Crying out in agony, he hauled himself up and bent his knees, so that the soles of his boots were pressed flat against the windowpane. Then—clinging on with what was left of his reserves—began to hammer on the glass with his heel.

At first the pane simply reverberated in the frame, and for a moment he thought he was about to be thwarted, right here at the end—but then the glass gave a satisfying *crack*, fracture lines spidering out from the site of the impact. He kicked again, and this time his foot went through, along with an attendant shower of broken glass.

Swiftly, he kicked away as many of the jagged edges as he could, and then lowered himself in through the opening, feeling the ragged shards scoring his back through his jacket as he twisted and dropped to the floor.

A moment later he was standing unsteadily inside the vestibule, his shredded fingers dripping blood.

Newbury glanced up at the burning carriage. The door was still hanging open. Inside, he could see the bulky shape of a revenant lurching towards him through the pall of smoke, its clothes smouldering, its flesh scorched and black. It was heading for the door, having picked up his scent.

Newbury reached for the door, and slammed it shut. "Oh no you don't," he said, his voice a dry croak. "You're staying right where you are."

He turned and ran.

The train was as empty now as it had been a few moments before, as he'd passed through in the other direction. As he ran, he called out for a guard, bellowing at the top of his lungs in an effort to gain attention.

In the third carriage he entered, he saw a man in uniform stepping out from one of the cabins, frowning at Newbury as he came hurtling along the passageway.

Newbury skidded to a halt, and grabbed the man by the front of his jacket. The guard looked alarmed, but didn't put up any immediate resistance, clearly terrified by Newbury's wild manner.

"There's a fire," said Newbury, between gulps of air. "Back there, in the last carriage. The whole place has gone up. It's full of revenants. You've got to stop the train before it spreads."

The man stared at him blankly, as if trying to comprehend what Newbury was telling him, to make sense of the terrible state of the raving man standing before him, clutching him by the front of his uniform.

"A *fire*," repeated Newbury. "Do you understand? You have to get the driver to stop the train."

Slowly, the man nodded, and then finally something seemed to register. He pushed Newbury away, and stirred into action. He closed the door to the cabin and set off at a run for the front of the train.

Relieved, Newbury set out behind him—although with a somewhat different destination in mind: He was going in search of Amelia.

When he found her a few moments later, she was not, as he'd expected, in dire need of rescue, but propped up in the dining car, alone and feverish.

She was sitting at one of the tables, her head lolling back, her eyes closed, and sweat beading on her forehead, pooling in the small of her throat.

He rushed to her side, cupping her face in his hands, checking her pulse. She was burning up. She'd evidently staggered there in an effort to return to their cabin, and found herself unable to continue.

He searched her hurriedly for scratches or other obvious wounds, fearing the worst. Had she encountered a revenant? Had she been infected? His heartbeat thundered in his ears as he checked her over, but he found evidence of only a few fresh bruises, and marks upon her wrists where they'd been bound.

"Amelia? Amelia!" He slapped her gently upon the cheek, trying to bring her round. "It's Maurice. What happened to you? Was it Mrs. Wren?"

At this she stirred, opening her eyes. She didn't seem able to focus on his face. She parted her lips, but no sound came out.

Newbury cast around, searching for a glass of water. There was an overturned bottle on one of the nearby tables that still appeared to contain some liquid. He grabbed it and held it to her lips, drizzling it into her mouth. She gulped it down thirstily.

"Don't... don't..." she mumbled.

"Don't what?" said Newbury, dabbing her forehead with a damp serviette.

"Don't go in there," mumbled Amelia. "Petunia... dead. Don't go. Infection. Don't..."

Infection? He studied her for a moment—the shallow breath, the flickering eyes, the prickles of sweat. This certainly wasn't the revenant plague. He had half a mind to disregard her warning—to go and investigate Petunia's cabin in the nearby carriage. If he could ascertain what they were facing, then perhaps he could work out how to help her. He started to get to his feet, but Amelia grabbed his hand. She squeezed it tightly, until it hurt. She really didn't want him going anywhere near the other carriage.

"*No,*" she said. "I got out so you wouldn't have to go in there. Stay here, with me."

"All right," said Newbury. "But not here. Let's get you back to our cabin."

Gently, he made a pillow in the crook of his elbow and scooped her up into his arms. She felt light and hot, like some drowsy, fey creature, and not the woman he had spent so many hours of intimate association with, helping her to heal; not his friend, whom he cared for deeply and profoundly, and hoped one day might become something akin to family to him.

The healing rituals were at an end, of course—there was no way now that he'd be able to retrieve the book. The cultist was dead, and the secret of what had become of it had died with him. He looked down sadly upon Amelia's upturned face as he staggered through the narrow doorway and out into the foyer on the other side, wondering how long she had. He could only hope that the work he'd already done would be enough to sustain her for a good while.

He felt the train judder beneath him, and realised that the driver had applied the brakes. Finally, they were stopping. They could make it off this dreadful train, and away to safety, to somewhere he could get help for Amelia, before continuing on to St. Petersburg for Veronica's new heart. He only hoped it would not be too late–for either of them.

Clutching Amelia close, he continued on to their cabin, where he laid her out upon her bed, fetched fresh linen and water, and remained by her side until the guards came calling to order them both off the train.

CHAPTER 30

It was only now, standing in the wintery splendour of St. Petersburg, that Amelia had a sense of how spectacularly her guidebook had misled her.

Back in England, she'd hungrily devoured the thing from cover to cover, and then again on the train to Dover, trying to get a sense of the place, of what to expect. She'd committed all sorts of facts and figures to memory—about the weather, the architecture, the language. None of them meant anything to her now. Oh, the details were all well and good, but what the author had singularly failed to put across was the sheer wonder, the spectacle—the *magic*—of the place.

Standing there, in the heart of the city, she was lost in an icy fantasia. It was as if she'd left the real world far behind her, and instead been transported to this vivid wonderland, where moustachioed policemen swung sabres from the backs of magnificent white bears; where every building, as far as her eyes could see, glistened with a hoary rime of frost; where ice sculptures of dancing sprites—all angular and inhuman—caroused across the plazas, or nestled in the shadowy mouths of side streets as if waiting for the light to fade before springing fleetingly back to life. Even the frigid air *smelled* different. She filled her lungs with it.

Overhead, diffuse storm clouds, smudged by an inky thumb, released their burden upon the provinces to the east, and all around her people hastened towards their destinations, heads bowed against the chill.

Amelia started at a mechanical rumble from behind her, and turned to see a palanquin, embellished with golden fretwork, borne along by two bull-like automatons. Steam rippled from their brass nostrils, and the ground shook with the thunder of their passing. A thin, furtive-looking man peered out from inside the bizarre transport, like a sinner unwilling to surrender the safety of the confessional. She wondered what secrets he was hiding.

Out here, in this fabulous place, she felt *alive*—more alive than she had in years. Her encounter on the train had changed her, in ways she was still trying to understand. She'd regained her senses somewhere after Hrodna, aboard a smaller, local train.

Much of what had happened in the aftermath of Petunia's attack was lost in a bizarre fever dream—in which she'd imagined blossoming vines enveloping the entire train, curling through the bodies of all the passengers, with only her left in the middle of it all, untouched by the bizarre growths. It was as if her body had resisted them somehow, had burned them out with a fever. Nevertheless, she couldn't help feeling that they'd *altered* her in some indescribable way. She felt better than she ever had—more vibrant and healthy.

Of course, Newbury had found out about the fungus, and Julian Wren, after quizzing the train guards who'd opened up the carriage—or rather, the ones who'd found their fellow guards, who'd bloomed in the passageway after opening the door.

He'd explained that there was no way of knowing how long the effects of the fungus might last—or, indeed, if they might prove permanent. There was a possibility that the parasite had somehow altered the chemistry of her brain; that it had rejuvenated her, and banished her condition for good. Equally, though, there was the chance it might return at any moment, and if so, Newbury no longer had the means to help her—the book had been lost in the conflagration on the train.

All she knew was that the encounter with Petunia Wren had given her not just a new perspective, but also a new opportunity, and she planned to embrace it with all the vivacity she could muster.

Newbury had filled her in on the details of their onward journey. The train had eventually been stopped, and emergency services called to attend the stationary vehicle. The surviving passengers—Newbury and Amelia included— were unloaded and taken by trackless ground train to the nearest town, where they were held in isolation for two days, and received any necessary medical attention. Newbury had seen his wounds tended, and Amelia had been administered drugs to combat her dangerous fever.

She'd been delirious, but not unconscious, and recalled snatches of words and images: Newbury's concerned face, the flitting view of frozen countryside from her window, the taste of hot broth.

He'd nursed her en route, and when they'd switched trains at Hrodna, she'd been close to recovery, and the fever had broken. She'd grown stronger every day since, gaining confidence, too, and despite everything that had happened, she'd even found herself enjoying the relative calm of the remaining journey, untroubled by cultists, or revenants, or women bent on revenge.

Now, they were here, and it was as glorious and strange a place as she could have ever imagined.

"It's breathtaking, isn't it?" said Newbury, patting his gloved hands together to stave off the chill.

"I have no words," said Amelia. "Besides thank you."

He turned to her, and grinned. "Let's save that for when

we're home, and your sister is sitting up in bed and berating us both for the dangers we put ourselves through, shall we?"

Amelia laughed. "Oh, I never thought I'd say it, but that sounds wonderful."

"Well then, I see no reason to delay. We're not here to see the sights—as much as the place intrigues me. We have an urgent appointment, and an equally urgent requirement to return to England."

"So where are we going?" said Amelia.

Newbury removed a slip of paper from the pocket of his fur-lined overcoat—bought upon arrival at the nearest outlet—and unfurled it, regarding the printed address. "I think we'd better take a cab," he said, holding out his arm towards the oncoming traffic.

The workshop of Carl Fabergé was an august residence close to the heart of the city, a soaring townhouse in an expensive district, surrounded by similar properties that Amelia presumed must belong to the exceedingly well-to-do.

During the cab ride she'd felt dizzy with the wonder of it all, sitting glued to the window, drinking in everything from the enormous ice-and-clockwork swans that glided across one of the plazas, giddy children riding upon their backs, to the colourful minarets, which looked to her like gilded balloons, floating just above the rooftops of the city.

Newbury opened her door and helped her down from the cab, paid the driver, and then looped his arm through hers as they crossed the street to the address in question. A press of the doorbell set off a delightful whistle, accompanied by a tiny clockwork bird, which peeked its head out from a small aperture in the brightly painted door, regarded them both, and then retreated.

Amelia found herself grinning. She had no notion of

how Newbury had even arranged this meeting; how he had contacted Fabergé in the first instance to commission Veronica's new heart. She presumed he'd used his royal connections—perhaps even his relationship with the Queen herself—to broker the deal. She couldn't see how else he could have paid for such an undertaking.

She heard creaking footsteps from inside the house, and then, a moment later, the door opened to reveal a child-sized automaton, dressed in the black suit of a valet. It wore an intricate porcelain mask, comprised of scores of interlocking pieces that shifted with an odd mechanical whir, describing what she took to be a smile. The painted eyes were blue and staring.

She saw Newbury frown. "Good day. We have an appointment with Mr. Fabergé. I am Sir Maurice Newbury, and this is my companion, Miss Constance Markham."

The automaton inclined its head, and its features reset into a solemn expression. It beckoned them inside.

Newbury did as requested, and Amelia followed. She felt charmed by the little thing, seeing it as yet more evidence of the wonder of this unusual city, but Newbury seemed somewhat disturbed. She believed she could understand why.

The little automaton rocked unsteadily on its heels, and then scooted around their legs, heading off down the hallway and waving for them to follow. She noted that there were small wheels embedded in the machine's heels, and it slid easily across the polished floorboards ahead of them.

They followed the automaton deeper into the house. What had at first seemed like a typical—if grandiose—residential home, full of hat stands and mirrors and portraits on the walls, soon opened out to be so much more. The rear of the property had been significantly remodelled, walls removed and extensions erected, to create a workshop of incredible scale.

It was not that the place was big—Fabergé's work was

about precision and minutia–but more the oddities and marvels it contained.

At the heart of the room sat a balding man with a grey beard, whom she presumed to be Fabergé himself, nestled amongst a bizarre series of black metal arms. They stemmed from him like massive spider legs, attached to a control harness that appeared to be clipped around his waist and affixed to his back. He sat amongst these unusual structures as if in repose, a king upon his throne, whilst–to Amelia's amazement– the mechanical arms appeared to operate independently of one another, each of them assembling tiny jewelled eggs at innumerable workstations, which were placed at intervals around the edges of the room.

The intricacy of the work was incredible, and Amelia found it hard to believe that Fabergé was somehow controlling it all simultaneously from his seat of power, pulling the strings to make each of his mechanical soldiers march.

As if she needed proof, Fabergé turned his head to regard them, and all work instantaneously ceased, the mechanical arms falling silent and still. The effect was impressive, if somewhat eerie.

"Sir Maurice, I presume," said Fabergé, in precise, clipped English.

"Indeed," said Newbury. "It is good to meet you." He strode forward, offering his hand, and then withdrew it sheepishly when he realised Fabergé's real hands were otherwise engaged, encased in metal sheaths that–Amelia presumed– served as some sort of puppeteer's gloves.

"You are late," said Fabergé pointedly. "Two days late, to be precise. I do not approve of tardiness."

"My apologies," said Newbury. "Our train met unexpected delays."

"Yes," said Fabergé, with the hint of a smile. "I heard about the fire, and the revenant outbreak. One cannot help wondering whether you, Sir Maurice, might have had a part to play in that."

"Let us just say that I was anxious to ensure any delay was kept to a minimum," said Newbury.

Fabergé laughed. "Very well." He moved, and his brace of mechanical arms stirred. "Did you bring them?"

"I did." Newbury reached inside his coat and withdrew a sheaf of papers. "The schematics you requested."

"Most excellent," said Fabergé. "Give them to me."

Newbury held them out, and two of the mechanical arms clacked across the ground towards him, then rose into the air and snatched them out of his hands. They folded in around Fabergé, holding the papers up to the light and rustling through them hurriedly, passing the pages beneath his nose.

Fabergé's eyes glistened as a smile broke out upon his lips. "Very well," he said. "You have completed your end of the bargain. Here is mine."

Another of the arms looped around, this time bearing a plush red cushion. Upon it sat a small, brass, egg-shaped contraption.

"The heart?" said Newbury, plucking it tenderly from the cushion and cradling it in his palm. Amelia could see a number of small valves around the edge of the device, as well as a series of tiny cogs and wheels, whirring quietly behind an inlaid glass panel.

Fabergé nodded. "It is a delicate instrument. Its inner workings are perfectly balanced. You must take care to return it to England without incident."

"Oh, I think there has been enough incident already," said Newbury. "I shall guard this with my life."

"Your 'Fixer' will know what to do," said Fabergé.

"Thank you," said Newbury. "I can't tell you what this means to me."

Fabergé raised an eyebrow. "I have the schematics I requested. I *know* what it means to you."

She saw Newbury frown, and then take a handkerchief from his pocket and carefully wrap the heart before sliding it into a pouch in his overcoat.

Amelia started as Fabergé's arms suddenly resumed their odd, mechanical dance. It was clear they'd been dismissed.

"Good day to you," said Newbury, but Fabergé was already lost in his work, a hundred mechanical fingers each tending to their tiny, elaborate constructions.

Newbury took Amelia by the arm and led her to the door, and then out into the cold afternoon.

"Is that it?" she said, when the door had closed behind them. "We came all this way, just for that?"

"It's enough," said Newbury. "We have the heart. We didn't come for pleasantries."

Amelia nodded. "What was it you gave him?"

Newbury took a moment to consider his reply. "Payment," he said. She could tell by the look on his face that whatever the payment was, it had cost him dearly.

"Well, I suppose it's back to the train station?" she said. "Although I must admit—the prospect of another long train journey doesn't fill me with rapturous glee."

Newbury laughed. "I concur. How about we consider a different mode of transport for the return leg of our journey? Airship, perhaps?"

Amelia squeezed his arm in excitement. "I think that's the best idea you've had since all of this began."

CHAPTER 31

❦

The waiting room at the Fixer's house was perhaps the most depressing place that Amelia had ever set foot. It was so clinical and soulless, so neat and immaculate, and not at all the sort of place where one would want to sit and await news of a loved one's battle for her life.

Not that she could imagine the sort of place where anyone would *want* to do such a thing.

The space had been dressed to resemble a comfortable living room, with a crackling open fire, a chesterfield sofa and matching armchairs, a drinks cabinet—but the stark white marble floor gave the place a clinical air, and the clacking of Newbury's shoes as he paced back and forth was beginning to drive her to distraction.

She was tired and emotional—she knew that—and all she wanted was for this terrible wait to be over. They'd been there for hours already, having come directly from the airfield, their luggage sent home in a cab. The journey had proved blissfully uneventful, and as the days had passed—and her strength had not ebbed—she had even begun to enjoy herself. Unbeknownst to Newbury, she'd even risked mingling with the other passengers on the airship's observation deck, fearing that if she didn't, she might never have put that particular demon to rest. She wasn't yet ready to believe that everyone in the world was out to get her—and she was independent enough, and *stubborn* enough, to ensure she didn't start.

Newbury had kept to himself during much of the flight, and while he was clearly healing—the effects of the ritual were beginning to ebb, and his wounds were closing up nicely—the reality of Veronica's situation was becoming all too real to him. Amelia had felt it, of course—while they'd been fighting their way across the Continent to reach Fabergé, there had been something they could do, some means to assist in her recovery. Now, they had done all they could, and all that was left was hope.

Newbury had never been one to get by on hope alone—she knew that. He needed to be active, to be out there, helping people, doing his bit. That's what made him the man he was. And so, unable to *do* anything, a fug had settled upon him, and she could see the results of it now, in the way he hung his head and ground his teeth, how his fingers picked nervously at the hem of his jacket, or his incessant pacing. She knew it was testament to how much he cared for her sister, but she wished he'd allow himself just a moment of respite. He'd done all he could; now it was in the hands of the Fixer.

She looked up from her lap. Newbury was at the window, peering out through the net curtains. "Where's Charles?" he muttered. "He should be here by now."

They'd sent word to Bainbridge, of course, almost as soon as they'd stepped off the airship, but they'd yet to hear word.

"I imagine he's been detained by important police work," said Amelia. "He'll be along when he can, I'm sure."

"Hmmm," said Newbury. He resumed his pacing.

"Of course, he's in for a bit of a shock when he does arrive," said Amelia.

"Because of Veronica?" said Newbury.

"Well, yes, hopefully. But I was referring to *me*."

Newbury seemed to take a minute to catch on. When the thought finally struck, he stared at her, wide eyed. "He thinks you're dead." He rubbed a hand across his chin, considering their options. "Perhaps it's best we keep you in one of the side rooms for now," he said. "Out of his way."

"No." Amelia shook her head.

"No?"

"That's right. *No*. I've been dead long enough, Sir Maurice," she said, "and I refuse to remain dead any longer, at least to Veronica's immediate circle of friends. My condition is… apparently in remission, and I feel the time has come to show my face to the world again, even if I must do so under an assumed identity." She straightened her back and met his gaze, defiant.

Newbury smiled. "Well, if you expect me to argue with you, you'd be wrong. But I'll allow *you* to take it up with your sister." He glanced towards the sound of footsteps from the hallway. She saw him swallow.

The door creaked open on hinges that were well overdue an oil, and a man in a leather smock stood in the opening, a stern expression on his face. Blood was smeared across his shirtfront and arms, and Amelia could see horrific-looking tools poking out from little pockets in his apron. "She's awake," said the Fixer.

"Then it *worked*?" said Newbury.

"Of course it bloody worked," said the Fixer. "Why do you think I'm standing here smiling?"

"But you're…" Newbury trailed off, shaking his head. He glanced at Amelia. "Go to her."

Amelia nodded. She got to her feet, suddenly anxious. "We should go together."

"No. This is *your* time, Amelia."

"Very well." She followed the Fixer out of the room, and along the hallway to another small room.

"In there," he said. "But remember, she's weak. It's going to take some time before she's back on her feet. If she's tired, let her rest."

"All right," said Amelia. She had no idea what to expect. She took a deep breath, and stepped through the door.

Veronica was lying in bed at the far side of the room, propped up on what appeared to be a small mountain of pillows. She was wearing a white linen nightgown, with the blankets pulled up to cover her wound. Her hair was tied back in a taut ponytail, and her cheeks were flushed. She turned as Amelia entered the room, and her mouth parted in a broad smile. "Amelia! You're here!"

Amelia ran to her side, wishing she could sweep her up in a tight embrace, but instead took her sister's face in her hands and kissed her brightly on the forehead. "Of course I'm here. Where *else* would I be?"

"Well, from what I hear, halfway across the world having all sorts of adventures!" said Veronica.

Amelia offered her a wry smile. "So you've heard."

"Some of it. The Fixer's quite a talkative chap, really, when you get to know him."

"Humph!" said Amelia, rolling her eyes and laughing. "Well, I hope he didn't spoil all the best bits."

"Oh, only that you and Sir Maurice went gallivanting to St. Petersburg to fetch me a new heart, and that you encountered a little trouble on the way."

"A *little* trouble…" said Amelia.

"Go on, I want to hear it all," said Veronica.

"You're not too tired?"

"I've been asleep for weeks. It's the least you can do."

"Oh, the *least*!" Amelia propped herself on the edge of the bed and took Veronica's hand as she recited her tale.

Veronica listened intently, shaking her head and squeezing Amelia's hand when she learned about Petunia Wren, and the fungus, and everything that Amelia had been through while Newbury dealt with the cultist and the revenants.

"Oh, Amelia," said Veronica, when she'd finished her story. "I'm so terribly sorry."

"Whatever for?"

"For everything you went through, of course! All because of me."

Amelia shook her head. "I did it because I wanted to do my bit, to help save you. Sir Maurice could never have managed alone."

"But Petunia Wren, thinking you were me... seeking revenge for what *I'd* done." Veronica looked pained.

"Don't you see? We were *lucky* it was me, and not you. If she'd managed to get to *you*... well, you wouldn't be here now," said Amelia.

"You might have died. I've seen what that fungus can do," countered Veronica.

"I feel better than I ever have, Veronica. My condition... it's *gone*. Sir Maurice says it might yet come back, but I don't think it will. Whatever that fungus did to me, I'm *grateful* for it. Isn't that the best revenge against people like Petunia Wren? To defy them, to live on? Just as you're doing, with your brand-new heart."

"You've grown wise all of a sudden, Sister," said Veronica. "I'm so grateful, and so proud." She laughed. "So tell me, Constance Markham, where did that come from?"

"I don't know... I just sort of blurted it out, and it stuck."

"It's a good name. It suits you."

"I'm thinking of keeping it," said Amelia.

"Now *that's* a conversation for later," said Veronica. She looked suddenly tired. "Now go and fetch Newbury, would you? I'm feeling sleepy, but I'd like to see him before I get some more rest."

"Of course." Amelia leaned forward and kissed Veronica on the forehead again. "It's good to see you, Sister."

"Not as good as it is to see you," said Veronica, with a smile.

CHAPTER 32

"Did you really do all of that?"

He was sitting by her bedside on a stool he'd brought from the other room, his hands folded upon his lap. He hadn't taken his gaze from her once since he'd entered the room, and she had the odd sensation that her new mechanised heart was quickening, even though she was sure that was impossible.

"All of what?" he said, with a smile.

"You went all the way to St. Petersburg, risked all of that, for me?"

"Do you even have to ask?"

"No. I just…" She stopped for a moment to catch her breath. "Maurice, you gave me a *heart*."

Newbury grinned. "Your sister had a lot to do with it, too, you know."

"I know. She told me. About the Cabal, about Petunia Wren… I've missed so much." She looked away, suddenly morose.

"What is it? Tell me what you're thinking? I can see there's something on your mind."

She met his gaze. "It's just… everything that's happened to her, to Amelia. It's all because of *me*. Those horrors she went through at the Grayling Institute, her life trapped in Malbury Cross, and now this, being mistaken for me, having to go through all of that…" She reached out her hand, and Newbury took it. "I just wonder if I do her more harm than good; if she'd be better off without me. And now there's all this 'Constance Markham' business, too, and I just do–"

"Stop." Newbury reached over and gently put his finger to her lips. "You're her *sister*. You mean everything to her. You're all she's got. And don't you even think about trying to take that away from her." He smiled. "All those years, locked away in those terrible institutions… is it surprising that she wants a little taste of the world? And why shouldn't she?" He looked wistful. "You should have seen her, Veronica. She did you proud."

Veronica put her hand on Newbury's arm. He felt warm and familiar, comforting. "I'm not the only one she's got," she said. "She's lucky to have you. We *both* are."

"That's more like it," said Newbury, laughing.

Her smile was fleeting. She swallowed, unable to dispel the shadow she could feel settling over her mood. "There's something else I need to tell you," she said.

"Anything."

She was silent for a moment, and she had a notion she could hear the faint ticking of her new heart, like the workings of a distant clock, measuring out the seconds of her life. "It's Sir Charles. I know you're not going to want to hear this, Maurice, but he's mixed up in something. Maybe something terrible. I saw him handing files to Professor Angelchrist. He denied it when I confronted him about it. I'm worried he no longer has your best interests at heart."

"Oh, Veronica," he said, his face creasing in concern. "I'm so sorry. You've got it all wrong."

"Yes, I thought that's what you'd say. That's why I went to get proof. That's when it happened, you see. That's when…" She trailed off. He knew exactly what she meant.

"No, that's not it." He looked pained. "It's all my fault. I should have told you. I was trying to protect you."

"Told me *what?*"

"You see; I *know* what Charles and Angelchrist are up to. But it's dangerous. More dangerous than anything we've been involved in before." He looked over his shoulder to make sure they weren't being overheard. "It's this new agency, Angelchrist's so-called Secret Service. They know everything the Queen is up to, about the Grayling Institute, about August Warlow and his boltheads, *everything.* They're working on a project, an initiative…" He stopped suddenly, catching himself. "But we can talk about that later, when you're better."

She wanted to tell him no, to carry on, but she knew he was right. If things were as dangerous as he suggested, then the Fixer's house wasn't the safest place to discuss it. And besides, she was feeling so tired. "So Sir Charles didn't have anything to do with the Executioner? All that business with the assassinations?"

"Charles? No, of course not! That was the Prince of Wales."

Veronica looked up at him, confused. "The Prince of Wales!" She sighed. "I've been such a fool," she said.

"No. Never that. But next time, *talk* to me. I only have your best interests at heart, Veronica. I care about you so very much. I…"

There was a rap at the door.

Veronica sighed. "Yes?"

The Fixer entered the room. He was still wearing his bloody smock, and Veronica wondered if he ever took the thing off. "Sir Charles Bainbridge is here to see you both," he said.

Newbury glanced at Veronica. "Do you want to see him? I can explain everything if you'd rather not."

"No, no. Of course I want to see him," said Veronica. She nodded to the Fixer. "Ask him to come in."

He inclined his head, and left.

"You were saying?" said Veronica. She still had hold of Newbury's hand.

"It'll keep," he said. "Until you're well. Then we can talk properly, about the future."

Veronica smiled. "Yes, let's do that."

There was another rap at the door, this time louder, and made distinctive by the use of a cane.

"Come in, Charles," called Newbury. "I hope you've brought flowers."

Bainbridge blundered through the doorway, looking somewhat sheepish. "Flowers? No time for ruddy flowers, Newbury! The woman's had a new heart installed–I wasn't about to stop for a chat with the posy girl on the way here, now was I?"

Newbury caught Veronica's eye, and they both laughed.

Bainbridge crossed to her bedside, took her hand in his own, and kissed it. His bristles pricked her skin, and his lips were icy cold. "Miss Hobbes. I can't tell you how relieved I am to see you looking so well. We all feared for your safety. I… well, I don't know what we would do without you. I don't know what *I* would do without you."

"I'm thankful to say that you won't have to," said Veronica. "At least for a while."

"And you, Newbury–you've caused quite a stir," said Bainbridge. "All that business on the train, with the revenants and those ruddy acrobatics. You're the talk of the White Friars. And have you told Miss Hobbes about that woman, Wren, and what she was up to? She knows all about that sorry business of old."

Newbury grinned. "Yes, she knows all about it, Charles."

"Good, good…" said Bainbridge. He seemed distracted. Veronica could see that there was something else troubling him.

"What is it, Sir Charles. Speak your mind."

He looked down at her, and shook his head. "No, it'll keep. It's too soon to be troubling you with my burdens, Miss Hobbes."

She sighed. "Look, you're here now, and if you don't tell me, I'll only lay awake and fret."

Bainbridge glanced at Newbury, who nodded his agreement.

"It's the Queen. She's summoned all of her agents. You, too, Newbury, once you're done here."

"To what end?" said Newbury.

"That's just it. She's declared outright war. She's drawn up a list of all the Secret Service agents, and we've been ordered to dispose of them."

"Dispose of…" said Veronica. "We're not assassins!"

"We're whatever she wants us to be," said Bainbridge. "But this time she's gone too far."

"Angelchrist?" said Newbury.

"In hiding," said Bainbridge, "but I fear it's only a matter of time. She'll winkle him out, Newbury, and then it'll be over. For all of us."

Newbury got to his feet. "In that case, we must act," he said. "It's time."

"Time for what?" said Veronica.

"For the Albion Initiative," said Bainbridge. "But it's no use, Newbury. We haven't had time. Somehow, she's got the names of all of our agents. There's no one left, aside from us."

Newbury glanced at Veronica, and then grinned. "Charles— come with me. I think it's about time you met Constance Markham…"

ACKNOWLEDGMENTS

A special thank you to all my patient readers, who have waited so long to discover what happened to Veronica after the terrible events of *The Executioner's Heart.* This one's had a long gestation period.

Thanks also to my editors, Diana Pho, Liz Gorinsky, Ed Chapman, Cath Trechman, and Miranda Jewess; to Cavan Scott for being an invaluable sounding board; to my family for their ongoing support and encouragement.

The soundtrack for this one was provided by Chairlift, Clare Maguire, Lyla Foy, David Bowie, Kate Bush, and Vaults.

Read on for another Newbury and Hobbes short story

∾ THE ∾
WORD OF MENAMHOTEP

BY GEORGE MANN

I

It always started like this: in a room with a corpse, the air thick with the iron tang of blood and stale tobacco. Policemen milling about treading valuable evidence underfoot, Bainbridge in a foul temper, and a head thick from the morning's first intake of opium.

Newbury sighed. Perhaps he'd fallen into something of a rut. So far, a cursory glance at the scene had failed to stir even an inkling of enthusiasm. He had no notion why Bainbridge had demanded his presence—the dead man appeared to have been shot, judging by the bloody hole in his chest, and there was little sign of anything of a more esoteric nature, besides a handful of vaguely obscure—and rather dry sounding—volumes of Ancient Egyptian history on one of the bookshelves.

"Well?" said Bainbridge.

"Give me chance, Charles. I've only just arrived."

Bainbridge muttered something unintelligible beneath his breath. Newbury dropped into a crouch beside the body.

The dead man's face was lily white and slack jawed, his eyes open and staring. A thin line of blood had dribbled from the corner of his mouth, stark and obscene, while more had drained from a wound in his chest, staining the front of his shirt and congealing on the oak floorboards beside him. He was lying on his side, as if he'd been attempting to roll over when his heart had finally given out. Newbury estimated he'd been in his mid-fifties, but had lived a reasonably adventurous life, judging by the leathery complexion and deep lines around his eyes. He'd been well travelled, but the loss of so much blood had deprived his cheeks of their earlier colour. "Foulkes tells me this is the third one you've found in similar circumstances this week," he said.

"Did he, now?" Bainbridge's moustache twitched with irritation. Evidently, he'd been expecting to reveal this troubling information to Newbury himself.

Newbury checked inside the lapel of the man's jacket. No wallet. "What did you say his name was?"

"I didn't," said Bainbridge. "He's Matthias Bright, an archaeologist. Quite famous in certain circles, apparently. Wrote some contentious papers challenging the accepted lineage of the ancient kings of Egypt. Caused quite a fuss amongst those concerned with such things."

"I think I recall something of the matter. Old Pyecroft at the museum was greatly put out by it all." Newbury appraised the dead man with new eyes. "How interesting."

"Hmmm," mumbled Bainbridge. "Not half as interesting as how he ended up on his drawing room floor with a quarter inch hole in his chest. It'll be more than a few fusty old professors getting uptight if we don't get to the bottom of this soon. Assuming, of course, that none of *them* are responsible."

Newbury frowned. "It's entirely possible, but in my experience, professional rivalry in academic circles is rarely cause for murder."

"Well, *someone* certainly took a dislike to him," said Bainbridge. "Although I'm damned if I can find any evidence of a third party. The door was locked from the inside."

Newbury glanced at the window. It was shut. So the assassin hadn't taken a shot from outside—not unless one of the policemen had already closed the window. "Any obvious connection to the other victims?"

"Parsons is looking into that now, although it seems reasonably obvious–they were all academics with an interest in antiquities. And Ancient Egypt in particular."

"And they were all shot in the same way?"

Bainbridge nodded.

Newbury studied the body again. "There's no exit wound."

Bainbridge frowned. "Yes, I noticed that. In fact, I was specifically looking for it. There's something strange about the exit wounds on the other bodies."

"How so?"

"The trajectory of the bullets entering the bodies and the angle of the exit wounds don't seem to make sense. It's as if the bullets ricocheted around inside the ribcage before exiting at high velocity."

"Which is a clear impossibility," said Newbury. "Did you recover any of the bullets?"

"No."

Newbury stood, stretching his back. "Anything else."

Bainbridge reached into his pocket and withdrew a small object, wrapped in a white handkerchief. He held it out to Newbury. "This is why I sent for you. We've found one at the scene of each murder. Practically identical, down to the dusting of white powder around the base."

Interest piqued, Newbury took the object and weighed it in his palm. It was about the size of a pipe bowl, and relatively light for its size. Slowly, he unfolded the handkerchief.

It was a scarab beetle, crudely rendered in plaster. Its carapace had been painted glossy blue. Bizarrely, it had inaccurately been given eight legs instead of six. He turned it over. There was a small, roughly hewn cavity in the unpainted base of the plaster, about the size of a thumb nail. The base was covered in white plaster dust.

"That's it?" he said.

"We found it on his desk," said Bainbridge, nodding. "Same with the other two. Any idea what it means?"

Newbury shrugged. "Nothing that I'm aware of. It seems like one of those cheap souvenirs you'd find in a souk. Only, even they wouldn't make the mistake of giving it eight legs instead of six." He ran the tip of his little finger around the edges of the hole in the base of the thing, frowning. "Can I hold onto this? I'll head home, do a bit of poking around."

"Of course." Bainbridge grinned. "But first..."

Newbury felt his spirits dropping. "No, Charles. Not today. I haven't the patience to face her."

"She's growing tetchy," said Bainbridge. They both knew that was a grave understatement—Newbury hadn't visited the Palace for weeks. "What do you expect me to tell her?"

"Tell her I'm engaged on the case," he said. "Tell her I'm chasing the dragon. Tell her anything you damn want."

"Be it on your own head," said Bainbridge, with a heavy sigh.

Newbury slipped the scarab into his jacket pocket, now neatly folded up in its handkerchief again. "I wouldn't have it any other way," he said.

II

Newbury had learned to detest the morgue. The acrid stench of carbolic, the sluices awash with blood and other foetid bodily fluids, the all-pervading aura of death.

It wasn't that he'd developed a sudden aversion to corpses—more that he supposed he'd just spent too much time here in recent months. Although, on reflection, it might simply have been that all the bodies he'd come to examine had proved so disappointingly *ordinary*.

Bainbridge was waiting for him in the foyer, leaning heavily on his cane. He straightened up when he saw Newbury duck inside out of the rain. "You're late," he said.

"Indubitably," said Newbury, brushing droplets from his coat.

Bainbridge shook his head. "The surgeon's waiting for us, down here." He indicated the way with a wave of his cane.

"Did he manage to retrieve the bullet?" asked Newbury, as they walked the length of the tiled corridor.

"Oh, he found something much more interesting than that." Bainbridge stopped before an open doorway, and ushered Newbury inside.

Matthias Bright's corpse was lying exposed on a marble slab inside, the flesh pale and waxy. The eyes were shut, and the chest had been closed with a ladder of thick, black stitches.

The room itself was tiled in the same white and brown porcelain as the corridor, and the accoutrements of the surgeon's art were everywhere to see—untidily scattered upon work surfaces, trolleys and shelves.

A gaunt surgeon was standing beside the slab. He was tall and thin, with a balding pate and long, bony fingers. He was dressed in a bloodied leather smock. He peered at Newbury from beneath heavy, hooded lids.

"Doctor Breal," said Bainbridge, from over Newbury's shoulder. "This is Sir Maurice Newbury. I'd like for you to explain to him precisely what you've just explained to me."

Breal nodded curtly, inhaled so that his nose emitted an alarming whistle, and then spoke. "Contrary to initial appearances, this man was not shot."

"Then what was responsible for the hole in his chest?" said Newbury.

"This," said Breal, taking a kidney shaped dish from the nearest trolley and holding it out to Newbury.

Inside was a small metallic object, about the size of Newbury's thumbnail. It resembled nothing so much as a small insect, with a series of fragile-looking legs extending from a brass carapace. It was presently on its back.

"I found it wedged in one of his ribs," said Breal.

"May I?"

"Be my guest."

Newbury upturned the dish and allowed the little device to tumble out into his palm. He held it up to the light. "It's a scarab," he said. "With eight legs."

"Quite," said Bainbridge.

"And if you'll note the rather vicious mandibles..." said Breal.

Newbury used the tip of his finger to turn the scarab over. "It appears as if they're designed to rotate," he said.

"Indeed," said Breal. "I believe the device used them to burrow into the victim's chest, piercing his heart and causing a slow and rather agonising death. It's quite ingenious."

Newbury returned the scarab to the dish, and glanced at Bainbridge. "I suppose that explains the exit wounds you noted on the other victims. If similar automata killed them, the devices will have exited the victims to avoid detection. They won't have been concerned with trajectory."

Bainbridge nodded. "That was my thinking, too. And it also explains the lack of a third party. They were targeted assassinations. We even have the delivery method."

"The plaster scarabs," said Newbury. "The small cavity in the bases. The automata must have been sealed inside, and dug themselves out when activated or triggered. A seemingly innocuous object suddenly becomes the tool of an ingenious assassination."

"So what are we dealing with?" said Bainbridge. "What's the significance of the scarabs? Did you find anything?"

"I fear not. I can find no mention of an eight-legged scarab in any of my books or files. I'll pay a visit to Aldous this afternoon, see if he can shed any light."

"Very well," said Bainbridge. "And I'll keep digging, see if I can't turn up a more definite connection between the victims. There has to be a reason they're all being targeted." He shook his head. "It's a rum business, Newbury. You think it's one of your lot?"

"My lot?"

"Some godforsaken cult, or some such. You know what I mean."

Newbury grinned. "It remains a distinct possibility."

"And what of Miss Hobbes? Where is she? I presume you'll be engaging her in all of this, too?"

"In time. She has some other business to attend to first."

Bainbridge sighed. "She's turning out to be as darn mysterious as you are, Newbury. I tell you, you're a bad influence on that girl."

Newbury laughed. "I rather think you underestimate Miss Hobbes."

Bainbridge shook his head, and then waved in the direction of the door. "Well, go on then. Go and see what Mr. Renwick can dig up. I'll call on you later at home."

"I'll look forward to it," said Newbury, with a grin.

III

Aldous Renwick was perhaps the most peculiar man that Newbury had the fortune to call a friend. Wild in appearance, with chaotic wisps of stark white hair, nicotine stained fingers and a grizzled, unshaven aspect, his most startling feature was his left eye, or rather, the device that had replaced it—a protruding mechanical lens that had, he claimed, been wired directly into his brain, replacing the original organ. It was a disconcerting object, shifting in its ball socket as if independent of both Renwick and his other, remaining eye; black and glassy save for a pinprick of orange light in its strange, fathomless depths. Newbury believed the device— or at least the surgical work that had been carried out on Renwick's brain during its fitting—to be accountable for the man's somewhat unconventional demeanour.

He was peering at Newbury now, over the top of a jar of the strange, pink brew he drank instead of more traditional beverages. They were sitting in the cluttered back room behind his bookshop, surrounded by the paraphernalia of a lifetime studying the esoteric and occult. "An eight-legged scarab, you say?"

"Yes, that's right." Newbury took the plaster beetle from his pocket and passed it over. He watched Renwick appraise it for a moment, turning it over in the palm of his hand. His mechanical eye whirred. He raised his hand to his nose, and sniffed. "At first I wondered if it was a mistake—a crude error perpetrated by someone trying to approximate the real thing, but then I saw what came out of it, and realised the error was intentional." Newbury had outlined their findings at the morgue upon his arrival at the shop. Renwick had immediately placed the closed sign in the shop window, locked the door, and ushered him through to his lair.

Renwick placed the scarab on his workbench and crossed to one of the bookcases that seemed to line every inch of the wall space in the room. He searched the serried spines, his fingers dancing over the cracked leather bindings. He found what he was looking for and pulled a book down, blew a cloud of dust from the pages, and returned to where he'd been standing beside his workbench. He opened the book and began leafing through.

Newbury waited patiently, a smile tugging at the corners of his mouth. He'd seen this before. Renwick was checking his facts before reciting his conclusions to Newbury.

After a couple of minutes, Renwick looked up from the old tome and peered over at him quizzically, as if he'd forgotten Newbury was there. "Menamhotep," he said. He held the book out, tapping the left-hand page. Newbury took it.

"Menamhotep?" He glanced at the image in the book. It was an engraving of a listing stone pillar, high on a windswept moor. The carving had been eroded through centuries of exposure, but the central image was still largely visible—an eight-legged scarab beetle, surrounded by other, barely visible runes and sigils.

"A lesser known goddess from early-Dynastic Egypt," said Renwick. "She typically took the form of an eight-legged scarab or a spider-headed woman, and was the overseer of fate, responsible for weaving the vast web of causality. No action went unrecorded by Menamhotep, who alone understood the connection between all living things. She had the power to bring lovers together, or steer them apart; to start or end wars; to ensure the long reign of a Pharaoh, or end it suddenly in bloodshed. From the centre of her web in the heavens she witnessed all things, past and future."

"But this engraving shows an English landscape."

"Ah, that's where it gets interesting," said Renwick. "See, Menamhotep was largely forgotten during the earliest days of the Old Kingdom. No idols have ever been found—just fragmentary records, a few passing references in hieroglyphic reliefs. Her cults faded, and she went largely unmentioned for nearly two thousand years. But then the Romans settled in Egypt, and for the briefest of moments—just a few months—her cult was revived, before once again passing into obscurity." Renwick sipped at his strange concoction, and gave a satisfied sigh. "By then, the Romans had settled in Britain, however, and from that briefest window of revival, brought the cult to our shores."

"So the cult flourished here while it died off back in Egypt?"

Renwick nodded. "For a while. It was taken up by the locals, who identified Menamhotep with an ancient pagan spider spirit of the woods. Over time, she became Anglicised. Worship continued into the Saxon period, but was abolished with the establishment of Christianity. By the year 900 she was all but forgotten, save for a handful of old monuments on Dartmoor."

Newbury tapped his finger against his lips, thoughtful. "Yet someone doesn't want to let her sleep." He folded the book shut and placed it on a wavering stack beside his chair, and then got to his feet. "Thank you, Aldous. You've proved as invaluable as ever."

Renwick smiled and inclined his head. "Glad to be of service." He picked up the plaster scarab. "May I?"

Newbury grinned. "Just don't tell Charles," he said, reaching for the door handle.

IV

♛

"We've established a clear connection between the victims." Bainbridge stalked into Newbury's drawing room, the bowl of his pipe in his hand as he stabbed pointedly in Newbury's direction with the mouthpiece. Rivulets of rainwater were still running down the back of his overcoat, dripping all over the floorboards. "We need to hurry."

"Charles, you're *wet*. Think of the books."

Bainbridge stopped before the fire and turned on the spot. He regarded Newbury through a wreath of smoke. "Listen, are you coming or not? I have a police carriage waiting outside."

"Coming *where*?" Newbury leaned back into the soft embrace of his sofa. His head was throbbing, and he was beginning to feel a little unsettled. The tainted cigarettes in the wooden box on the side table were calling to him, but the thought of Bainbridge's bombastic objection was enough to stay his hand. He took a swig from his brandy instead.

"To the British Museum. We need to find a man called Oleander Crow."

Newbury drained his glass. "Is this about Menamhotep?"

"Menamo-who?"

"The eight-legged scarabs. They're a reference to an Ancient Egyptian goddess called Menamhotep. An old cult that came to Britain with the Romans."

"Well that would certainly make sense," said Bainbridge. "It seems all the victims were part of an expedition to Egypt last year. They found something in the desert—a particularly noteworthy tomb, mummy and treasure and all that—but apparently there was an antechamber where the walls were covered in ancient hieroglyphs, reciting some previously unknown legends. They took photographs, and they've been working together to study the texts since their return. They were planning to publish shortly, having recently completed the translation work." Bainbridge exhaled a ruffle of smoke from his nostrils. "Crow was the expedition leader, and the only survivor of the four. At this moment he's either our chief suspect, or the next intended victim."

"I've known Crow for years. He's a good man. I can't believe for a minute that he'd set out to harm his colleagues," said Newbury.

"Then we'd best hope we can get to him before they do—whoever *they* are."

"Alright." Newbury pulled himself up out of the pit of the sofa, stretching his weary limbs. "I'll get my coat and meet you at the cab in a moment."

V

The British Museum was shrouded in a veil of mist and rain as the police carriage trundled over the flagstones and pulled to a halt outside the main entrance. It was approaching early evening, and the usual stream of visitors had evidently been dissuaded by the inclement weather–the grounds appeared deserted.

They clambered out of the carriage and, with heads dipped against the rain, sprinted for the cover of the main lobby.

"His office is in the basement, close to mine," said Newbury. He led the way across the marble concourse to the private stairwell that disappeared down into the gloomy belly of the museum. He hadn't visited his office here for some weeks, and knew that he'd have an enormous pile of paperwork to contend with when he did. Veronica, too, had been otherwise engaged with her sister over at Malbury Cross, leaving the running of the office to Miss Coulthard. He assured himself she'd have matters in hand, and resolved not to disturb her. At least, not if he could avoid it.

The passages beneath the museum were a warren, linking offices, study rooms and storage areas, as brimming with treasure as any buried tomb in the Saharan sands. They hurried along the tiled corridors, leaving a trail of dirty rainwater behind them.

"Here," said Newbury, indicating a door. Crow's name was printed in black on a small brass plate affixed to the door. Through the glass pane, he could see that a gas lamp was burning inside. He rapped on the door, and then tried the handle.

"Oleander?"

He stepped in, and Bainbridge bustled in behind him. The room as a small antechamber to Crow's main office, which he'd converted into a reading room, lined with books and scrolls, and with a small table and two chairs. Another door led into the adjoining office, where Crow was sitting hunched over his desk.

"Oleander?" repeated Newbury.

Crow looked up, peered myopically over the top of his spectacles, and then grinned. "Sir Maurice! Haven't seen you around these parts recently, what?"

Newbury crossed into the other room and shook Crow by the hand. He was a short man in his fifties, who'd retained a full head of dark hair that was nevertheless shot through with a startling streak of white, just above the left temple. His skin was tanned and lined, and his grip was firm. He was missing two front teeth, which he delighted in telling everyone had been lost during a fight with a Bedouin during one of his fateful expeditions. No one knew whether it was true, but Newbury had a sense that the truth more than lived up to Crow's telling of it; Crow was a man who'd seen things in his lifetime that most men could only begin to imagine.

"Oleander, this is Sir Charles Bainbridge, of Scotland Yard. We need to talk to you as a matter of urgency."

Crow sighed, removed his spectacles, and rubbed his eyes. "I presume with regard to the recent deaths of two of my colleagues?"

"Three of your colleagues," corrected Bainbridge.

Crow looked suddenly stricken. "Oh, no, not Matthias?"

"I'm afraid so," said Newbury. "He was found this morning. He died in the same way as the others."

"Which was?"

"He was assassinated by a tiny automaton of an eight-legged scarab, hidden inside a plaster decoration."

"An eight-legged scarab..." Crow frowned. He reached down and opened a drawer in his desk, and then took out a small plaster scarab, which he placed on the desk before him. It was identical to the one taken from bright's house that morning. Bainbridge glanced at Newbury.

"Where did you get that, Dr. Crow?" said Bainbridge.

"It arrived in the post this morning. There was no note. I assumed it was a little joke from Matthias—it relates to the work we've been doing, you see..."

"Regarding Menamhotep?" said Newbury.

"Yes, that's right," said Crow. "We've been translating a mythic cycle that we discovered in a tomb last year, during our most recent expedition. It's known as 'The Word of Menamhotep', and it's a creation myth—along with a series of accompanying rituals and incantations—referring back to pre-Dynastic Egypt, and a pantheon of gods that are mostly now forgotten, or later became transmuted into some of the more recognisable deities that you tend to hear about." He waved his hand. "As far as we're aware, the story hasn't been told for nearly four thousand years. It's a fascinating insight. The writings purport to be the recorded words of Menamhotep herself. Menamhotep was a minor deity, with little more than a cult following, really, so to find a text like this after all this time..."

"Where is the translation now?" said Newbury.

"Well, it's all here, collated in this folder." Crow indicated a large manilla file. "It's painstaking work. We've had to do it all from hand, from photographs. I'm in the final stages of collation."

"Bring it with you," said Newbury, getting to his feet. "We're taking you somewhere safe."

"What? Don't be ridiculous," said Crow, looking flustered. "I have work to do. Important work."

"Dr. Crow. Your life is at risk," said Bainbridge. "Consider this: whoever is responsible for the deaths of your colleagues knows where you work. And they've sent you that," Bainbridge pointed at the plaster scarab, "with the clear intention to cause you harm."

"But it's just a plaster decoration, as you said." Crow reached for the scarab and picked it up. As he lifted it, a plume of white dust billowed from the base. Puzzled, Crow turned it over to reveal a small cavity in the base. "What?"

"Up, now!" bellowed Bainbridge, grabbing Crow by the sleeve and hauling him roughly to his feet. Newbury reached over and grabbed the file, tucking it inside his coat. "We're leaving."

Crow flinched, and at first Newbury thought he was responding to Bainbridge's rather forceful grip on his arm, but then he noticed that the man was swatting at something on the back of his hand. "Charles! It's on him!"

Bainbridge twisted, releasing Crow, who stared at Newbury for a moment, clearly terrified, before holding up his right hand. There was a small, bloody hole in the flesh, and Newbury could see something moving beneath the skin. "What…what…?" he mumbled, confused and pained. He scratched at the wound, trying to prise the scarab out with his fingers.

"Hold him down, Charles." Newbury searched in his pocket for penknife. "I'm sorry, Oleander. This is going to hurt, but there's really no other option. We have to work quickly."

As Bainbridge grappled with Crow, pinning his hand to the table, Newbury moved in, the knife grasped firmly in his fist.

"No, no, no…what are you–" Crow broke off into a shrill

scream as Newbury dug the tip of his penknife into the back of the man's hand. Newbury could see the burrowing scarab forcing its way through the man's flesh, digging through muscle as it moved towards the wrist. If it got into his arm, Crow's life was forfeit—there was no way they'd be able to get it out of him before it had finished its work and punctured his heart.

Newbury twisted the handle of the knife, and then, keeping the pressure on, flicked the blade up and out, sending a hunk of bloody flesh—and the scarab—sailing across the room, where they struck the rear wall and slid to the floor. Dark blood welled from the wound, spilling out all over the desktop. Crow looked as if he were about to swoon.

"Hospital, now," said Newbury. "I'll see to the device."

Bainbridge nodded, shepherding Crow from the room, leaving a trail of dripping blood in their wake.

Cautiously, Newbury crept around the desk, his eyes tracking across the tiled floor. The ragged hunk of Crow's flesh—about the size of a postage stamp—was lying against the skirting board, sitting in a small puddle of blood. Beside it, glinting in the warm light of the gas lamp, was the tiny metal scarab. It was on its back, its legs scrabbling at the air as it attempted to right itself.

Newbury glanced at the desk, and his eyes fixed on a heavy glass paperweight, filled with blooming swirls of blue and yellow. He snatched it up and slowly approached the scarab. It remained on its back, still attempting to right itself. Dropping into a low crouch—careful to keep as far back as he could—Newbury raised the paperweight above his head, then brought it crashing down upon the scarab.

The porcelain tile fractured under the force of the blow, and Newbury's arm reverberated painfully, causing him to involuntarily release the paperweight. He rocked back on his haunches, clutching his forearm, while the glass semi-sphere rolled away across the floor.

He looked down. There, on a broken fragment of tile, was the twisted chassis of the scarab, tiny cogs and broken limbs surrounding it like a pool of spilled blood.

VI

♛

"Just the thought of something that small being so deadly," said Veronica. "It's enough to make you fear opening the post ever again."

She was sitting in the armchair by the fire in Newbury's drawing room, while Bainbridge paced, and Newbury leaned against the windowsill, smoking a cigarette. Elsewhere in the house, Scarbright—Newbury's valet—was hard at work crafting one of his culinary delights for dinner.

Oleander Crow had been safely installed at Bainbridge's house, under the watchful guard of Parsons, one of Bainbridge's most trusted junior officers. His hand was going to take some time to recover, but at least he was alive.

"It's really quite a clever conceit," said Newbury. "Easy to deliver, difficult to detect. And to build automata that *small...*"

"Really, Newbury. You can't tell me you *admire* the handiwork of these villains," said Bainbridge.

"I admire their methods, if not their actions," said Newbury.

"I must admit to being confounded by them," said Bainbridge. "My men are out there scouring every damn crevice of London, but so far, there's no obvious lead. We can find nothing related to this so-called Menamhotep, and try as we might, we can't establish a motive for anyone else connected to the expedition. There's no reason any of them would want any of the victims dead, and their alibis all seem to hold up. We'll keep going, of course, but it's damn frustrating when the answers fail to present themselves like this."

Newbury stubbed his cigarette out on the windowsill and crossed to the sideboard, from where he retrieved his copy of the evening newspaper. "If you'll forgive me, Charles," he said, unfurling the broadsheet and leafing through the pages, "I took the liberty of interceding. I decided a more direct approach might prove fruitful." He found what he was looking for, folded the newspaper open on the right page, and smoothed it down, tapping a small advert amongst the classifieds.

Veronica and Bainbridge had moved around to stand behind him, peering over his shoulder. The advert read:

```
TO THOSE WHO SEEK THE WORD OF MENAMHOTEP
WHAT YOU REQUIRE IS IN SAFE HANDS
TOWER BRIDGE, 7PM FRIDAY
SIR MAURICE NEWBURY
```

"Of all the foolhardy things…" said Bainbridge, trailing off. "Don't you see what you've done? You've made yourself the next target. What if they come after you here, with one of those *things*?"

"Perhaps," said Newbury. "But even so, it would flush them out. And why risk it? If they're after the translated pages, they have no guarantee they're here. Better to chance the meet."

"Surely they'll see it's a trap," said Veronica.

"I imagine so," said Newbury. "But at least we'll get a sense of what we're up against, and how important those translated pages really are to them. As Charles said, it's not as if we have any other leads."

"I don't like it," said Bainbridge. "Not at all." He tugged

thoughtfully at the edge of his moustache. "But it's done now. Assuming they see it, of course."

"They'll see it," said Newbury.

"So, tomorrow evening," said Veronica. "We're coming with you, of course."

Newbury glanced at her, and grinned. "I wouldn't have it any other way." He tossed the newspaper back on the sideboard. "We need to make preparations. We have to assume they'll come armed and ready for an ambush."

"Oh, we'll be ready," said Bainbridge. "I'll get word to Foulkes right away. Whoever these murderous devils are, we'll be waiting."

"Like a spider at the centre of a web," said Newbury, with a grin.

VII

♔

Newbury turned the collar of his overcoat up against the pattering rain. A thick mist had settled across the river, shrouding the opposing tower, hugging the road and swirling around their ankles. It softened everything, as if it were somehow dispersing reality itself, leaving Newbury with the odd sensation that he was floating, up there on a bridge between two worlds.

He stood with Veronica and Bainbridge, leaning against the rail, waiting. Bainbridge hadn't stopped checking his pocket watch, despite the fact that bells all across the city had only just finished ringing out the hour.

Newbury peered over the railing. Below, he could see the mast of a ship, jutting rudely from the mist. The river itself was utterly obscured.

"They're here," said Veronica.

Newbury turned to see a figure walking towards them from across the bridge. They were dressed in a thick, black overcoat, rendering them in near silhouette; a moving, shifting, shadow. As they drew nearer, he discerned that the figure belonged to a woman. She was wearing a hat, pinned neatly on the side of her head, atop a neat arrangement of thick, dark hair. She was pretty, with a coffee-coloured complexion and startling brown eyes. She'd had a hair lip as a child, which had been surgically corrected, leaving her with a charming, impish smile. She was carrying an umbrella like a stick, still folded away, despite the weather. "Sir Maurice Newbury?" she said, as she approached.

Newbury pushed himself away from the railing. "And you are?"

The woman extended her hand. Newbury took it. Her fingers were cold to the touch. "Mathilda Bathurst. I saw your advert in *The Times.*"

"Quite." He noticed Bainbridge bristling beside him.

"I believe you have something of interest to us."

"Us?" said Newbury.

The woman smiled. She carried herself with a supreme air of confidence. "My associates and I would very much appreciate it if you were to simply hand it over."

"Now look here," said Bainbridge. "I think you misunderstand. Three men are dead, and I have every reason to believe you and your *associates* are behind it. You'll be coming back to Scotland Yard with us to answer some questions."

Bathurst laughed. "Sir Charles, I'd heard you were an amusing man." She held out her hand to Newbury. "Now, the papers."

Newbury reached inside his coat, but withdrew only his battered silver cigarette case. He popped it open and took one, then returned the case to his pocket. He huddled over for a moment while he lit it with a vesper. "First, I want to know what you intend to do with them, and why they are worth the death of three men to obtain. Is it a simple act of suppression? Are you attempting to prevent their publication?"

Bathurst sighed. "Menamhotep wills it, and it shall be done," she said.

"Oh, how dreadfully disappointing," said Newbury. He

blew smoke from the corner of his mouth. "For just a moment, I thought you were going to be more than just another inane follower of an obscure cult."

"An obscure cult?" The woman scoffed. "You have no idea of the web we have weaved throughout this city. Of how long we have worked in the shadows, or the lengths we will go to, to see Menamhotep rise. Those papers are just the beginning." She glanced at Bainbridge. "You can take me in, incarcerate me, kill me, but within the hour another will stand in my place. Far better that you hand over what is rightfully ours. I might even allow you to live."

"You might allow *us* to live?" said Bainbridge, incredulous. "Come on, Newbury. Let's get this over with. I'm anxious to get out of the rain."

Bathurst took a step back, and at first Newbury thought she was about to turn and flee, but instead she made a gesture above her head, snapping her fingers. Almost immediately, two figures appeared from the mist behind her, shambling forward on stiff, ungainly legs. Within seconds, another four had appeared in their wake, marching across the bridge with the same stuttering gait.

"Revenants," said Veronica.

"No," said Newbury. "Listen." There was something almost mechanical about the newcomers, and as they moved, he thought he heard the whine of servos.

"These are the saved," said Bathurst. "Their spirits reborn after death. This is the power of Menamhotep."

Two of the figures had now lurched fully into view, and the full horror of the occasion became apparent. They were shambling corpses, their flesh embalmed and dried, smooth and stretched across their decaying bones. Their eyes were missing, their sockets dry and hollow, staring and unseeing. They were wrapped in trailing bandages and adorned with necklaces bearing eight-legged scarabs. They were mummies, either plundered from their resting places in far off sands, or somehow recreated here, on British shores, in a gross parody of the funeral rites of the ancients. Their skeletons had been wired to brass supports, their joints fixed with servos, and they lumbered in a terrible semblance of life, powered by the same technology that had driven the tiny scarab automata.

Bainbridge raised his walking cane. "Stand aside, Miss Hobbes." He twisted the head of the cane and the shaft began to unpack, levering apart to reveal a reinforced glass chamber within. The main shaft began to spin, generating a spitting charge of electricity, which crackled inside the glass chamber, causing the very tip of the cane to spark and crackle. "Foulkes," he bellowed, and Newbury heard running footsteps from behind, as the six policemen came charging in, revolvers loaded and ready.

"You can prevent all of this, Sir Maurice, by surrendering the file," said Bathurst. "What happens here is your responsibility."

"Fire!" bellowed Bainbridge. The police revolvers barked, and four of the shambling mummies seemed to stutter for a moment, before continuing their ponderous, onward march. "Again!" called Bainbridge, and the shots rang out in quick succession, like snapping dogs. Once again, the mummies stumbled, but continued on their way.

Bathurst laughed. Newbury was beginning to wish he'd brought a weapon, rather than relying solely on the police. He cast around for something he could use against the automatons, but there was nothing to hand. He'd have to think on his feet.

The first of the things was nearly on top of them. Bainbridge stepped forward, brandishing his cane. "Call them off, Miss Bathurst," he said, his voice level.

Bathurst said nothing as the mummy took a further step towards Bainbridge, raising its hand as if to take a swipe.

"Have it your way, then." He jabbed at the thing with the tip of his cane, piercing the dry flesh of its gut and causing the electricity in the glass chamber to discharge. Lightning crackled across the mummy's entire frame, arcing between its remaining teeth, causing the servos to spark and the long-dead flesh to ignite with a sudden *whoosh*.

The mummy took two more stuttering steps forward, and then collapsed in a burning heap, its wired joints juddering, raindrops fizzing on its superheated frame. Wretched black smoke curled from the remains of its flesh, causing Newbury to wrinkle his nose in disgust.

The rest of the police had surged forward, and were now concentrating their fire on one automaton at a time, which appeared to be paying dividends, as another of the things went down while Newbury watched, and the police swiftly reloaded and began their assault on a third.

Bainbridge placed his foot on the smoking corpse and wrenched the end of his cane free. He twisted the head again, causing the spinning section to re-engage, and the charge once more began to build inside the chamber.

Newbury glanced at Bathurst, weighing his options. There were still three automata unengaged by the police, and while Bainbridge moved to tackle another of them, Newbury didn't fancy his chances against the others unarmed. He knew they would intercede if he tried to make a move against the woman. Veronica, on the other hand, had begun edging along the railing, evidently with a view to heading Bathurst off if she tried to make a break for it. He decided to remain where he was for now. He had the file, after all, which might prove to be their only leverage if things went awry.

"I'm impressed," said Bathurst. "I can see I'm going to have to engage a little more in the way of persuasion." She rapped the end of her metal-tipped umbrella against the ground three times in quick succession, and then smiled at Newbury mischievously.

Somewhere beneath Newbury's feet, something made a sharp scratching sound. He glanced down, half expecting to see the ground suddenly erupt around him, but all remained still, quiet.

He heard Veronica gasp, and turned to see her falling back from the railing, where an enormous black beetle had begun clambering up over the side of the bridge, its eight mechanical legs stabbing at the ground as it fought for purchase, scratching at the stone. It was about the size of a police carriage, with a fat, bulbous shell of glossy plates, and two twitching mandibles jutting from the front where its mouth should have been. Two men wearing goggles and black robes were strapped to its back in a leather harness, riding it as one might ride a horse. It was monstrous, an engine of destruction, built to the design of the eight-legged scarab so synonymous with Menamhotep.

"Veronica, run!"

Close to where the machine had emerged from under the bridge, Bainbridge was yanking his cane from the ruins of another mummy. He glanced up, just as the scarab dragged its bulk over the edge of the rail and dropped to the ground a few feet from him, its mandibles clacking as it advanced. He twisted, raising the cane, but the charge was spent, and there wasn't time for it to replenish. He backed away, glancing for support from the other policemen. "Foulkes!"

Bullets pinged off the armour plating of the scarab's head, and the man in the front of the saddle slumped suddenly, a fine spray of blood misting into the air where a bullet caught him in the throat. He listed to one side, gurgling, while the man behind him took up the controls, and the machine lurched forward, its mandibles grasping for Bainbridge.

Bainbridge swung his cane like a club, battering at the mechanical proboscis, but the shaft simply rebounded off the brass, and he staggered back, narrowly avoiding the burning mess of the mummy he'd just despatched.

As Newbury watched with a sense of dawning horror, the machine skittered forward–surprisingly agile now that it had cleared the railing–and scooped Bainbridge up in its mandibles, swinging him violently from side to side as he grappled to prise himself free.

Unsure what else he could do, Newbury pulled the file from inside his coat and ran to the edge of the railing. He thrust his hand out, over the sea of mist and the swirling river below. The file fluttered in the breeze, which threatened to wrench it from his fingers.

"Stop!"

The sound of gunfire and ricocheting bullets ceased. The scarab stopped shaking its head. Only the steady advance of the mummies continued, accompanied by the gently whining of their servos. The driver of the scarab looked down at Mathilda Bathurst, who was standing by the vehicle's feet, watching Newbury with a curious expression.

"You realise if you let go of that folder, we'll have no reason not to kill your friend," she said.

Newbury glanced at Veronica out of the corner of his eye. She looked as if she were getting ready to make a play for Bathurst. He shook his head, and, frustrated, she held her ground. "And you realise that if you *do* kill him, I'll destroy the only copy of this file in existence."

"Then it seems we're at something of a stalemate," said Bathurst, with a grin.

"Let him go, and you can have the file," said Newbury. "No tricks. Just a straight exchange. We give you the file, and we all walk out of here."

"How do I know you can be trusted?"

"You have my word."

Bathurst laughed. "I trust you see the irony in that?" She nodded to the scarab driver, and he operated a lever, releasing the mandibles and causing Bainbridge to slump heavily to the ground. He crumpled onto the wet road. "The file," she said, holding out her hand.

"Tell your followers to back off, first."

Bathurst sighed, and with a wave of her hand, dismissed the two remaining mummies. They turned ponderously, and then shambled off into the mist on the other side of the bridge. Newbury waited until they had gone.

"And *that,*" he said, nodding his head to indicate the scarab.

"Go," said Bathurst. The driver–still operating the controls over the slumped form of his dead colleague–turned the machine around, and clacked off into the rainswept night. Bathurst lifted her umbrella and pressed the tip against the back of Bainbridge's neck.

Slowly, Newbury lowered his arm and stepped away from the railing. He took two steps forward, and then stooped and laid the file on the ground. Raindrops were pattering upon its surface, staining the card. Soon, the pages inside would be unreadable.

"Back away," said Bathurst.

Newbury took three steps back. "Now let him go, and we'll retreat from the bridge."

"Sir Maurice," said Foulkes from somewhere behind him. "We can't just let her get away."

"We can, and we will, Inspector. I won't forfeit Charles's life for *this.*"

"Very wise," said Bathurst. She lifted her umbrella away from Bainbridge's neck and beckoned to Veronica, who came forward, stooping to Bainbridge's side. Slowly, she helped him up, collecting his cane, and together they staggered towards Newbury.

"All right, Foulkes. Tell your men to back away now." Newbury came forward to help Veronica, shouldering some of Bainbridge's weight. He was dazed, and bleeding, but alive.

"You heard him," said Foulkes. The reluctance was plain to hear in his voice.

Together, the six policemen retreated in a line, refusing to take their eyes off Bathurst until the thickening mist had enveloped them.

Newbury watched as Bathurst hurried over and crouched to collect the folder, which she swiftly slid under the protection of her coat. Then, opening her umbrella and resting it nonchalantly on her left shoulder, she turned and walked away.

"Until next time," said Newbury.

She didn't look round.

VIII

"You shouldn't have allowed her to get away. It's unconscionable."

"I'm pleased to see you're back to your old self, Sir Charles," said Veronica, passing him another brandy. He was slumped in the armchair by the fire at Newbury's house, wearing a brooding expression. The doctor had been and gone, and warned him under no uncertain terms that he needed to rest up for a few days. He'd suffered a few bruises—mostly to his dignity, it seemed—but otherwise he was quite well.

"You allowed her to get away with three counts of murder," Bainbridge continued, his eyes following Newbury as he paced around the room. He looked furious. "And now you're damn well smirking about it, too!"

"I did no such thing," said Newbury.

"Then what do you call allowing her to walk away with the bloody prize, then?" He caught a glimpse of Veronica scowling at him, and softened. "Look, I'm grateful for what you did. Of course I am. But surely Foulkes could have taken steps on the bridge. A well-placed bullet to slow her down and she'd be in custody now. At least then, justice would have been done."

"You heard her, Charles. Her little speech about the cult. We underestimated them, badly. Look at the resources they have. That *machine*…not to mention those walking cadavers. I believe she was telling the truth when she claimed that someone else would be waiting in the wings to take her place if she fell. Bringing her in wouldn't have made the slightest bit of difference. They'd still be out there, and the people who are truly responsible would be free to carry on as if nothing had happened."

"Isn't that true now?"

Newbury shook his head. "No. Because now we have a name, and a face, and a sense of what we're dealing with. Now we can go after the real prize. We can dig them out, drag them into the light, and discover what they're really up to. Then we'll make them pay for the crimes they've committed, too."

Bainbridge nodded. "Alright. I see your point." He smiled. "What was it you said, earlier? 'I'm not sure I agree with your actions, but I admire your method'."

"Something like that," said Newbury, laughing.

"But what about the file?" said Veronica. "Surely there was more to it than a simple creation myth. There has to be a reason they wanted it so badly and were prepared to kill the men involved in translating it. You mentioned rituals and incantations—do you think they're going to try to use them?"

"It won't do them much good if they do," said Newbury.

"Because it's all poppycock," scoffed Bainbridge.

"No," said Newbury, a little more emphatically than he'd intended. He crossed to one of his bookshelves and took down a leather folio. He opened it and withdrew a sheaf of pages covered in neat, spidery scrawl. "Because I kept a few choice pages back as insurance."

Bainbridge guffawed. "I'd love to see the look on that woman's face when she realises."

"I'm not so certain, Charles. We made an enemy today. She didn't seem the type to let things rest. This is tantamount to a declaration of war."

"Then war it shall be," said Bainbridge.

Veronica crossed the room to stand before him. She put a hand on his arm. "And when the time comes, we'll face it together. This time, we'll be ready."

"Hear, hear," said Bainbridge. "Now get over here and fetch me my pipe, would you, man? It's time you admitted I was right."

Newbury raised an eyebrow. "You were?"

"Yes. About it being one of your lot. A cult. You can't deny it now, can you, eh?"

Newbury sighed. He looked at Veronica. "You know, I think he might have a point."

"I suppose there's a first time for everything," she said, laughing.

ABOUT THE AUTHOR

George Mann is the author of the Newbury and Hobbes, The Ghost and the Wychwood series of novels, as well as numerous short stories, novellas and audiobooks. He has written fiction and audio scripts for the BBC's *Doctor Who* and Sherlock Holmes. He is also a respected anthologist and has edited *The Solaris Book of New Science Fiction* and *The Solaris Book of New Fantasy*. He lives near Grantham, in the UK.

GEORGE MANN
THE AFFINITY BRIDGE
A Newbury and Hobbes Investigation

Welcome to the bizarre and dangerous world of
Victorian London, a city teetering on the edge of
revolution. Astounding new technologies abound;
airships soar over the capital, trains rumble through
the streets, and clockwork automatons carry out menial
tasks. But beneath this dazzling veneer lurks a
sinister world...

Ghostly policemen haunt the alleyways of Whitechapel,
cadavers rise from the dead, and now an airship has
crashed under strange circumstances. Mystified by a
series of grisly murders, Scotland Yard call upon the
brilliant Sir Maurice Newbury, Gentleman Investigator
for the Crown, and his recently appointed and
unflappable assistant, Miss Veronica Hobbes.

So begins the first thrilling adventure of
Newbury and Hobbes, in a steampunk London
you will never forget.

GEORGE MANN
THE OSIRIS RITUAL
A Newbury and Hobbes Investigation

Death stalks London and the newspapers proclaim
that a mummy's curse has been unleashed. Sir Maurice
Newbury, Gentleman Investigator for the Crown, is
drawn into a web of occult intrigue as he attempts to
solve the murders. And he soon finds himself on the trail
of a rogue agent—a man who died to be reborn
as a living weapon.

Meanwhile, Newbury's able assistant, Miss Veronica
Hobbes, has her own mystery to unravel. Young women
are going missing from a magician's theatre show. But
what appears to be a straightforward investigation puts
Miss Hobbes in mortal danger.

Can Newbury save his assistant, solve the riddle of
the mummy's curse, capture the deadly man-machine
and stop the terrifying Osiris Ritual from reaching its
infernal culmination?

GEORGE MANN
THE IMMORALITY ENGINE
A Newbury and Hobbes Investigation

Gentleman Investigator for the Crown, Sir Maurice
Newbury, has brilliantly solved a number of near-
impossible cases for Queen Victoria along with his
assistant, Miss Veronica Hobbes. But while all appears
well on the surface, Newbury has an increasingly
uncontrollable secret…

What was once a flirtation with the lure of opium has
turned into a full-blown addiction for Newbury. Hobbes,
along with Newbury's dear friend Bainbridge, the chief
investigator at Scotland Yard, try to cover for him as
much as possible, but when the body of a well-known
criminal turns up, Bainbridge and Hobbes drag Newbury
from an opium den to help them with the case. The body
is irrefutably that of the criminal, but shortly after it is
brought to the morgue, a crime is discovered
that bears all the dead man's hallmarks.

Newbury and Hobbes will come face to face with
their hardest and darkest investigation to date.
These are no copycat killings… But how can a dead
man commit a crime?

For more fantastic fiction, author events, exclusive
excerpts, competitions, limited editions and more

VISIT OUR WEBSITE
titanbooks.com

LIKE US ON FACEBOOK
facebook.com/titanbooks

FOLLOW US ON TWITTER
@TitanBooks

EMAIL US
readerfeedback@titanemail.com